KEYS
of
LIFE

KEYS of LIFE

Book Three

EVIL REDEEMED

Carolyn Schield
Tom Vorbeck

ACKNOWLEDGEMENTS

Special thanks to our outstanding copy editor, Alexandria Arnold, for her incredible patience and great talent. Her dedication over the years inspired us to continue with our dream. Her tremendous courage and honesty were much appreciated.

Tom and Andrew Aker produced another stunning cover. Our families and friends supported us and many thanks for your wonderful generosity and love. Our father and mother deserve credit for encouraging us to follow our dreams.

We couldn't do it without our test readers Sandra White and Kay Gambill. We give a great big thanks to Jennifer and John who encouraged us. Kay Gambill took on the added responsibility of proofreader and helped edit our book and thank you so much Kay for an excellent job.

Marty Johnson gets a round of applause for his gorgeous illustrations in the book and front cover. His art work is phenomenal and so creative.

A shout-out to all the staff at the Fairfield Inn at Wentzville for their great accommodations and taking such good care of us. Sienna Book Club thanks for your support.

Tom and I have been blessed with wonderful families and friends. Thanks to all of you, we did it, again.

CONTENTS

PROLOGUE

Cordy decided the only thing to do was get drunk. She grabbed the tequila bottle and poured a shot. She turned on the television and raised her glass. The broadcaster described the amazing light show in New Orleans' Jackson Square. Cordy had to admit the whole thing was surreal. Wind blowing and lightning sparking the sky, she remembered the laser beam shooting from the Orion sword.

Cordy trembled as she thought of the static electricity crawling around her body as she held onto the Sword of Water. The tequila burned her throat, and her whole body felt the familiar warmth flowing through her. She poured herself another shot as the commentators declared that a miracle had saved New Orleans from a disaster of biblical proportions.

Her emotions were all over the place. Uriel had told her she was the chosen one — called to help save mankind from De Villiers' greed for power — but she didn't want to be a hero. The quiet life of helping sick animals and teaching karate seemed like heaven now. Her life would never be the same. Her great-grandfather's voice filled her mind as she remembered that she was from a line of great warriors dating back to the Crusades, during which Templar Grandmaster Saunhac fought to protect the treasures of the Pure of Heart.

Recalling her great-grandfather's death brought tears to her eyes. She, Ash, and the chief were retrieving Pure of Heart artifacts in Nova Scotia when they came under attack by the Dark Watchers. Bob had come to their rescue with a helicopter extraction. Cordy had already been hoisted to the rescue helicopter. As she watched the chief's and Ash's ascent, the chief was shot in the chest by a Dark Watcher. Knowing that he was dying, the chief cut himself from the rope to save Ash and plunged into the freezing ocean. Cordy and Ash followed him into the deep waters to rescue him. When Cordy reached him, the dying old man tore a necklace from around his neck and handed it to her. Dangling from it was the legendary Solomon's ring with the Star of David carved on it. He motioned his good-bye and dropped to the bottom of the sea.

Ash later explained the ring's significance. Legends suggested that Solomon used the ring to build his famous First Temple where the Ark of the Covenant was housed. He also told her that the powerful relic made all of the angels and animals obey anyone who wore the ring.

Cordy fingered the ring and thought to herself, *how many died for this? De Villiers will kill anyone who stands in his way of obtaining the ring and the Keys of Life. My parents, the chief, and Sister Agnes died fighting to protect me and the world.*

Thinking of her late ancestor, the Templar Grandmaster Saunhac, she remembered a stained-glass scene at the St. Louis Cathedral in

New Orleans. It showed him with one eye bandaged, kneeling as Saint Louis accepted a key as his reward for winning the city of Damietta. To Cordy, the key symbolized the precious treasures of the Pure of Heart, known as the Keys of Life. It seemed to her that Templar Grandmaster Saunhac was kneeling in service to protect them. These gifts, from the beginning of time, were to protect Earth and her children from mass extinction. This was exemplified when Uriel gave Noah the Keys of Life before the great flood. It was obvious that their powers were immense, and De Villiers coveted them. The greedy madman of the Dark Watchers had killed so many to possess them.

They had escaped for now, but De Villiers would continue to hunt them down. Marriage and a quiet life were out of the question for Cordy while De Villiers ruled over the Dark Watchers. Jon and Ash were crazy for asking her to marry them during a gun battle. It had to be the shock from the lightning bolts hitting their brains. Nobody had time for love in the middle of a war. Her head told her to be logical, but her heart ached for a kiss from the one she loved. She gulped down another shot.

The broadcaster showed earthquakes, volcanoes, and severe weather hitting all parts of Earth. No one knew what was causing the devastation. Scientists noticed the same phenomenon happening on planets all over the solar system. Solar flares had increased, and Earth's magnetic poles were shifting slightly farther from the North and South Poles. Governments all over the world brought in top scientists to figure out what was triggering the chaos.

Everyone was at a loss as to how to stop this disaster befalling mankind and all the animals. They predicted an extinction-level event if conditions weren't altered.

The Guardian had warned them this was going to happen. The Keys of Life needed to come out of hiding to help save the world.

De Villiers, the newly crowned Dark Watcher Grandmaster, killed Sister Agnes and her great-grandfather Chief Saunhac of the Mi'kmaq so he could get his hands on the keys. They had protected these treasures for years and kept them from his grasp. No one was safe with De Villiers as head of the Dark Watchers. Cordy grabbed the tequila bottle and sucked it down.

Cordy realized how lucky she was to have valiant friends such as Ash, Bob, and Master Wong, who stood by her side through this war. All of them would sacrifice their lives to save Earth's children. She understood the Guardian's mission over the millennia and realized her career as a veterinarian showed her heart's compassion for all living things, making her a perfect fit for a Pure of Heart. A plan formed in her head and she realized what needed to be done.

I am a descendant of the Templar Grandmaster Saunhac. Just as he showed his service to protect the keys, so will I. De Villiers must be stopped at any cost! So, let it be written, so let it be done!

Cordy raised her glass and gave a Mi'kmaq war hoop.

CHAPTER 1

Kneeling at the Altar

Cordy knew they had a long way to go in this battle of good versus evil. Something was making her sick to her stomach. Was it the fear of losing one more of the Pure of Heart team or was she just hungover from the night before? Her head felt like the Mi'kmaq pounding war drums. She rolled over and thought, *this is what a tequila sunrise really is, and it's not pretty. I feel like I'm going to die.*

The sun wasn't up yet, but Cordy knew she had to get going. As she got out of bed the reality hit her: it was definitely a hangover. The tequila was still talking to her. As she walked across the room to get dressed, she looked in the bathroom and just one look at the porcelain altar made her fall to her knees and begin worshipping. The sounds that came out of her were as if a wild animal was dying in the wilderness.

Ash and Jon heard the disturbing sounds coming from Cordy's room. Thinking someone was killing her, they kicked the doors adjoining their rooms to Cordy's to break the locks. They ran in to find a sickly Cordy hugging the toilet. With a pale face and bloodshot eyes, Cordy screamed at them, "Get out and stay out!"

Jon apologized, "I am sorry, cherie, for interrupting but it sounded as if you needed help. I'm worried about you after seeing you so sick. Can I get you anything?"

Cordy gave him a death stare. Jon did an about-face and scurried from the room.

Ash looked down at Cordy. She had never looked so fierce. He didn't run but he understood why Jon did. He reached over and grabbed a washcloth and put cold water on it and handed it to her.

Cordy's anger bubbled up. "I don't need any help. I can take care of myself, mister-lying-on-the-blond-bombshell-naked-in-the-middle-of-the-night. Don't think I'm ever going to forget that scene."

She turned her head and started to wretch violently. "I swear I will never drink tequila again!"

Ash tried not to smile. "I always said that when I was down on all fours, but it will pass. Tequila goes down easy but comes up hard."

"Ash, I'm sorry for treating you so badly."

"I forgive you." Ash filled a glass with water and handed it to her, so she could rinse her mouth.

As Cordy rested on the floor, she reflected that it was nice having someone there for her. Ash wasn't afraid of taking care of a sick woman. After her parents were killed in a plane crash, Cordy had always been on her own. Waves of emotion washed over her. Tears welled in her eyes and streamed down her face as she thought, *this man has broken the wild mustang and tamed me.*

Cordy was summoning the strength to stand when she felt a rumbling all around her. "Do you feel that shaking?"

Ash shook his head. "It's probably your stomach."

The room started shaking and the mirror in the bathroom split in two. A rumbling growl surrounded them. Ash pulled the weak Cordy up against him.

"We're having an earthquake. Run!"

The two ran down the stairs watching cracks form in the walls and tried not to lose their balance. They reached the door and spotted Master Wong in the middle of the lawn with a sword in his hand.

Cordy pointed to her elderly teacher. "He's holding the Sword of Earth."

Ash saw him, too, and wondered what he was doing with it.

An hour earlier, the elderly man had been meditating — which he did every day — when he noticed the Sword of Earth glimmer and shake on the dresser. He ignored it, but the Sword of Earth did it again. He closed his eyes and a vision of a lovely woman dressed in a beautiful red, satin kimono with white cranes appeared before him.

"I am the Guardian. You must take the Sword of Earth outside now, my old friend."

He opened his eyes and dressed. Master Wong wondered if it was a dream or a warning. Everyone was asleep, so he grabbed the Sword of Earth and walked onto the manicured lawn.

Master Wong watched the plantation house shake and the trees sway. The sound from the ground brought a deafening rumble. It was a major earthquake. He knew the power of the Sword of Earth could produce and prevent earthquakes. The sword connected with the tectonic plates of Earth. He raised the arm that held the Sword of Earth and waited.

CHAPTER 2

The Earth Moved

Bob and Julia woke up snuggled against each other. Julia had never been so happy in her entire life. She felt her whole body tingle when Bob's lips met hers and his strong arms wrapped around her. If he thought he was sleeping in this morning, he was in for a surprise. She rolled on top of him, kissing his neck ever so lightly and then his lips. The lovers lay naked under the sheets, feeling the electricity as their bodies came together. Bob's eyes twinkled with mischief. "Hello, wife," he whispered in her ear, softly rubbing her back.

Julia smiled back, "Hello, husband. I like the sound of that. You ready for a morning workout?"

Bob winked. "Oh, I'm always ready. Can't you tell?"

The two let their passion consume them, oblivious to everything in the room. They didn't notice the increased shaking of the bed, nor did they realize a light was shining from the Guardian of Earth's crystal ball, which had been covered by a pillow on the other side of the room.

The Guardian, a beautiful woman inside the crystal ball, anxiously cried out, "Bob, I am receiving alarming information. Do you feel it?"

Bob heard her but only had his mind on one thing and yelled out, "Oh yeah! I can feel it!"

Julia chimed in with a "Yes!" The bed rattled more and more. The dainty porcelain angel figure danced on the nightstand as the lamp fell off the table and crashed to the floor. Bob and Julia didn't notice it. Nothing existed for the lovers except the exhilarating feeling of desire.

The frustrated Guardian yelled, "No kidding, Bob. I'm registering a 6.8 earthquake on the New Madrid Fault Line. You need to warn the others and find shelter now!"

Bob and Julia looked at each other in shock as the little angel tumbled to the floor.

The chairs fell, and the table toppled over. Paintings on the wall crashed to the floor. The lovers' eyes met, as they realized a huge earthquake was in progress.

"What the hell!"

Screams of alarm rang throughout the house as everything shook violently. Bob scurried to put his pants on and Julia grabbed his T-shirt.

The Guardian's urgent voice cried out, "You must get out before the house falls in!"

Bob saw the cracks climbing up the walls as plaster on the ceiling dropped around them.

Julia grabbed the crystal ball and Bob rushed to push her into the hallway.

Randy was still in his room reading a newspaper when the shaking started. The walls cracked and parts of the ceiling split and fell around him. Realizing he was in danger, he pulled on his pants and grabbed the bags loaded with the Pure of Heart treasures. He threw open the door just as Bob and Julia headed for the stairs. He ran after them glumly thinking, *there goes my deposit!*

Jon felt the tremors and knew instantly it was an earthquake. He went in search of Sam, his little sister. He ran to her room and found her on the wrought-iron balcony wondering what was going on outside. Trees were being uprooted and cracks were forming in the ground on the lawn. Sam's eyes filled with surprise as she saw the fear in Jon's face. Time slowed down in that moment. Her biggest fear was to see her brother killed in front of her and in that instant, she realized it was his, too. The iron railing pulled loose from the shocks and Sam felt the floor drop from under her. Gravity pulled her down and her arms flailed in the air. Her brother reached and grabbed her hand just as the balcony collapsed. Sam screamed as she dangled off the edge while Jon held tightly to her hand.

"Don't let me go, Jon."

He fell to the gyrating floor holding her with all his strength, but he continued to slip closer to the edge.

"Never, little sister. If you die, I die."

Hearing Sam's screams, Peter Woo and Chris rushed into her room and went to Jon's aid. They grabbed and pulled the terrified, dangling Sam back into the room.

Chris knew instantly what was causing the shaking. He had lost many friends in Haiti from an earthquake a few years back. Memories of that disaster were still vivid in his mind. His friends and family were killed from concrete buildings burying them in their collapse.

"We've got to get out of here! It's a death trap!" Chris cried. All of them flew down the stairs with chandeliers dropping in front of them.

They all ran for the door and found Master Wong on the lawn holding the Sword of Earth. Ash, Cordy and Randy were ahead of them by a few feet. When everyone was out of the house and on the lawn, the elderly man raised the Sword of Earth and pointed the blade downward and, with all his force, plunged it into the ground.

A shock wave released, and an electric pulse spread through the ground, knocking everyone to their knees. The tremors stopped. An incredible stillness filled the air.

Jon hugged his sister. "Sam, are you, all, right?"

She smiled up at her big brother. "A few scratches, but I'm alright. What the hell happened?"

The Guardian's solemn voice rang out, "The New Madrid has awakened. It is only the beginning."

CHAPTER 3

Map of the Lost Tribes

Ash tried to break the tension. "Now, that we've got your attention, a meeting has been called."

Everyone's eyes turned to him. The stately mansion that had stood before them was now destroyed by the earthquake. Trees had fallen, and the concrete was cracked. Randy and Chris were covered in dust and knocked to the ground.

Jon smiled at Ash. "You're not that good, Ash. I would like to know what the hell happened just now."

Everybody gathered in a circle around Master Wong as he lifted the Sword of Earth from the ground. The gleaming sword had relieved the pressure built up by the tectonic plates pushing together. Richard the Lionheart had wielded this same sword during the Crusades after finding it in Jerusalem near Temple Mount. The sword had rested with the Lionheart in the abbey where his effigy stood until Ash, Cordy, and Jon found it. Its power to rule Earth was seen by all that day.

Randy looked at the news coming in on his phone. The earthquake had started as a powerful 6.8 on the seismograph but it lasted only a few seconds. Experts were puzzled over how quickly the shocks stopped. Many lives were saved because of it. The property damage was immense, but the human toll was surprisingly low.

The crystal ball that Chief Saunhac had given Cordy started to shine and then projected a holographic image of a beautiful woman in a white robe. They all recognized her at once as the Guardian. She reminded them, "Remember that I am the Guardian placed here long ago to protect the precious life on Terra, or what you call Earth. Behold the star map before you." She stretched out her arm and a design of the solar system appeared with the planets revolving around the sun. She pointed to an unknown object near Neptune.

"The Wanderer has returned."

Jon, the astrophysicist, saw the planet's large elliptical orbit. "I've heard of this planet. Cal Tech discovered something like this. It's a huge object and has the mass of eleven earths. How long is the Wanderer's orbit around the sun, Guardian?"

"About 25,000 years," the Guardian replied. "Terra and the other planets are being affected by the Wanderer's orbit. I've seen the disasters brought by this event and recorded it in my database. I detect the poles shifting, which might cause flooding and Earth crust slippage.

"Over time, the Pure of Heart has protected the treasures and knowledge of the ancients from such catastrophes. The pyramids built around the world were created for this day. They are a network connected to Terra. You have all the tools except for one. The ancient ones left the tools to help all of life survive. The Keys of Life are these tools. The Pure of Heart has been instrumental in saving life on Earth from extinction. You must prepare and protect mankind from the impending doom."

Master Wong added, "Sister Agnes told me that a map drawn by early European explorers was sent to Rome. She said Chief Saunhac told her that the Native Americans' sacred resting places, cities, and temples were marked. Sister Agnes said that the famous North American Saint Rose Duchesne knew about the legends because she worked with the different tribes in the area. The Acadians lived in the area and protected the secret. The Mississippi River was used to transport supplies and helped the Pure of Heart communicate to each other. New Orleans played an important part as you all well know."

Jon nodded. "The Lafitte family has played their part through time. We will do our best to save the world."

"I remember a dusty old file called the Map of the Lost Tribes in the Nephilim archives," Julia said. "I thought it was just a story. I may still have the file. If I'm not mistaken, the map went to the Vatican, where early explorers' maps were collected. Bob, it looks like we're going to Rome for our honeymoon. We're going to need an expert to help us."

Bob smiled. "I love pizza, so it sounds good to me. Randy will hold down the fort while we're gone."

"Brother Michael is the man for the job," Ash said. "I bet he has connections to get you into the map room. All we need is a photograph of the map. I'll call Nova Scotia and have Brother Michael meet you. As the legend goes, one of the Lost Tribes of Israel consisted of a great sea-faring people who took the treasure of Solomon's Temple with them."

Randy jumped in. "I can rig you with a hidden camera in your watch and eye glasses. The Vatican doesn't allow pictures. You'll need new passports and papers to get you through customs. I'm on it."

"Well, we have a plan at least," Cordy said. "Bob and Julia will go to Rome to meet brother Michael and get a picture of the Map of the Lost Tribes. Randy will go to New York and use the Pure of Heart resources to try to create small arks all over the world. We will use Noah as our mentor. He gathered and built the ark, filling it with provisions to ensure mankind's survival. We will do the same. Food, water, and survival equipment will be needed to send to every country in case we fail. Linda's friends in the Diplomatic Brat Corps could help us and warn people. The Pure of Heart will create survival locations to prepare for upcoming disasters. The Diplomatic Corps designates will let us know what they need to survive at each location. We will send them all the help they need. The rest of us need to find a place to lie low for a while."

Peter Woo spoke up. "We should head to Saint Louis. We have friends there."

"We could float up the Mississippi River undetected," Sam added. "After the Lafitte family was told to quit the outpost in Galveston, some of the family moved to Alton, Illinois. Our great ancestor Jean Lafitte had a wife and settled there. As a result, we have many friends on the Mississippi barges. They would never reveal our presence to the Dark Watchers."

The Guardian started to fade, speaking softly, "Many types of catastrophes have brought mankind to the brink of extinction. The story of Noah and other Great Deluge stories of various civilizations describe the catastrophic flood. Plato described the Lost City of Atlantis. Today, there are many concerns for global disaster. The Wanderer is just one.

"The treasure of the Lost Tribes will help prevent Earth's poles from shifting. Its power is immense. However, I cannot tell you what it is or where it is. I fear if one of you is captured, all will be lost. So, it is up to you to find the treasure and stop the impending disasters. For all of time, the Pure of Heart has saved the world from the brink of extinction. The world is in your hands. Save as many as you can!"

CHAPTER 4

Human Shields

The Jackson Square miracle was being replayed on every television station. As the Pure of Heart united their swords to thwart the hurricane, De Villiers, leader of the Dark Watchers, watched in awe of their power. His father and teachers had talked about them. He had studied them and their legends for years. But to see them in action was something else. He had to possess them!

Dark Watchers across the world were in a state of panic. The plan had been that the destruction caused by the hurricane would devastate stock values and ruin the Lafitte family's financial empire. Instead, Lafitte's stocks were up, while the Dark Watchers had lost billions. They weren't happy about it. De Villiers didn't care what his minions felt, what he really wanted was the Pure of Hearts' treasures, at whatever the cost.

De Villiers called Mindy, his assistant, to report on the progress of their plans. Mindy walked in wearing a low-cut skin-tight black dress accentuating her curvaceous figure and shapely legs. Although she looked like every man's dream, she was one of the deadliest assassins among the Dark Watchers. On his orders, she had infiltrated the Children of the Nephilim organization while under the management of the now-deceased chairman to spy and steal their secrets. De Villiers used this information to hire all the remaining members of the defunct Nephilim corporation into the Dark Watchers. Her next task was tracking down and capturing Cordy and Ash.

"Oh, that awful rash is gone. You must feel so much better," Mindy said.

De Villiers seethed with anger as he thought of the voodoo curse that Chris, the descendant of Queen Marie Laveau, had put on him. He had made a voodoo doll in the image of De Villiers and placed it in poison ivy in retaliation for De Villiers using his own black magic to cause Chris a permanent leg injury. The rash was gone now, but Chris would pay for the agony he put De Villiers through.

Mindy sat on De Villiers' desk and seductively crossed her legs. Isis, his faithful cat, jumped into his lap. Stroking his precious feline's back, he asked, "What news do you have?"

Mindy replied, "Did you see the latest news on the New Madrid Fault?"

De Villiers' eyes met hers. "Yes, I saw it, the reports of the strange phenomenon that caused the earthquake to diminish. It had to be the Sword of Earth. Do you have any idea where the Pure of Heart are hiding?"

"My team is on it," she assured him. "The problem is roads, bridges, and telecommunications are out, so getting information is difficult. But I have my people searching for them."

"How's our other plan progressing? Time is running out and the cataclysm is getting closer. Are we prepared?"

Mindy smiled at him. "We've got the Neanderthal program and the kidnapped Pure of Hearts located together in our prison bunkers. We could leak out information that their friends are our prisoners. They'll come to save them and then we capture them. The Pure of Heart won't try to blow us up because we have hostages."

De Villiers stroked Isis on the head and she purred. "I want you to keep watch and hunt them down. Leak the information about our hostages. We need to have a backup plan just in case they slip our grasp. I've learned one thing and that's not to underestimate them."

Mindy showed him a security video on her tablet. In bunkers deep in the ground, men, women, and children were in jail cells. They were kidnapped Pure of Heart from the area. Dark Watchers guarded them. "We're keeping them sedated so they don't get any ideas. The bunkers have enough food and water to last a year."

De Villiers smiled. "I'm pleased, Mindy. They're our insurance policy. Now, we just need to get the Pure of Heart treasure and we will be in business. The problem is time is running out. The awakening of the New Madrid is just the beginning."

"I have to ask why we need the Neanderthals. They've assimilated well, but why do we need them?"

"We've discovered that most Europeans and Asians have one to two percent Neanderthal DNA. This suggests that Neanderthal interbred with modern man. I want to preserve their blood in the event that we incur an ancient plague. We may need their antibodies to develop vaccines to guarantee our survival."

Mindy's eyes met his. She had to ask. "Are the Nephilim's children the Neanderthal? They are bigger and stronger than humans.

I can see them called giants. I've seen how big they are in the videos sent by our scientists."

De Villiers smiled. "Genesis 6:4 talks of the offspring of the 'sons of God and daughters of men.' So, it would seem so or at least that's why the Children of the Nephilim resurrected them. They called them the 'offspring of Orion. At the cathedral in Chartres, a stained-glass window depicts the story of Noah where a giant holding a club named Orion stands in the presence of smaller humans. It seems the legend was known even in the days of the Crusades. My family knew and so did the Saunhacs. It's been a secret for a long time and many times evidence of it conveniently disappeared."

"Bring Cordy's friends to me. If we're going to survive, we need them. They need to be alive if possible."

"I'm on it. All our people are on alert. The Pure of Heart will slip up, and we'll find them." She poured a glass of Scotch for each of them and handed him one. De Villiers raised his glass in a toast.

"Here's to us. History books will write of how we saved humanity."

Mindy's glass reached her lips and she smiled. "Napoleon said, 'History is written by the winners.'"

CHAPTER 5

Star Charts

As Mindy drank, De Villiers pulled out the dossier on the Pure of Heart gathered by the Children of the Nephilim. Using computers, they had access to birth records around the world. Comparing birth records to star charts, the chairman and his minions could discover potential Pure of Heart. Any possible Pure of Heart would be put on a list and supervised. The committee would decide who would live or die. The same tactic was used by Herod in the Massacre of the Innocents, in which the first-born males were killed to stop them from fulfilling the prophesy of the three kings. Mindy could gather data from the dossier for their pet project of killing the Pure of Heart as long as birth dates weren't forged like Cordy's had been. Sister Agnes had changed Cordy's birth date by a day, thus hiding the fact that she was a possible Pure of Heart.

Astrology is based on the idea that there is a connection between the planets, the star systems, and the individual. Many ancient people believed an astral universal force or heavenly power influenced our destiny. They believed the twelve Zodiac signs and the stars could chart the course of a child's life and give insight to the future. For example, a child born in the House of Aries would be influenced by Mars and had the potential to be a great warrior. Gemini was an air sign and children born under an air sign would have high intellect and thoughtfulness. A child born under a water sign such as Cancer would have an emotional tendency with tears of joy and sadness being the water of life. A child born under a fire sign such as Leo would have a temperamental nature and be full of pride. Earth-sign children would be practical.

Many French Cathedrals such as Chartres have stained glass windows from the 1100s depicting the Zodiac. Blanche Castile, Saint Louis, and Queen Eleanor of Aquitaine recognized the interconnection of the heavens with everyday life and considered it sacred knowledge given to mankind. They brought in their astrologers for their interpretations of the stars. They used this knowledge in dealing with rival kings and queens.

Julia Villiers' impressive dossier stood before De Villiers. She was a distant cousin of his, just as was the dead chairman. De Villiers' family split up centuries ago, with some becoming Dark Watchers and the others joining the Children of the Nephilim. They believed one day their families would head both organizations. Little did they know De Villiers would take over both. His star chart signaled his intelligence and his ambition. His father saw the potential of his son and placed him in the best schools in England.

The former chairman realized the necessity of having a Pure of Heart obedient to him. Studying star charts, he discovered the potential of a little girl named Julia. He killed Julia's parents and abducted her. Through years of abuse and brainwashing, Julia forgot who she was and transformed into Ellen, the chairman's soon-to-be top assassin. Ellen became his edge in building his organization and eliminating his competition. What the chairman hadn't seen in her star charts was that Ellen would eventually become his worst nightmare and would ultimately destroy him and the Children of the Nephilim.

De Villiers had also seen Julia's start chart. He felt certain that the chairman had misinterpreted part of her chart. The charts only gave a person a glimpse. An interpreter could make a very big mistake. He could see that Ellen was a killer, but for whom?

On the command of the chairman, Ellen was sent to kill Chief Saunhac, the leader of the Pure of Heart. Since De Villiers was not certain of her ultimate allegiance, he saw his chance to arrange her assassination as well. His minions would assist her in the killing of the chief and once he was dead, they would assassinate Ellen. However, before Chief Saunhac died, he spoke to Ellen and prompted her to remember who she really was — Julia, a Pure of Heart. With the rebirth of Julia came the death of Ellen.

"I never understood the fascination with the star charts," Mindy remarked. "Doesn't anybody have a chance to be a Pure of Heart if they want to be?"

"You're right. Anybody can be a Pure of Heart but those marked have the greatest possibility. Ancient wisemen saw the connection between the stars and mankind. Seers were called in to help see the future. Astrology is an ancient teaching which I learned from my father. I want those whose names are marked in the dossier to be gathered up as soon as possible. They will be my hostages and my bait. Cordy and Ash won't be able to resist rescuing them. When they come, we'll spring our trap."

Mindy smiled. "I assume my star chart is in there, too."

De Villiers smiled. "It is, and it shows your potential to be a secret agent. Your greatest strengths are your dedication and loyalty. Your devotion to the one you love is unquestioned. It's written in the stars."

Mindy leaned over and kissed him. "We know who I love the most."

He began to let his hands roam all over her. He whispered in her ear, "Yes, we do."

CHAPTER 6

Until We Meet Again

Everybody grabbed their belongings and got ready to depart. Randy ordered two helicopters to land on the grounds of the southern mansion. Sam arranged for a barge to be waiting for them on the Mississippi River.

While they were waiting, Julia got on her computer to search the files that she had obtained from the Children of Nephilim's database. "Yes! I remembered correctly. I found evidence that the map exists in the map room of the Vatican. Legend says that people from Ancient Egypt settled in North America prior to Columbus. They say ancient treasures were buried there. The secret map is hidden in the Vatican map room for safe keeping. Could they be the children of the Lost Tribes?"

She showed the file to Ash. "The Guardian is right. The map does exist. It's been hidden because it doesn't fit well with the history we've been taught."

Ash browsed the file. "The Egyptians or the Lost Tribes may have found a way to America and left their treasure here, near the Mississippi. Many scholars have compared the Mississippi with the Nile. The name Isis — that of the Egyptian goddess — can be seen in the middle of Mississippi. And then there are town names along the river named Memphis, Cairo, and Thebes —just like in Egypt."

Jon chimed in, "My gut is telling me you need to also keep an eye out for the connection of the Wanderer while you're at the Vatican. Pope Urban VII locked up Galileo, one of the greatest astronomers of his time, for revealing how the Earth revolved around the sun. It may be important."

Bob smiled. "I'm thinking this should be easy. All we need is to get a photo of the map. Randy fitted me with these eyeglasses and a watch that can take pictures. Honey, how do you like me in my new glasses? Sexy, huh?"

Julia grinned back at him and whispered, "You're right. It does kinda turn me on!"

Everyone laughed because to them. Bob looked like a nerd.

Ash said, "Okay, we've verified the map exists. Let me call Brother Michael."

Ash called his parents in Nova Scotia. He told them about the map of the Lost Tribes, explaining that they needed Brother Michael's help to retrieve a picture of it.

Brother Michael held a special bond with Ash's family. Long ago, the monk, saved Ash's father's life by hiding him and giving him sanctuary at Mt. Carmel Monastery. He kept him hidden for years, from even Ash and his mother, until they too needed sanctuary to escape the Dark Watchers.

While hiding from Dark Watchers, Brother Michael explained to Ash the power of the golden ankhs, the Keys of Life that Ash had brought from Egypt. He twisted the ends of the ankhs and to Ash's surprise, seeds streamed into Brother Michael's hand. Brother Michael explained that the seeds were held in reserve in case a cataclysmic event threatened the world food supply.

"Hello, Brother Michael. We need your help."

"Yes, Ash, how can I be of service?"

"My friends need to get into the map room at the Vatican. I was wondering if you had any contacts there?"

"I do have an old friend who could help. He happens to work in the Vatican. He could obtain the proper credentials and clearance for your friends. I would be happy to go to Rome to make introductions and help your friends. It will give me an opportunity to see the paintings of Michelangelo, Raphael, and Bernini one more time. Also, I've heard that the Vatican map room is fascinating. I will get packing and rendezvous with your friends in Rome."

"Thank you, Brother Michael."

Ash turned to the group, "Brother Michael is on board. He'll meet you in Rome."

While everyone finished discussing the details for the map expedition, Cordy had her own secret mission. She packed up her treasures and searched out Randy, who was waiting for the arrival of the helicopters. He was on his way back to New York to hold down the office until Bob returned.

She handed him a manila envelope. "I want you to take these legal papers with you. I have some very important instructions for you when you get to New York."

He laughed. "What is this? Your will?"

Cordy smiled back at him. "As a matter of fact, it is, so you better wait 'til you get to New York to open it. And keep it quiet until Bob comes back from Rome. He's got enough on his plate."

Randy saw the seriousness in Cordy's eyes. "I'm on it. Your project has the highest priority."

The helicopter flew in closer to land and Randy boarded while the others waved good-bye. He said to himself, *she doesn't think she's going to make it and preparing for the worst.* He wanted to tell Bob but Cordy ordered him to be quiet. Randy knew she was right because Bob would refuse to hear any talk about death. He waved back to a smiling Cordy and his friends. He was going to miss them.

Cordy found Jon in his room packing. She handed him an envelope.

"What's this?"

"It's the shares I acquired from the Lafitte Corporation buy-out. I signed it all back to you. You're boss of the Lafitte businesses again. My family says thank you for all of your help. The Lafittes and the McDermotts have been allies for centuries. Let's keep it that way."

Jon opened the envelope. He never had been so surprised in his life. Cordy had saved his family's fortune and businesses.

Jon reached over and gave her a light kiss on her cheek. "Merci, my family seems to be always in your debt. Thank you, Cordy. You're the most amazing woman." Another helicopter could be heard in the distance.

"I've got to see Bob and Julia off." She turned and left him stunned with the gift she had given him.

Bob handed his bags to the copilot and Julia hugged Cordy. Bob gave Cordy a bear hug, too.

"You take good care of her, Bob."

"Aye, aye, cupcake. I promise we will find the map. You be careful."

Ash shook Bob's hands. "I'll take care of her, Bob. Don't worry."

Bob smiled. "Thanks, Ash. That makes me feel *so* much better. I'd keep practicing your shooting if I were you."

Bob boarded the helicopter as Julia waved to their friends and they headed to Rome.

Comrades, all of them, Bob thought. They were the best damn team he'd ever fought with in his entire career.

CHAPTER 7

Under the Radar

When Randy landed in New York, he knew it was going to be a different work environment without his boss. When Bob and Julia were in town, it felt as if they were Randy's bodyguards. They were very protective — almost worse than his parents. With the couple in Rome, Randy wasn't prepared for the heightened security Bob put in place during his absence. He felt like he was back in a United States intelligence agency again. He looked out the window of the company helicopter and saw two black SUVs with eight armed body guards waiting for him. When the door opened, four of the bodyguards came running and surrounded him as he got into the SUV. Damn, it was like he was the president of the United States on Air Force One.

"My name is Mr. Bear," one of the bodyguards said. "Bob said that I'm to protect you with my life and not to let anything happen to you. He said you're in control of the company in his absence. I'll take you to the office."

"Should I call you Bear or Mr. Bear?

"My friends call me Bear. So may you."

"I would like to go to my apartment before going to the office."

"No can do. Bob had us move all your stuff to the 98th floor. He had it converted into penthouse apartments. All the work was done in secrecy. Looks like you've been promoted."

"Well, then, to the office it is."

When they arrived, Randy was greeted by Jeannie, one of Randy's first hires. She looked excited to see him. "Bob promoted me to office manager and said you're the boss of the company."

"Well, that was my job," Randy said.

"Oh, Randy, things are changing around here so fast. Bob made you CEO. He's still the president but you're the main decision maker now."

"Well, hold on to your hat because I have news. Cordy is no longer the owner of the company. She signed it over to Bob. I think she feels something terrible is going to happen to her. She wanted Bob to have the company and now he's gone.

"Jeannie, I am so glad Bob picked you to be part of my support team. It's good to have a trusted friend by my side during these trying times. What have I missed while I was gone?"

"Follow me to your new office, sir."

"Wait a minute Jeannie, I've told you a hundred times not to call me sir. Come on, Bob wouldn't let me call him sir. He said after he left the Navy he never wanted to say sir again. Just call me Randy. The promotion doesn't change anything. If you ever see me getting arrogant, call me out and remind me to be the Randy you know."

"Yes, sir, just joking with you." They laughed, and it broke the tension between them.

As they rode the elevator to the 98th floor she briefed Randy on everything that was happening. When they got to his office he couldn't believe his eyes. An opened door led to a luxury penthouse apartment with an incredible view of New York. Jeannie already had his name and title on the door. This was unusual for the company. Bob really didn't believe in special treatment for management. All the extra dollars went to working projects. Bob must have felt security could protect him if he were on site.

"I put all your mail on your desk, but pay attention to the brown manila envelope — it has a strange return address."

Randy sat down and rifled through the envelopes and pulled out the suspiciously large brown one. Jeannie was right. It looked strange. It had a picture of the three wise monkeys with descriptions under each one — see no evil, hear no evil and speak no evil.

"Jeannie, did this go through our regular screening for possible contaminants?"

"Yes, I had it checked twice."

"Well, here goes."

As he started to open it, Jeannie cautioned, "Do you think that's wise? If you want you could go to the hall for safety, and I will open it for you."

Wow, she would risk her life to protect me.

"No, that's OK. I think danger comes with the job, but I would like *you* to step out just in case."

"Randy, you know me better than that. I will always be at your side through everything."

"Well, then go out in the hall and ask Bear if he could come in." She turned and walked out and sure enough she came back with Bear.

"Bear, I have a suspicious package that needs to be opened." Bear put on rubber gloves and walked over without hesitation. He took special care with the package and opened it. Looking inside, he said. "We're clear," and then he shook out the contents onto the desk.

Randy cautiously looked at the stack of papers. On the front of the stack, a note was written: YOUR PHONE WILL RING IN A FEW SE-CONDS AND IT WILL BE FROM AN UNNAMED CALLER. ANSWER IT.

As Randy thumbed through the rest of the papers, he saw some that looked funny because they just had sets of numbers. Others had names of banks and account numbers. There were some pages that had only company names on them.

Randy's cell phone rang. and he quickly answered it, "Hello, this is Randy, with whom do I have the pleasure of speaking with?"

A female voice came through the other side of the phone. "I am the head of a secret organization that was set up by the Diplomat Brat Corps in honor of Linda, Ash's friend who died for a better world. We call ourselves The All-Seeing Eyes because we have eyes everywhere. We see the evil and we hear the evil and we will speak about this evil to you and only you. What you have in front of you is the first installment of information from the Dark Watchers' net-work. Knowledge is power. We have set up our organization based on one of the most powerful women of her time, Eleanor of Aqui-taine. She had great knowledge and knew how to use it in a world of powerful men. We have computer geeks, and we know how to use them. We work behind the scenes. The first group of numbers is latitude and longitude coordinates for over a thousand Dark Watcher hold-outs, weapons stores, and food banks.

"The second group of papers contains the names of banks that launder their money and the last group is a list of global companies in which they have a controlling interest. This information should keep you and your team busy for a while.

"We know all about the Bear. He has a great record. You couldn't be in better hands, and Jeannie, you rock, girl. Your new office manager would take a bullet for you, Randy. She's a keeper."

As the girl was speaking, Randy reached into his top drawer and pulled out the Stones of Truth. Ash had brought them back from Egypt. One stone was engraved with the heart of Osiris and the other, the head of Ibis. They were used to determine if someone spoke the truth. If they moved together, the speaker was being truthful. If they were lying, the stones moved apart. Randy placed the stones two inches apart. He whispered, "O, Keeper of the balance, let her heart be revealed. Is everything she is saying true?"

The stones moved together. "You speak the truth and your heart is true," Randy said. "Well, I'll be!"

"Well, I need to get off this line. Don't try to find out who I am. Keep a lookout in your mail. You will know what to look for on the outside of the envelope. Remember this: it's up to you to keep this top secret." Randy heard a click and she was gone.

"Well I think we just hit the lottery, Jeannie. Let's get to work planning our next attack. Oh, and Jeannie, you inherit the Stones of Truth. The magical stones can tell the heart of any man or woman. Their secret power will help you know if someone lies in their interviews or reports. Now that you are the new office manager, you have the responsibility of keeping them safe. Use them wisely and guard them with your life.

Jeannie smiled. "Well, you did have me worried having rocks in your desk."

Chapter 8

Roman Holiday

Brother Michael packed as fast as he could and tried to hide his excitement. He loved his friends Aziza and Han, but he needed a change of scenery. He had spent years studying ancient texts at Saint Catherine's Monastery near Mount Sinai and loved the life of solitude. He was an archaeologist and had enjoyed the quiet life of a scholar at the monastery for most of his life. A house filled with babies was not for him. He called his close colleague and friend, Father Antonio, who lived in Rome, and told him he was coming to visit. They hadn't seen each other for five years but on the phone, it was like they had been separated only yesterday. Brother Michael told him his friends would need a place to stay and everything was to be top secret. Father Antonio had connections in the Vatican and would help them get the access they needed. As an added bonus, the father said he had an idea of where the map of the Lost

Tribe could be located. All was arranged. His friend would await him in Rome.

Han saw how happy his friend was when he heard the call from Ash and wished he could go, too. Aziza grew bigger and was entering her nesting stage. Every day the two elder men worked getting prepared for the twins who would come soon. Ash's mother's pregnancy was going well, but Aziza needed her husband to be with her. Han dreamed of reading some of the ancient manuscripts kept in the Vatican but knew his place was with his wife during this crucial time. Mary, the housekeeper for the late Chief Saunhac, helped Aziza and her kindness was much appreciated. She made their transition to life in Nova Scotia so much easier but still Han knew Brother Michael longed for his libraries.

Brother Michael would be taking another friend with him to Rome from Nova Scotia, Grey Smoke's prodigy named Wapek. The name Wapek was Mi'kmaq for white. He was the eldest pup of Grey Smoke's litter. His father was the chief's wolf dog. Brother Michael helped train Wapek to be a service dog, keeping them both busy, and he came to love the dog with all his heart. Cordy's grandfather Bill stopped by to visit them and helped Brother Michael get the papers for a service dog. What better way to get through security but with a service dog, the men figured. Randy had sent him the glasses he needed to take pictures of map.

Ash's mom gave him a hug. "Thank you for saving my family. I want you to know how much I appreciate all you have done for us."

Brother Michael smiled at the pregnant woman beaming up at him. "I feel like I'm family. You've never let me doubt it."

Han clasped his friend's hand. "You are family. You are my brother."

The car pulled up to take him and his well-trained companion to the airport. Han, Aziza, and Mary waved good-bye to him and wished him luck on his journey.

They flew in Cordy's private plane. Brother Michael started doing more research about the Lost Tribes of Israel. Many of the documents talked of myths and legends left behind by the scholars of the past. Some of the earlier explorers thought the Native American tribes were possible descendants of the Lost Tribes of Israel. Archaeologists today have found no evidence of this theory but many religious scholars in the past believed in it. Legend said that after the destruction of the Temple in Jerusalem, the Lost Tribes would be found and they would play a part in the last days of Earth.

Explorers such as La Salle, Marquette, and others sent back reports to Rome with a map of the tribes' sacred lands and settlements. The Mississippi River had many similarities to Egypt's Nile River. Brother Michael studied in Egypt knowing full well the importance of water to the ancients. Water was key to life and its spirit was revered amongst the tribes. They placed their sacred lands near the waterways. Some believed water was a powerful energy which helped grow crops and cleanse the land.

Father Antonio had investigated the Gallery of Maps, which was created by geographer Danti of Italy. He'd not discovered any documents pertaining to North America in that room, but he felt a small office which held copies of archived maps from the New World could be found in a vault that could be accessed through the once-secret staircase of Pope Urban VIII's chapel. The office was the size of a big closet but contained a vast database. A secretary worked there. The files were photo copies of the originals from the Vatican libraries. It was designed to be easily accessible to scholars. The problem was that only clergy scholars were allowed access.

Brother Michael and Father Antonio fit the requirements, but Bob and Julia did not. A plan was being formed on how to get them into the small office.

Brother Michael read reports that the vault and staircase had been recently renovated. Pope Urban VIII had created a passageway between Sixtus the V's apartment and that of Julius II. He wanted his own private chapel and created the Secreta Scala, also known as the secret stairway. The Apostolic Palace was filled with secret chambers and passageways but known only to a few. Pope Urban VIII had the great painter and architect Pietro Cortona decorate the chapel.

Pietro Cortona descended from a long line of masons and painters. His reputation through Italy was well known and he became the head of the Guild of Saint Luke. The guild exists today, and many famous artists have been members of the illustrious famous organization. The monk's instincts told him the Pure of Heart would leave a clue near where the map was located.

Pope Urban VIII had many controversies during his reign but one of his biggest was with Galileo. The great astronomer's fatal mistake was making fun of Pope Urban VIII in his petition, which placed Galileo in prison for the rest of his days. The "father of science" had made an incredible telescope which allowed him to see the moons of Jupiter. Galileo discovered sunspots, comets, and the phases of Venus. The century-old battle between science and religion continued for many years after Galileo's death.

Ancient man looked to the stars for signs of the future. Ancient astronomers would produce horoscopes for many of the kings and queens. Brother Michael knew many extinction-level events such as the disappearance of the dinosaurs were blamed on anomalies of the heavens such as an asteroid hitting Earth. Galileo knew how

Earth related to the other planets and the sun. Special powerful forces were at play and sometimes collisions and tremendous explosions occurred in an ever-changing galaxy.

Brother Michael leaned back in his seat and closed his eyes while Wapek slept at his feet. He would be in Rome in a few hours and then the treasure hunt would begin. The academic grinned and thought, *what a wonderful Roman holiday.*

CHAPTER 9

Carpe Diem

Bob was dressed in a black business suit, and Julia looked out the airplane window at the eternal city of Rome below them. They weren't normal tourists because they packed a few goodies in their bags. Both were armed for battle. Julia wore a wrist camera as a back-up to take pictures of the Lost Tribes map. One can never have enough resources on a mission. Murphy's law seemed to always play a part in her assignments. She wore a silk tan and black dress showing off her great figure. Bob looked at her three-inch stilettos and smiled.

"Are you going to be able to run over cobblestones in those shoes? I don't know what kind of trouble to expect. Maybe you should sit this one out and wait for me at the hotel."

Julia smiled back but there was fire in her eyes. "Where est you go my husband, I go est. These heels won't slow me down. They have a special feature you might like." She pulled off her shoe and clicked the side. A tiny razor-sharp knife blade sprung out from the heel.

"Now that's a sexy pair of shoes," Bob said. "I like the way you think, dear."

The two newlyweds clinked their champagne glasses together and whispered, "Salut!"

The clear blue sky and Italian sun shone as they got off the plane. The couple put on their sunglasses. Their limo was waiting for them. Bob ordered their chauffer to a convent in Vatican City where Brother Michael was to meet them.

"Have you met Brother Michael?" Julia asked. "Can you recognize him?"

Bob put his arm over her shoulder in the back seat. "I met him in Nova Scotia with Ash's crazy parents. He seemed like a nice guy. I'll recognize him."

Julia looked out the car window. "I had a memory of the chairman last night. It's weird how the memories I'd repressed are coming back to me. I remembered how he killed my parents and how he abused me as a child. I was terrified of him. Julia was frightened of him but not Ellen. I'm not afraid anymore. I've seen the light, as some would say.

"You know Bob, you fell in love with Ellen and she fell in love with you that day in the elevator. She's a part of me just as much as Julia, and what endears you to me is that you love us both. I remember you at my bedside in the hospital. You never left me. Julia emerged out of the fog and there you were, holding the light guiding my way.

"Chief Saunhac brought me back too. What an amazing man! I still can't believe the sacrifice he made for me. I won't let you down. If anything happens, I want you to know I love you. You're the best thing that ever happened to me." She turned and kissed him lov-ingly.

Bob gazed back at her. "How could I forget that elevator ride? We were both fed up with those sanctimonious idiots at the meet-ing. Yes, it was Ellen at the meeting, but I always believed tender-hearted Julia warned me they were going to kill me if I stayed. You have an incredible inner strength and intuition. I recognized a true fighter when I met you. I love you, too. Don't you ever forget it."

Julia kissed him again. "I know but if I catch you flirting with any Italian girls, I'll kill you."

Bob laughed. "Roger that."

The chauffer announced, "Santa Maria Convent."

Bob looked out the limo window. "What the hell, he brought a wolf with him to Rome. You've got to be kidding me." Julia couldn't believe her eyes as she looked out her window.

Outside the ancient Roman villa-turned-convent and church stood an elderly monk holding the leash to a huge white wolf-dog and a suitcase. Brother Michael looked like a blind man being led by his service dog. He wore the dark glasses with the high-tech camera that Randy had given him. The door opened, and the wag-ging dog jumped in and barked a greeting to Bob and Julia. Brother Michael shook hands with Bob and smiled at Julia as the door shut.

"Bob and Julia, how nice to see you. I hear congratulations are in order. Are we ready for an adventure?"

"Can I ask who your friend is?" Julia asked.

"Of course. Let me introduce Wapek, my service dog. As you can see, he's very friendly. He's a wolf-dog, a mix between gray wolf and Siberian husky."

Julia reached over and petted the gorgeous creature with the softest fur and bluest eyes.

"He's gorgeous. Where did you get him?"

Wapek licked Julia's hand. Bob reached over and petted him, too.

"You know his father, Grey Smoke, Bob. He's part of his litter. He's been a great companion and is a certified service dog. I've been training service dogs in my spare time. We're going to need him to get through security. In the Vatican, no pictures are allowed so a blind priest with these special high-tech dark glasses won't be suspicious. The cameras in the glasses are top notch.

"My friend has procured us all the needed papers, but I will need both of you to change before we reach the Apostolic Palace in the Vatican. I brought your clothes. Randy helped me with your sizes."

Bob petted Wapek's furry head again. "I remember Grey Smoke. He saved our asses in Nova Scotia. Grey Smoke and his pack took out the Dark Watchers. I think it's great he's a service dog. You're right, security should let us through easier."

Julia opened the bag with their clothes and raised her eyebrows.

"I'm supposed to be a nun, and I believe you're a priest." She pulled out her long black habit with a veil and his white collar and black cassock. They both laughed at the absurdity of it.

"I know it's funny for both of you but remember. you're in Rome. Father Roberto and Sister Joan will be your names. You're both here for an interview at the Vatican. The real Father Roberto and Sister Joan have been delayed so my friend has all the badges ready.

"After security, we will meet my friend who is the administrator of the Vatican archives. He will take us to where the map of the Lost Tribes should be located.

"These should help us get through security."

Brother Michael handed Bob the dark glasses. "Father Roberto is blind, so you will wear these instead of the glasses Randy gave you back in the States. They have been outfitted so you can take video and camera shots. Everyone at the home office and headquarters will receive your photos and will be watching. They'll be able to communicate with you as well in the event that they have questions."

"I bet I hear lots of laughing when they see our outfits."

"Brother Michael, close your eyes."

Julia and Bob put on their costumes. When they arrived at the Apostolic Palace, the door of the limo opened and Father Roberto, wearing dark glasses and holding onto Wapek's leash emerged, followed by Sister Joan and Brother Michael.

"Carpe Diem, my friends. All the world's a stage. Men and women are mere players. Let the performance begin."

CHAPTER 10

Book of Enoch

In the late hours, Ash sat with the Book of Enoch and its variations before him. He contemplated how for centuries it was considered a mysterious book. It was forbidden by some churches as it was considered non-canonical. Others such as the Ethiopian Tewahedo Church considered it sacred. The book of Jude in the New Testament referred to Enoch. The Essenes hid away the Dead Sea Scrolls which contained parts of the Book of Enoch in the caves of Qumran when Rome confiscated many of their precious relics. One wondered if they saw far into the future the coming destruction of Jerusalem and discovery of their precious books.

Ash opened up the Book of Enoch and began reading a section about the War of Heaven:

The Watchers, or holy ones, came down from Heaven to watch men. A war sprang out because a group took the daughters of Eve as wives and had children. Hybrids, known as the Children of the Nephilim, were the result. They were evil offspring and were considered dangerous to humanity. A rebellion resulted as the Watchers split into two factions. One faction could not give up Eve's daughters and allow mankind to remain in peril and possible destruction. They obeyed the rules of the Lord of Hosts and worked for the survival of mankind. The other faction defended the Nephilim way of life and all of its evilness, creating human technology that led to weapon production and sorcery. The door to heaven was closed to those who betrayed the Council of Heaven.

Upon finishing the section, Ash realized that the Dark Watchers and the Light Watchers took their names from the Book of Enoch. He also realized that just like long ago, he and his friends were fighting a war to save Earth and her children from destruction.

Ash continued reading and made notes of facts and his impressions: Enoch must have been a Pure of Heart. Uriel took him up to heaven to give him knowledge regarding the sun, moon, stars, and planets. He was instructed in mathematics and given a solar calendar so that he could calculate the cycle of seasons. He was given treasures to help the Pure of Heart in their fight against the Children of the Nephilim. He traveled through a triangular-shaped portal to help testify in the trial of the Watchers. Later, Uriel would assist Noah, Enoch's descendant. Sacred knowledge was given to save life not destroy it.

The giants must have struggled like the rest of mankind in a hostile environment. One of the lessons the giants didn't learn was that size doesn't always matter. Goliath, at first, wielded his sword in defense of his people but soon became cruel and arrogant. He was taken down by a much smaller young man with a stone and a sling. A courageous heart and brilliant mind can overcome and defeat huge obstacles!

The Book of Dreams, one of the chapters within the original Book of Enoch, talks about Enoch's visions of the future and the Great Deluge. It also explains that the treasures of the Pure of Heart were protected and housed in the Temple for the day when they would be needed. But, when invaders entered the Holy Land, the treasures of the Pure of Heart were removed from the temple and were secreted away. Many seeking the treasures didn't realize that only a Pure of Heart could wield them. Many tried and were met with death. De Villiers knew this about the treasures — that only a Pure of Heart can touch them. That's why he needed the Pure of Heart to accomplish his goals.

The Book of Enoch was written in the second century B.C. and for centuries only a few knew of its contents. Do we have technologically superior protectors from the past who created the Guardian? Enoch, a Pure of Heart, was shown the stars by the angel Uriel. Many of the Pure of Heart treasures were hidden in locations tied to the stars and the sun.

Ash murmured, "It's all here. Enoch describes the battle of good and evil since the beginning of time. Sometimes it's a skirmish. Sometimes it's a battle. Sometimes it's a war. With De Villiers and his hunt for the Pure of Heart and their treasures, we're in an all-out war. We must discover what we need to find the treasures and stop De Villiers once and for all."

CHAPTER 11

Secret Staircase

Swiss guards stood at attention outside the doors of the palace. Through the large metal doors and past the guards, a smiling elderly priest rushed to embrace his friend.

"Brother Michael, I'm so excited you have come and bring such wonderful guests. It is such an honor."

"Let me introduce to you Father Antonio, my good friend and fellow colleague. We attended college together. These are my dear friends, Father Roberto and Sister Joan, from the Angelic Missions. Their good works are known to you. Wapek is Father Roberto's faithful service dog and companion."

Father Antonio placed the security badge around Bob's neck and then over Julia's. "Please follow me. Brother Michael has told me you have little time so let us proceed."

Bob hit the button on the side of his glasses to film while Randy, back in New York, taped the film footage from Bob glasses. Julia clicked on her wristband camera for back up. Father Antonio walked over to the Swiss Guard and presented all of their documents.

Father Antonio explained, "Father Roberto is blind and requires his service dog. Brother Michael is their assistant and my friend. We are in a bit of a hurry as Father Roberto and Sister Joan are scheduled for an interview and the television crew is waiting for them."

The Swiss Guard inspected the papers. Since the papers were in order and Father Antonio was highly regarded, the three clerics and the snow-white dog were waved through rather than having to pass through the metal detectors. Not wanting to arouse suspicion, they strolled into the Sistine Chapel as if they were tourists. Above them, on the ceiling, was Michelangelo's magnificent painting, *The Last Judgment.*

"This is where popes are elected," Julia said. "The dimensions of the Sistine Chapel are the same as Solomon's Temple. What a coincidence that Cordy wears Solomon's ring."

Bob turned his head and looked at her. "The Keys opened heaven's doorway. Ash found the Keys of Life in Egypt. Can the keys open it? I bet De Villiers wants to open the doorway." He stared at Julia. "We are talking about heaven, right?"

Julia nodded. "Yes, it's written in Matthew16:18-19. Look at this fresco. Peter is carrying a key in his hand. Solomon's Temple is the octagonal building in the background. The stories of the creation of Adam, and the Great Flood are depicted also up above our heads. It's the story of mankind."

Brother Michael smiled. "Saint Catherine of Alexandria is above us, too. How beautiful she is. Ash saw her holding a crystal ball in her hand in her painting. Is it a coincidence that the Guardian is connected with the crystal ball the chief gave to Ash? My research work in Alexandria was my dream, but I'm in heaven here in Rome. We appreciate your help, my friend."

Father Antonio nodded. "The Pure of Heart has played their part over the course of time. The paintings above have recorded man's struggle to survive. Let us continue on our journey, shall we?" He pointed to the other rooms past the golden doors.

They walked on to the Raphael Rooms, where the *School of Athens*, depicting the great philosophers of the time, was hanging. Plato, Socrates, and Aristotle as well as Pythagoras were painted in rich color for all to see.

"This is astounding!" Brother Michael remarked. "Thank you so much for giving me this precious gift. The men standing in this painting represent the great minds of mankind through history."

"I want you to see something we recently discovered in our renovations," Father Antonio said. "It has to do with your work. Follow me."

They walked on further to the Borgia Apartments where Father Antonio pointed to a painting called *The Resurrection*.

"Now look at Pinturicchio's fresco. It was painted after Christopher Columbus's return from the New World. Some scholars believe that the figures in the background are images of Native Americans. Many believed Columbus's trip had remained top secret in Spain during the time this painting was produced but it seems Pope Alexander VI knew all about it.

"The Lost Tribes map is another example of how information leaked out and found its way here. We have kept the Lost Tribes map in a secret place, but we have access to a copy of it."

With his glasses, Bob took a close-up view of Pinturicchio's fresco for the peanut gallery back home. He could almost hear their excitement as he scanned the painting. Ash would have loved to have been there with them.

They entered a smaller room decorated with frescoes when Bob heard a whisper in the corner of the room. A familiar face in a Swiss Guard uniform stared at him. "I see the sign of the Pure of Heart on the fresco above the archway. Get closer, Father Roberto."

Bob's surprised face made Julia look closer at the handsome red-haired Swiss Guard. Bob never talked about Uriel but then Bob didn't talk much about his past.

"What a coincidence. Uriel, is that you? I didn't know you worked for the Swiss Guard. Let me introduce you to my friends. Uriel and I met at Chief Saunhac's funeral. You're a man with many talents."

Brother Michael and Father Antonio smiled at Bob's friend. Uriel petted Wapek and the dog licked his hand. Julia didn't know what to think. She looked at Bob, who seemed genuinely happy to see this mysterious redhead.

"What about this painting?" Bob moved closer, so all could see it.

"Ah, Father Roberto, the painting is above the secret staircase of Pope Urban VIII. This room is his chapel. The painting was done by Cortona. He was head of the Saint Luke's Guild. The name of this particular work is the *Deposition of Christ*."

Uriel whispered to Bob, "Notice Mother Mary's hands are the same as the hands of Christ in Caravaggio's painting *The Taking of Christ*. You're in the right place, my friend. Duty calls so I must leave you all. I hope you find all of Rome's treasures. Till we meet again! Arrivederci, Father Roberto and lovely Sister Joan."

Father Antonio went to the wall and clicked a small wooden heart carved in the paneling. A panel opened slowly.

"Follow me. We shall take the secret staircase to the archives office." They went down a narrow staircase and entered what looked to be a closet. Inside was a small office where one gray-haired priest sat working at his desk. He smiled when he saw them.

"Hello, Father Antonio, and welcome Father Roberto, Brother Michael, and Sister Joan. What a beautiful dog."

"My friends, this is Father Lorenzo. I told him that you were coming and what you wanted to see. He's located the copy of the Lost Tribes map."

They all shook hands and gathered around his desk. Before them was a yellowed copy of a map of the New World. It displayed the Mississippi River and the East Coast shore line.

Brother Michael pointed to the document. "This map is unique because it shows the sacred lands of all the tribes and their names. This is truly amazing."

Bob got as close as possible to the map to scan it with his wristband camera. Julia pretended to adjust her veil and did a back-up recording as well. Randy sent Bob a signal through his glasses letting him know the transmission was coming through clearly. The team back home was getting an eyeful.

Several tribes and their lands were recorded on the map — Huron, Algonquin, Choctaw. There were other markers, too, that would need to be researched. He was certain that once Ash saw the video recording of the map that he would go into Mr. Archaeologist Historian mode and get the answers they needed.

Father Antonio said, "I'm sorry Father Lorenzo, we must bring our visit to an end. It is time for us to go." Thanking Father Lorenzo for his assistance, Bob, Julia, and Brother Michael shook his hand and followed Father Antonio out of the room.

As Father Antonio led them out of the room a man rushed up to them and urgently said, "We must hurry. The interview with Father Roberto and Sister Joan begins in seven minutes!"

CHAPTER 12

Surrounded by Evil

No one knew the Dark Watchers better than Jon, but even he thought it'd be a miracle if he could get Master Wong, Peter, Chris, Ash, Sam and Cordy up to St. Louis undetected. Bob and Julia had left for Rome and Randy was at headquarters in New York. Jon knew the toughest job lie ahead. How could he keep them alive?

Sam could see the struggle in her big brother's face. He always felt as if he had to be in control. He didn't like relinquishing responsibility to his little sister especially when situations were so dangerous. However, daylight was burning, and it was time to go. Sam had just gotten a call from a friendly Dark Watcher who told her De Villiers' men knew where they were. They had only thirty minutes before the men would arrive.

Sam looked at her big brother. "Get over it! You know I can get us all to St. Louis without getting anyone killed. You're on my turf now, Jon."

"You don't understand, little sister. I feel this will be the most dangerous trip of our lives."

"Oh, big brother, do you remember the day I started working for the family? It was my seventeenth birthday. You told me that every day could be my last but that you guaranteed me that it would be the adventure of a lifetime even if it only lasted a few days. Three weeks later, we had a shipment taken and I was pushed overboard by one of the crew. I floated in the Gulf of Mexico all night with two dead bodies on either side of me. As the sharks started to feed, I could only think about how it could be me next. But as the sun came up, there you were pulling your boat up next to me with the biggest smile on your face. Do you remember what you said to me? You said, 'Hey, sister, sister, how was the night shift?' Do you remember what I told you?"

"Yes, you said, 'just another day on the job.' I was never so glad as when I pulled you up out of the water and your legs were still there. Sam, I think this time we're going to get real bloody."

"Hey, just another day on the job. I know my turf, Jon, so when I tell you to run, you run and when I say stop, you stop. I'm in charge of this mission!"

"OK, I get it, Sam."

"You get it. Oh, that's just great, he gets it."

"OK, I'll do it. I'll do it."

"Men, what are you going to do with them? Well, you should go and pack, brother."

"You know I've already packed and my things are in the car. I noticed your stuff was in there last night. When has a Lafitte not been ready to run?" They both laughed.

As the rest of their group came downstairs Sam started to bark out orders. "We needed to leave two minutes ago. Let's get a move on it, everyone." She winked at Ash. "We're in two cars. Jon, Chris, Master Wong and Cordy are in the first car. Everyone else will go with me in car two."

Like, I didn't see that coming, Cordy thought to herself.

Sam's phone rang. "Hello, this is Sam. Speak. OK, so everything is on schedule. We'll be there in five minutes.

"Jon it's time to roll, so stay close. We're just going down the road to the town of St. James. The boat is waiting for us. Try to keep up, brother." Everyone hustled to their assigned vehicle. The cars flew down the driveway at breakneck speed.

It was only four miles to St. James. Before they knew it they were unloading at a boat marina. Standing at the end of one of the walkways, one of Sam's employees held the rope to her Moggaro 700 water jet. It had fourteen seats and could outrun anything on the river. The name on the back of the boat was "Who's your Momma."

Jon grinned. "Well, little sister, looks like you're in competition with my boat, Who's Your Daddy." Everyone was loaded and the vibration of the engines starting was enough to make them all think this would be a ride they weren't going to forget.

Peter came up to Sam and pulled her to the side. "Sam, I think I should stay and take one of the cars and lead the Dark Watchers away from the group."

"Peter, you know that would mean death."

"Not necessarily, Sam. I'm sure I'll be able to get away."

Sam could sense something was wrong, but she couldn't put her finger on it. "Peter, I'm the captain of this team, and I said get in the boat now!"

Sam started to power out into the main current of the mighty Mississippi River, pulling on the throttle. The boat took off like a rocket! She turned back to look at Peter. He was as white as a ghost.

What she couldn't know was that when Peter was just eleven years old, his parents had to flee China after the Dark Watchers found out their son was a Pure of Heart. He made such a scene at the ship yard because he didn't want to get in the shipping container. There was a picture of a dragon painted on the outside of the container. Peter didn't understand that it was the only way they were going to get out of the country.

His father had sold everything they had just to save him. When they were in the container and the door was shut, the dock worker spray painted a large X on the outside. They were marked for death.

Peter remembered the swinging motion of the container as they loaded it on the ship headed for America. They had food, water and light, but it was unbearably hot. The bathroom consisted of a five-gallon bucket, and the trip lasted seven days.

When they pulled into San Francisco and felt the ship come to a stop, they felt as if they had a new lease on life. As the crane operator came across the container that had the X on it, Peter's life was changed forever.

The operator pushed the container into the ocean. It hit the water with such a force that his mother was killed instantly. As water flowed into the container, his father franticly tried to open the doors, but they were locked from the outside. Then he felt the container hit the bottom, resting on the sea floor with the locked doors facing upward.

His father took off his belt and looped it over one of the bars on the door that kept the doors closed. His father knew they were running out of time and in Mandarin, directed at Peter to hold on to his belt and find any air that might get trapped.

When Peter grabbed onto the belt, he realized that his mother's lifeless body was floating next to him. He started to cry but he saw his father shaking his head no. The flash light his father was holding was about to go out; it kept blinking on and off.

As the container filled with water, Peter's father handed him the flashlight. Peter realized that his father wasn't planning on making it. His father reached up and patted him on the head and then pushed himself down into the water. Peter saw air bubbles come to the surface. When the bubbles stopped, he knew his father was gone. His eyes filled with tears, but he pushed them back. He knew he was going to join them soon.

Peter's head was pushed to the corner where a small air pocket allowed him to breathe just a little while longer. When he started to get groggy, he knew that he was running out of oxygen and wouldn't be able to hold on. His father's black belt was the only thing Peter could see in the small bit of space providing life. He was just about gone when the bucket that they used as a toilet bumped into him. It was floating because the lid was still in place. He reached into his pocket and pulled out a pocket knife. Peter punched a hole in the bucket's lid and put his mouth over it and breathed in the foulest air he could imagine but it gave him more time.

The shipyard had gotten word of the container falling overboard and dispatched one of the several contracted salvage companies. To keep the shipping lane and the port free from debris the contractors had to remove containers as soon as possible. On that day, the contractor was William McDermott's company, from Montreal. Two divers went down to connect the cables so they could pull it up. Peter was surprised to feel the container start to move again. It took about fifteen minutes to make it to the surface. Peter ran out of air just before the container was lifted out of the water.

The salvage company wanted to get the water out as fast as they could because they now owned the contents. When they opened the doors, they found Peter and the lifeless bodies of his mother and father. One of the divers was an ex-Navy SEAL and had some EMT training. He checked the bodies for a pulse but didn't expect to find one on any of the victims.

First the man — nothing. Then the woman — nothing. When he tried Peter, he could feel a faint hint of one and called out for help. He cleared his airway and rolled him onto his side and pounded on his back. Peter began spraying sea water out of his mouth and nose, taking in large breaths of air. He was going to live, but at the same time, his heart was broken. He vowed never again to love any human like he did his parents.

The captain of the salvage operation called back to corporate to find out what they should do with the boy. Bill McDermott told them to take him to an orphanage in San Jose, California, and give the boy to a nun by the name of Sister Agnes. She would know what to do. And she did. She called her dear friend back in St. Louis, Master Wong. He was the only person she knew who spoke fluent Mandarin.

One week later, he flew out and picked up Peter and took him home. Master Wong never married but God blessed him with an adopted son. Peter had never gone near water again until today and it shook him to his core, bringing up memories as if it were yesterday.

Ash remembered a time on the Nile River, when an old man and his grandson helped him escape and suspected he was with an army of Pure of Hearts headed to do battle. *I bet that old man didn't think I was going to live one day after he dropped me off,* Ash thought.

Ash jumped up and went to Sam. "I was thinking, Sam, that we should lay low when everyone is looking for us. I had an old man teach me how to stay alive and it worked the first time."

Sam smiled at Ash. "You're right. I have to get up the river to the town of Union in the next twenty minutes to meet up with my secret hide-out."

"You have a secret hide-out?"

"You'll see, Ash man, I won't let anything happen to that ass of yours. I like it too much. Now my brother on the other hand said if you got left behind it wouldn't hurt his feelings at all. But I think I'm falling in love with you and so you aren't going anywhere. If the vet doc doesn't want you, well, you can have a backup plan." She winked at him.

Back at the crumbling plantation house, the Dark Watchers surrounded the mansion. A few men ran in, but they came out disappointed that their prey had gotten away. The commander figured the only way they could have gone was north. He bellowed, "If we can catch them, the sky's the limit in reward money. Let's hit it!"

The cars flew down the driveway and turned north on Highway 18. They knew the prize was close at hand.

Sam knew every minute was going to count so she never let up on the throttle. As the boat rounded the bend of the river, they could see a very large barge just up ahead. Sam picked up her radio and said, "Shamu, are you there? Come in Shamu. Are you there?"

"This is Shamu. Is that you, Little Orca?"

"Yes, this is Little Orca. Shamu, are you ready for Operation Jonah?"

"No, we have to slow down and stabilize our speed. We'll be ready in five minutes."

"Sorry, Shamu, we have to go now; no time left on the clock."

"Boss, you know we've only done this once before and it almost got you killed."

Sam looked back at everyone on the boat and said, "Don't worry, I've got this. Shamu, get ready in one minute. If you look off to your port side, you'll see me."

"Little Orca, we are a go for Operation Jonah."

With that, Sam took the speedboat and drove straight toward the front of the huge barge. Everyone let out a nervous scream and held on. The front of the barge began to open and the rush of the water was so loud that the only thing anyone could hear was the sound of their own heartbeat.

Sam got back on the radio and said, "We're lined up and slowing down. We'll be ready for lock on my mark."

She counted down while two large lifting arms grabbed on to the speed boat and lifted it out of the water as the barge doors were closing.

Jon shouted, "Yes, little sister."

Everyone gave Sam a round of applause.

Ash had to admit that it was the coolest maneuver he had ever seen, been involved in, and survived.

"Wow, I mean, wow!"

Cordy was just thinking, *show-off.*

The water was drained out of the chamber and two of Sam's staff helped unload everyone out of the speed boat. When Mr. Wong passed Sam she asked him, "What's Peter's problem?" Mr. Wong told her about what happened to Peter when he was eleven and how he never went near water ever again.

Sam was the last one out and Jim, her employee of many years, said, "Boss, that was balls-to-the-wall cool. I was the only one who said you were going to make it."

"Well, thanks for the vote of confidence, Jim." She shook his hand and noticed that she was shaking.

"No, boss, I made so much money on the bet. You're the best."

Sam headed down the line of barges to get to the towboat and command center. The rest of the group was to get settled in for the trip north.

As the Commander of the Dark Watchers came up to the bridge on Highway 18 at Union, Louisiana, there was no sign of any movement of the Pure of Hearts. He slammed his hands on the dashboard of the car and let out a yell, "How could they just vanish into thin air?"

CHAPTER 13

Slow and Hard

Ash was standing in the hallway of the barge with a lost look on his face. He knew that the Mississippi played a critical role in finding what they needed to stop all these crazy vibrations on earth. Julia and Bob needed to come through with the map or all would be lost.

"Hey, quit just standing there like a zombie," Jon said. "Help me with some of this gear we need to get stowed and to our bunks before the barges start to turn." They walked down the hallway to the next barge closing the hatch behind them. When they entered the next barge, they couldn't believe their eyes. It was like walking in to a spaceship. Everything was hi-tech; the living quarters were spacious and bright.

"This is a case of looks can be deceiving," Ash said. "You have a banged-up barge on the outside and on the inside, a communications hub. James Bond would be proud."

Peter came running up to Ash. "You should see all the cool gear they have in here — and a big screen TV in each stateroom. This thing has a bar, fire place, hot tub and sauna room. Lafittes know how to live the good life, I'll give them that."

Chris beckoned out, "Peter, follow me! Wait until you see the dining room in the next barge." They were greeted with white linen tablecloths over tables set with silver. It was better than any five-star hotel restaurant. Master Chef Phillipe, who had trained at one of the top culinary arts schools, approached to take their order.

Ash walked by Master Wong's stateroom and could see him deep in meditation. When he went by Cordy's stateroom, she was passed out on the bed with a trashcan next to her. *I guess the tequila hasn't worn off yet. The motion of the water must not be helping any.* Ash reached in and pulled the door. As he shut it, he said, "Good night, my love." Cordy rolled over in her bed and smiled and then let out a sickly moan.

Ash tossed his gear on his bed and just stood in the middle of his stateroom rubbing his head. Jon poked his head into Ash's room and saw a man who looked like he had the world on his shoulders. "Ash, what can I do to help?"

He looked up at Jon. "I need room."

"You are standing in your room."

"No, I mean I need room."

"You mean you need space to be left alone"

"No, I mean I need a lot more room, like a conference room to spread out all my stuff. I need to look at everything until it comes into focus. I'm missing something, I need to slow down and take a hard look at everything."

"Oh, thank God, Ash, I thought you were having a meltdown.

You scared me. Follow me, I know where there's a conference room." They grabbed his stuff and Ash followed Jon. They had to go into the barge that was two away from the living quarters. Just as they entered they heard a voice come over the intercom, *All lock down for turn. All lock down for turn.* A red light glowed next to the barge door.

"We will need to stay in this barge until they give us the all clear."

Jon walked down two more doors and opened the door to a conference room that would hold up to twenty-five people. "Ash, will this work for you?"

"You're the best. This is just what I need!" Ash went to the large whiteboard and started drawing and making a list. Jon went over to the bar in the corner and pulled out a bottle of red wine and a bottle of white and opened them both. He poured two glasses. Ash looked over at him.

"I don't want any wine, Jon."

"Monsieur Ash, they are not for you but for me alone. I will drink the white at the beginning of the turn and the red at the end of the turn. I know my sister is up in the bridge driving the towboat and, well, you can see how she drove the last boat we were on." Both Jon and Ash broke out in laughter.

CHAPTER 14

Ancient Secret Revealed

Ash spread his books and artifacts across the conference table. Jon sat in the corner chair with his bottles of wine. Ash looked at Jon and shook his head.

"Jon, sometimes when I think, I talk out loud, so just don't pay any attention to me."

"That's OK. Sometimes when I get drunk, I start to sing pirate songs, loudly."

"Interesting. Is that just before you go and plunder some booty?"

"Now, Monsieur Ash, be careful of what you say." Jon pulled out a sharp knife from his boot and with great precision, started to peel an apple he had brought from the kitchen.

"I didn't mean any disrespect, Jon."

"No, no, I just meant the word 'booty' means something completely different today than what you are thinking. I think of plundering a lot of booty everyday but since we left France, I have come up empty-handed."

Ash kept his eyes on the table and started to get a grin on his face. *That meant that Cordy had not been lured or succumbed to Jon's French charm and traps. His prey still eluded him.*

The barge finished its turn and straightened out. Sam's voice came over the intercom. "All clear. It's OK to move around but all guests must stay below, only staff may go on deck."

Ash dove into his books and studied the items they had already accumulated. He started a list on one of his legal pads.

Why did they hide Cordy and me?

Before he could get to question number two a familiar voice came from behind him, but the bright light in the room was a dead giveaway.

"Ash, my friend, why have you not reached out to me before now?"

"Uriel, you always make a great entrance, but I didn't ask for help."

"Yes, you did, you put down a question that no one would be able to answer but me." He handed Ash a pair of sunglasses.

"Thanks, Uriel. You're right. It just doesn't add up."

"Well, let's get started, Ash. Pick up your Bible." Ash had his father's King James version.

"Turn your Bible to Genesis 5 and read 22 and 24."

Genesis 5
²² And Enoch walked with God after he begat Methuselah three hundred years, and begat sons and daughters:
²⁴ And Enoch walked with God: and he was not; for God took him.

"OK, Ash, what did Enoch do?"

"He walked with God."

Uriel pointed. "Ash, let's put that whiteboard to use. Write down *Enoch walked with God.*" As Ash was writing, Uriel decided to brighten the mood. "Oh, Ash, by the way I decided to bring an old friend of yours with me. His first name is Jack and his last name is Daniels. He's a gentleman I think." Uriel pulled out a bottle from under his coat and took a swig.

Ash's head whipped around, and he could see a well-needed gift. "I love Gentleman Jack. Thank you, Uriel. It couldn't have come at a better time." Ash grabbed the bottle from Uriel and tilted his head back to take a long draw on the miracle elixir.

"You're going to need more of this before our conversation ends. Let's continue. OK, Ash, now comes Antar, the head of the Nephilim. Turn to Genesis 6 and read 2, 4, 5, 7, 8, 9, 11, 12 and 18."

Ash started reading as he sipped between verses.

Genesis 6
² That the sons of God saw the daughters of men that they were fair; and they took them wives of all which they chose.
⁴ There were giants in the earth in those days; and also after that, when the sons of God came in unto the daughters of men, and they bare children to them, the same became mighty men which were of old, men of renown.
⁵ And God saw that the wickedness of man was great in the earth, and that every imagination of the thoughts of his heart was only evil continually.
⁷ And the Lord said, I will destroy man whom I have created from the face of the earth; both man, and beast, and the creeping thing, and the fowls of the air; for it repenteth me that I have made them.

⁸ But Noah found grace in the eyes of the Lord.

⁹ These are the generations of Noah: Noah was a just man and perfect in his generations, and Noah walked with God.

¹¹ The earth also was corrupt before God, and the earth was filled with violence.

¹² And God looked upon the earth, and, behold, it was corrupt; for all flesh had corrupted his way upon the earth.

¹⁸ But with thee will I establish my covenant; and thou shalt come into the ark, thou, and thy sons, and thy wife, and thy sons' wives with thee.

"OK, Ash, what does this say to you?"

"Antar was a busy guy. He had relations with the daughters of men and took whoever he wanted as wife. After that, there were giants on Earth and they had relations with the daughters of men and had children. Some of these men became mighty and famous, but their hearts were evil. Earth became filled with violence and corruption. God saw this evil and declared he would destroy mankind. Noah was different. Noah found grace in God's eyes because he was just and walked with the Lord. As a result, when God sent the great flood, Noah's entire family was spared. Noah, his wife, their three sons and their wives entered the ark and waited for the flood to end."

Ash started drawing a family tree of stick people on the board for fun, he made an ugly Antar with a tail. Uriel laughed. "I see you're a better archaeologist than an artist. OK, Ash, what did Antar do?"

"He had children that became mighty, famous men and were evil."

"What was Noah?"

"Noah was a just man who found grace with the Lord and he walked with God."

"OK, Ash, turn to Genesis 7 and read 7, 21, 22 and 23."

Genesis 7
7 And the Lord said unto Noah, come thou and all thy house into the ark; for thee have I seen righteous before me in this generation.
21 And all flesh died that moved upon the earth, both of fowl, and of cattle, and of beast, and of every creeping thing that creepeth upon the earth, and every man:
22 All in whose nostrils was the breath of life, of all that was in the dry land, died.
23 And every living substance was destroyed which was upon the face of the ground, both man, and cattle, and the creeping things, and the fowl of the heaven; and they were destroyed from the earth: and Noah only remained alive, and they that were with him in the ark.

Ash drew a picture of a big boat on the whiteboard and took another swig. He was feeling warm and mellow now. Uriel grabbed the bottle from him. "It's my turn now. OK, Ash, what happened in this text?"

"Everything was destroyed except Noah and the ones who were with him."

"OK, Ash, read Numbers 13:13 and 33 then Deuteronomy 2: 10 and 11 and lastly, 1 Samuel 17: 4 and 51."

Numbers 13
13 And the Lord spoke to Moses, saying, 2 "Send men to spy out the land of Canaan, which I am giving to the children of Israel; from each tribe of their fathers you shall send a man, every-one a leader among them."
33 There we saw the giants[d] (the descendants of Anak came

from the giants); and we were like grasshoppers in our own
sight, and so we were in their sight."
Deuteronomy 2
¹⁰ The Emims dwelt therein in times past, a people great, and
many, and tall, as the Anakims;
¹¹ Which also were accounted giants, as the Anakims; but the
Moabites called them Emims.
1 Samuel 17
⁴ And there went out a champion out of the camp of the Phil-
istines, named Goliath, of Gath, whose height was six cubits
and a span.
⁵¹ Therefore David ran, and stood upon the Philistine, and
took his sword, and drew it out of the sheath thereof, and slew
him, and cut off his head therewith. And when the Philistines
saw their champion was dead, they fled.

"OK, Uriel, where are you going with this?" Ash implored.

"Settle down, Ash. We're getting there. Think of all of the scrip-
tures we've reviewed as a whole. What do you surmise?"

"Enoch walked with God. Antar and the Nephilim were evil and
violent. Noah walked with God and everything was destroyed except for Noah and the ones that were with him. Later Moses sent
men to spy out the land of Canaan and they saw the giants. And
lastly, David and the giant Goliath battle."

"So, the question you have to ask yourself, Ash, is when God destroyed everyone on earth except Noah and his family, how did
Antar's giant Nephilim come to be here after the Great Deluge?"

"Oh, my Uriel, God killed off all the evil and violent people on
Earth, but he saved Antar's seed."

"And how did he do that?"

"Antar's DNA was in the eggs of Noah's sons' wives. That means all people born after the flood are Antar's descendants. When he kills a Pure of Heart, or anyone else for that matter, he's actually encouraging the Children of the Nephilim to kill his descendants. For thousands of years, he has been an accomplice to the murders of his own children, the Pure of Heart!"

"Bingo! You won the prize."

Ash looked up and Uriel was gone. Jon had been sleeping in his chair the whole time. Both bottles were empty. *I need to tell Cordy. This explains so much.*

CHAPTER 15

Lights, Camera, Action

Father Antonio's surprise was obvious to the television producer. "We were not to do the interview until tomorrow."

The well-dressed middle-aged producer begged him. "We are running out of time. I heard from one of the guards that Father Roberto was here with Sister Joan. Please, my friends, give me ten minutes."

Father Antonio and Brother Michael froze.

Julia smiled at the producer and, in fluent Italian, said, "We would be happy to do the interview. I will interpret for Father Roberto because he has a very different accent and is hard of hearing."

Bob and Brother Michael decided to follow Julia's lead. Father Antonio was relieved they didn't cause a scene.

Bob whispered, "OK, so what did you say, and what am I supposed to do?"

Julia looked adorable even in her nun's habit. "Follow my lead, darling."

Bob wasn't used to taking orders on a mission, so this was a new role for him. But he wasn't ready to give any argument to his wife in this precarious situation. "Alright, Sister Joan, lead on."

The stage was set, and makeup applied to Bob and then Julia. The microphones were placed on their clothes. Lights flooded the stage, and the director led the way.

Bob and Julia went to their chairs as Wapek lay at their feet. They sat across from their interviewer, a very young and handsome man named Mario Lombardo. He was famous; his program was watched by millions all around the world.

Brother Michael and Father Antonio sat nervously and removed their rosaries from their pockets. Prayers were in order. Father Roberto didn't speak Italian very well — in fact, not at all.

Mario smiled and in Italian announced, "Ciao! My friends. We are here with Father Roberto and Sister Joan of the Angelic Missions. They are participating in the Better World Project Conference. The project is global. Its goal is to bring a better life for all the children of Earth. Father Roberto, would you please explain why you have come here today?"

Bob waved to the camera. "Ciao!" He then proceeded to act like he spoke Italian and waved his hands in an expressive way speaking with passion, but it was gibberish and ended with a "Mama Mia." Mario sat there not understanding a word while the film crew gazed on in a mix of disbelief and amusement.

For the first time in his career as an interviewer, Mario wasn't able to understand a word that had been said except for the "Mama Mia." He didn't know how to react. He looked in desperation to Sister Joan. This interview was turning into a disaster.

Julia quickly explained in perfect Italian for the audience and Mario, "Father Roberto's accent is difficult to understand since he comes from a very isolated village in the north of Italy. In his early years, he was a sinner who lusted for women, drank, and led a wicked life until he was blinded in an accident from a brick hitting his head. He felt it was a sign from God to change his ways. The sinner had awakened and decided to join the priesthood to serve mankind. His journey took him far and wide. Father Roberto found a generous sponsor whose heart felt the same.

"His benefactor believes in the Better World Project so much that Father Roberto has been authorized to deliver a check for ten million dollars. Father Roberto will continue the work for clean water, food access to all, and protection of the environment for everyone even the animals of the world. Mama Mia, what a wonderful project this is."

Everyone in the room was in shock over the amount of the gift. It took a few moments for Mario to process the wonderful news. In that moment, he realized that he had gone from the most disastrous interview of his life to the greatest.

Mario excitedly jumped out of his chair and ran over to shake Bob's hand.

"Magnifico! Magnifico! Father Roberto and Sister Joan!"

The TV producer announced, "Finito"

Julia whispered for to Bob to write a check as the head of the Better World Project rushed over to collect it. "Grazie!"

Bob looked at Julia with a smile, "Ten million dollars? Not two million, but ten million? I knew you would be high maintenance."

Julia smiled and whispered, "I'm worth every penny. Plus, it's for a good cause and a tax deduction."

The delightfully charismatic Mario whispered in Julia's ear. "Sister

Joan, I noticed your lovely Italian stilettos under your habit. They are exquisite. May I ask why you became a nun?"

Julia spoke softly, "Off the record, Mario, these heels are my favorite and so comfortable. I, too, like Father Roberto suffered from lust, but as you can see, I quit that bad habit and replaced it with a good one."

Mario smiled. "Affascinante and grazie."

Father Antonio and Brother Michael motioned them to follow and everyone waved good-bye as they left and headed for the back door to escape.

CHAPTER 16

It's a Miracle

Bob, Julia, and Brother Michael said their goodbyes and thanks to Father Antonio and headed for the limo when Wapek started barking at the vehicle. He pulled on the leash with a jerk.

Bob had worked with service dogs before when he was a Navy SEAL, and he noticed how agitated Wapek acted. He took his hand and pulled Julia back. His intuition told him to get behind the concrete wall to the right of them. He yelled to Brother Michael and Father Antonio to follow.

"Get back! Something's wrong!"

He had no sooner uttered the warning when the limo exploded. A huge smoke cloud rose from the burning of the vehicle. Screams filled the air as people ran in every direction. Debris scattered all over the cobblestones. Brother Michael spotted a group of men heading for them.

"We've been spotted. Follow me."

They ran through the streets. After several circuitous routes, Brother Michael stopped in one of the doorways of a small church. "We need to split up. Wapek and I will head for Ponte Sant'Angelo to draw them away. You hide here. I will lose them on the way there. You must hide, now!"

Before Bob and Julia could disagree, Brother Michael ran down the street. Bob and Julia went into a church. A confessional stood on the side of the room.

"I think we need to go to confession," Bob said. "What do you say?"

"I like it," Julia answered.

Bob entered the empty priests' stall and closed the door. He opened the screen, thinking he'd see Julia sitting there, but instead found an elderly man waiting for a priest to hear his confession.

"Bless me Father, for I have sinned. I am American, and it's been a long time since I have confessed."

"What is the trouble, my son?" Bob hoped this would be a short list.

"Father, I have had trouble with making love. I think if I let you know my lustful thoughts then I may be forgiven. I've tried everything, Father, and nothing has worked."

Bob wondered where Julia was and tried to get rid of this sinner. He pulled out his gun and placed it on his lap.

"Have you tried medication, my son?"

"It doesn't work, Father. I've cheated on my wife and ever since, there is nothing. I need to be forgiven and to do penance."

Bob heard the surprise in the voice of the elderly man. "Oh my! You must wait your turn, signorina! Oh, I'm so sorry, Sister, please come in."

Julia whispered to the confessor, "I am not a nun. There are wicked men chasing me. Please help me."

"Of course, my child," Bob said. "We will help you. How many men are we talking about?"

Julia sat on the man's lap. "Father, I believe two."

The elderly man felt a stirring through his body as they talked.

The Dark Watchers scoured the church but found no one so they headed out the exit door. They had caught sight of Brother Michael and the dog heading for the Ponte Sant'Angelo.

"I believe, my child, they have left. Thank you, my son, for your good deed to the lady," Bob said. "You are forgiven. Go in peace."

Julia jumped out and Bob grabbed her hand. They ran like the wind down the aisle and out the side door. As they opened the door, they heard an ecstatic cry of the confessor. He threw his arms up to heaven, "It's a miracle!" The elderly man felt something below that he hadn't in years. Bob and Julia smiled at each other.

They caught up to the two Dark Watchers and followed them from a distance. Julia took off her shoes and handed one to Bob.

"I told you these were great shoes." The small razor sharped knife popped out of the heel.

"I want to shoot them. C'mon, let me shoot them. My SEAL buddies would laugh at me if I kill them with a shoe."

Bob tried to get a good grip on the shoe and gave Julia an exasperated look.

"Shut up, it's quieter this way," she said. "You take the one on the right. I'm taking off this habit, too. They'll be looking for a nun, not a tourist."

"Good idea." He pulled off his collar and robes. The business suit underneath would blend in better.

They both snuck up behind their targets. Bob grabbed the bigger man around the neck. His friend ran to help him, but Julia jumped on his back. She learned from experience that the quicker the carotid artery was sliced, the sooner the victim bled out. She cut his throat with expertise. Her husband's technique was a bit rougher and took longer. She almost jumped in to help, but he gave her a ferocious look warning her back.

"I got this!"

Bob wasn't used to killing a man with a shoe. With exasperation he flung the shoe to the side and killed him the old fashion way — he strangled him. Bob dropped the Dark Watcher to the ground and grabbed the communication device the Dark Watcher carried and turned up the volume. They could hear the remaining Dark Watchers running after Brother Michael and then the grim news.

"We've got the monk and dog. Hurry up! We're on the Ponte Sant'Angelo."

CHAPTER 17

Cat and Mouse

Sam came in and in one fluid motion, swung her backpack on the table, threw herself into a conference table chair and slammed her work boots on the table top. She unbuttoned her shirt, took it off and dropped it to the floor. Underneath was a white ribbed tank with a white lacy bra peeking out. Neither one was containing her womanhood from spilling out the sides.

Ash told himself, *don't look! Don't look!* But his eyes wouldn't listen.

Drawing his eyes back to her face, Ash could see how tired she was. Compassionately he said, "Sam, you look exhausted."

"I was up on the bridge making sure we weren't being followed. Everything is looking good."

"I'd like to go up on the bridge some time and see the river for myself."

"Well, Mr. Ash, I can make that happen. I kind of like the thought of you being on top — but only at night. You see, there is a certain rhythm to the river and if anyone were to see you, they would know that you're not a river man. You don't move like a river man, and you don't look like a river man."

"Nighttime will be just fine."

Sam went over to Jon and took the second bottle of wine out of his hand then smacked his head in a loving sisterly way. "Hey, get up and get out brother, brother. Can't you see I have better things to do here?"

Jon whipped his head around with a murderous look. "You could get yourself killed doing that sister, sister."

He had a very stern look on his face. *I could never hurt her,* he thought. Then a small smile came to his face. "I will leave you two love birds." He ran out of the conference room before Sam could get another swing at him.

"And you, Ash, you can take off those sunglasses. If you're going to stare at me, I at least want to see your eyes."

Ash forgot he had on Uriel's sunglasses. When he took them off, his face was flushed red. "I'm sorry, Sam. So, so sorry."

"Well, I'm headed to bed. You're more than welcome to join me, Mr. Ash."

"I need to stay and work on the task at hand. The conference room is just perfect for me."

"Can I ask you a question? What's the biggest snake in the world?"

"Oh, that would be the anaconda."

"Well, then, it looks as if your anaconda is trying to get out. I think the way you're looking at me, I should take it as a compliment but if you're not going to take it out and let me play with it, then you need to cover it up with something. I'm getting ready for bed with or without you."

Sam walked over to the door in the middle of the conference room and opened it to what looked like a presidential suite. She took off her tank top and bra facing away from Ash and then dropped her pants and revealed a lacy white thong. Looking over her shoulder she taunted, "Cover it up or come on in!"

Ash reached down and grabbed Sam's shirt off the floor and held it over his crotch. "I am so sorry. You are so attractive, and it just happens. I can't, I don't."

Ash was admiring Sam's curves as she crawled into bed and lay down on her stomach. *I need, I need I need to get out of here now!* He turned and ran out of the conference room and stood out in the hall taking deep breaths. *I think I understand what Jon was talking about. I definitely wanted to plunder some booty, but it's Cordy I love, and nothing compares to Cordy standing in the moonlight by the window. She took my breath away.*

Cordy started to wake up. The bed was so soft. It was the best sleep she had had in a long time. She took a shower and got into some clean clothes. She went to look for everyone else, but they were all sleeping. Jon had his door open and was sprawled out in his string bikini underwear.

Cordy knocked on the door and inquired, "Jon, do you know were Ash is?"

Jon let out a growl. "Come to bed and keep me warm."

"Why don't you crawl under the blanket?"

Yeah, not a bad idea. "He needed more room, so he's in the big suite in the barge behind us."

"What do you mean the big suite?"

"You know, the captain's suite — Sam's room." Then Jon smiled into his pillow because he knew he had just started what they called in America a shit storm.

Cordy ran down the hall. *I hope I'm not too late.* She bumped into one of the crew. "How do I get back to the next barge?"

"Go to the hatch on the corner hall, and the light should be green."

Just as Cordy got to the hatch a voice over the intercom said, *Lock down for turn*, and the light turned yellow. Cordy hurried up and opened the hatch and went to the next barge just as the crewman was getting ready to lock it from the other side. *All lock down for turn,* was repeated and a red light lit up next to the barge door.

Ash was in the other corner hallway and had just crossed over to the sleeping quarters.

Cordy ran down the hall and asked one of the crew how to get to the captain's quarters. "Go down to the second door on the left. It will say conference room on the door." She ran down, knocked on the door, but no one came. Cordy reached down and tried the door knob and it was open. *Think, girl! Think! Do you really want to do this? Hell, to the yes, here I go!* Cordy swung open the door and yelled out. "OK, you ass man, where are you?"

But no one was there. The light was on and she could see all of Ash's things all over the table. But no Ash. Cordy walked up to the door and saw Sam in a thong lying on her stomach.

Sam let out a moan. "OK, this better be good. Who is it?"

"It's Cordy. I'm looking for Ash. Have you seen him?"

"OK, this is weird. You are staring at my butt. It's bad enough when a man does it. You know I can feel it." Sam rolled over snarling. "No rest for the weary. Throw me my T-shirt." Cory picked it up and threw at Sam.

"Thanks, OK, now you're looking at my breasts. This is just great. What can I do for you?"

"Sorry, but they're hard to miss. I'm looking for Ash. Was he here?"

"Yes, he just left a minute ago. He is coming back tonight. I promised him I would let him be on top."

"That son of a bitch. I'm going to kill him."

"Hold on, missy, I didn't say that right. I just woke up, remember? He wanted to go up on the bridge and look at the river, but I told him that the only time he could go up was at night."

"So, you and he didn't...?"

"Oh Cordy, no, we didn't, but not because I didn't try. I pulled out all the stops. I showed him the goods. I was hot. I mean, really hot, but then he went to the left and then to the right and then he turned and ran away as fast as he could just like a little rabbit."

Cordy began to smile. She walked up to Sam and gave her a hug and turned and walked out of her room. Sam shook her head, *Maybe now I can finally get some sleep.*

Cordy went out in the hall with tears running down her face. She looked up to heaven and said, "Well, Great-grandpa, he is my little rabbit."

CHAPTER 18

Neanderthal Program

Mindy swiped her badge and pressed a button on the elevator panel. The Children of the Nephilim used this underground bunker for their experimental program of cloning Neanderthals from ancient DNA found in caves in France. The scientists working on the secret project had produced seven specimens so far and she was there to investigate their progress.

The Children of the Nephilim's mission was to resurrect their long-lost ancestor and use them to build an army. She scanned their reports. The Neanderthals were bigger and stronger with huge appetites. Their metabolic rates were higher than humans, so they burned more calories.

The clones also had a heightened sense of smell which allowed them to detect someone who had Neanderthal DNA. The seven of them tended to be tribal. They fought amongst themselves but had never killed each other. All seven worked together but they did have a leader. The biggest surprise was that they were very intelligent and able to handle the high-tech equipment given to them.

The Children of the Nephilim believed the clones carried special antibodies needed for the future. They predicted that an ancient virus could emerge and while modern mankind would have no immunity, the Neanderthals would survive. In fact, the Children of the Nephilim wanted to unleash a virus on the world, anticipating only they would have the cure.

The elevator door opened, and a handsome Dr. Max Howard smiled at the beguiling woman dressed in a skin-tight black dress. "Mindy, what a surprise to see you. I didn't get word from your office until this morning that you were coming. You look stunning as usual. I'm at your service."

"Cut the crap, and let's get down to business, Max. I'm here to check on your progress. Give me the latest report. I hope for your sake that you're on schedule. De Villiers has been quite testy these past few weeks."

"Follow me. It's best for you to see for yourself."

They entered a room with a see-through glass mirror. "We can see them, but they can't see us."

Seven very large men stood at attention. At first, they appeared to look like other men except for their large size. Their heads and chests were larger, and their average height was around seven feet tall. Max pointed to the tallest, who looked like he was eight feet tall. "He's the leader.

"They have a pecking order and are very territorial as well. Their intelligence exceeds all expectations."

"Do they obey orders?"

"Yes, and they understand our language but seem to have developed a sign language amongst themselves."

"Have they killed humans?"

"Yes, They're very good at it."

"How they been doing out in the field?"

"They're operational and effective."

"What's their longevity?"

"Not as long as you and me. We estimate life expectancy at five to ten years."

"Do they have any weaknesses besides their short life expectancy?"

"They are slow runners. Otherwise, they are excellent marksmen and fighters."

"What's the name of the biggest one?"

"We call him Goliath."

Mindy laughed. "Does he know the story of how the Pure of Heart, David, cut off Goliath's head?"

"Yes, it was part of their programming."

"What's the others' names?"

"Orion, Hercules, Balor, Aegir, Atlas, and Jolly."

Mindy smiled. "Jolly, I like it."

"He's the funniest one of the bunch. He makes them laugh."

"Excellent work," Mindy said. "I want them ready for a special assignment. I'm relieved my report will make De Villiers very happy. He doesn't take disappointment well these days."

Dr. Howard opened the door and escorted her down the hall. The facility was filled with researchers and private military contractors. "I have to ask a question, Mindy."

"I noticed the extra food and provisions brought in. Are you expecting some sort of catastrophic disaster?"

Mindy turned to him, "I can't tell you that, Max. It's top secret.

But, all the scientists agree it's just a matter of time before a disaster hits. Better to be prepared, right?"

Dr. Howard gazed at Mindy. "Right."

Mindy, entered the elevator and pushed the button to go back upstairs. "Don't worry, Max. We've planned for every possibility."

CHAPTER 19

Man's Best Friend

Brother Michael ran with Wapek, weaving through the streets. The sun was starting to set, and darkness was coming. The dog and elderly man hurried toward the bridge with statues of angels looking down on them. The ancient Ponte Sant'Angelo bridge crossed the Tiber River and led to the Castel Sant'Angelo where Michael the Archangel stood on top, holding his sword. Brother Michael stopped in the middle of the bridge and Wapek growled as the three-armed men holding chains walked toward them. They blocked his way to get to the other side. A few tourists strolled along the bridge, but scurried away when the men gave them menacing looks. Brother Michael started to retrace his steps, but three more men blocked their way back. They were trapped. Wapek growled and showed his fangs. The dog crouched low and barked, warning the men that he was ready to defend his friend.

Three of the Dark Watchers rushed the dog and wrapped a chain around his furry neck. The dog tried to attack them, but the steel chain choked him. They grabbed Brother Michael and wrapped the same chain around his legs.

"Please don't hurt my dog. I beg you. Let him go."

The leader came up to the elderly monk and grabbed him by his robe. "Where are they?"

Brother Michael shook his head, saying, "I don't know."

"Wrong answer, Brother. Throw them over the bridge and keep looking for the other two."

Brother Michael looked up and saw a statue of an angel holding a sword looking down on him. He folded his hands the same way as Mary did in the Cortona painting in Pope Urban VIII chapel. "A sacrifice must be made. Let it be."

The men grabbed the chained dog and threw him off the bridge first, and then they pushed Brother Michael over the rail. Dog and man fell into the cold water of the ancient Tiber. Wapek tried to swim to the top, but Brother Michael's weight tightened the chain and choked him. The elderly man pushed himself to Wapek and tried to pull the chain off his neck. They were both drowning as their lungs burned for air.

The Dark Watcher leader leaned over the bridge and saw nothing but water. No bubbles surfaced to the top, indicating there would be no survivors.

"One more Pure of Heart is gone. Search everywhere for the other two and bring them to me. We must report back to De Villiers with the good news."

Bob and Julia watched the horrible scene from a distance as the men left the bridge.

"No man or dog is left behind on my team. You stay here and

cover me. I'm going to go down to the river bank and search for them downstream."

"Be careful, Bob!"

"Oh, you're starting to sound like my mother. If I run into anybody, I'll throw your shoe at him."

"Your mother sounds like a smart woman." She hugged him tightly.

The dark, cold water surrounded Brother Michael and Wapek. They sank deeper and deeper into the murky water. Finally, Wapek's wiggling and Brother Michael's pulling at the chain on his neck allowed the dog to squirm free. The drowning dog swam to the top to get air. Brother Michael struggled to pull the chains off his feet but was unable to loosen them. The monk struggled for air but to no avail. His body became still and lifeless. The dog dove down and grabbed the man's robes and pulled and pulled to bring him to the safety of the shore. Weakened, Wapek crawled onto the rocky bank dragging the body of his dear master.

Bob headed down the riverbank and found the monk lying on his back with Wapek on top of him. Bob couldn't believe what he saw—the dog had managed to drag Brother Michael, still bound with chains, to the riverbank.

He heard Wapek softly whining. Bob gently moved the dog and spoke softly, "Easy boy. Good boy." Brother Michael seemed to smile at Bob but he knew the familiar fixed stare of death looking at him.

"He's gone, Wapek. We have to leave him."

The dog licked the monk's hand, trying to get him to respond. Bob's voice cracked with emotion as he pulled the dog in his arms. Tears filled his eyes. The reluctant dog didn't want to move from his master's side.

Bob carried the dog over to the tearful Julia waiting up the bank.

It was a miracle the dog had survived. She petted the whining dog and checked him for any broken bones. Miraculously, the dog had only suffered bruises.

"It's amazing he's alive."

"Brother Michael saved him. He's with the angels now. The guy had the biggest smile on his face. I'm telling you, I've seen a bunch of dead guys in my time, but nobody was smiling. Freaky stuff."

"We need to get a hold of Randy and tell him to inform the police where Brother Michael's body is located, and we need to let everyone know we have a man down. We got the pictures of the Lost Tribes map, but I hope it was worth the price we paid to get it."

"We can't go to the airport. They'll be watching for us. We need to get out another way."

Wapek licked Bob's face. "I love this dog."

Julia smiled. "I always wanted a dog. Looks like we've got one. I think Brother Michael would be happy about us keeping him."

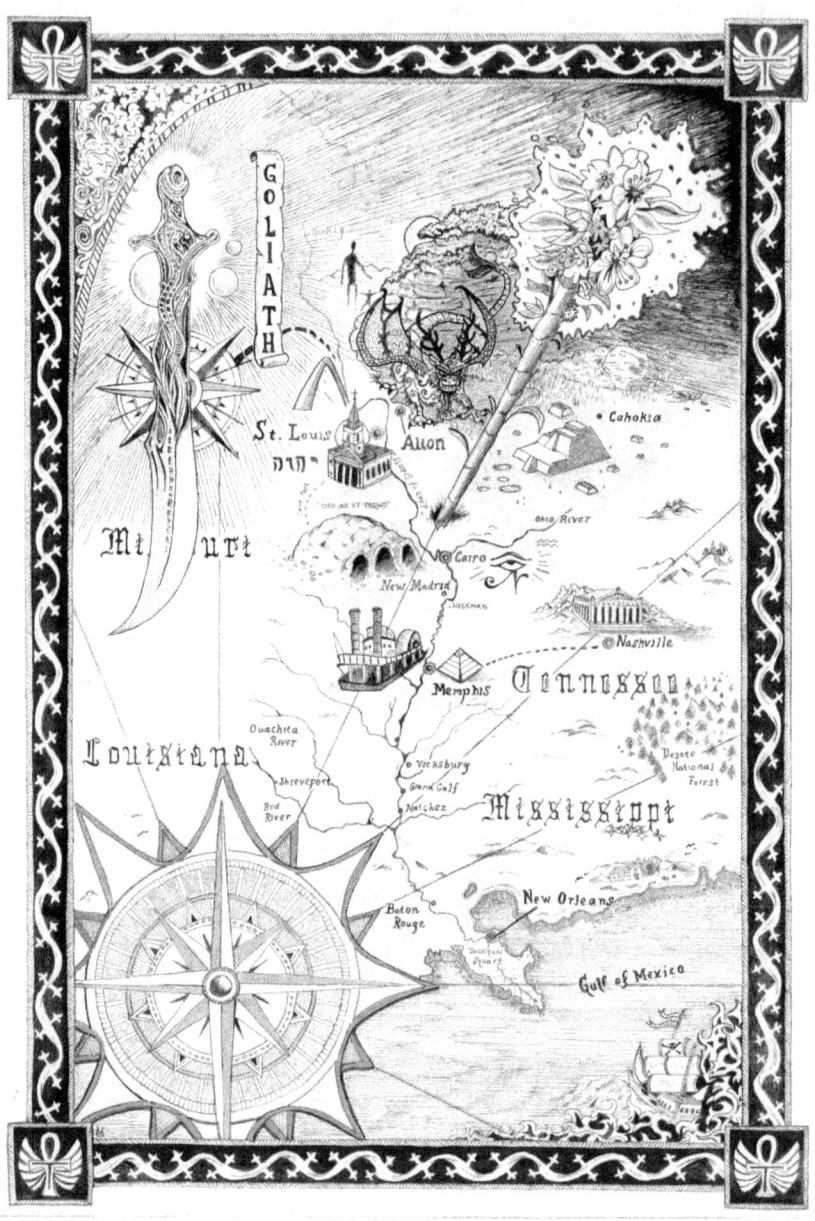

CHAPTER 20

Pillow Talk

When the all clear was called and the green light illuminated, Cordy went to find Ash. She was almost skipping down the hall when she saw Jon and Ash standing outside Jon's room. The smile on her face got even bigger.

Jon saw her coming, but he was confused. *Something must have gone wrong. I thought she would be angry after she saw Ash and Sam together.* Then he asked Ash, "Did you see Cordy down in the conference room just a little while ago?"

"No, I thought she was sleeping, but when I looked in her room she wasn't there. I need to find her."

"Well, don't look now, but here she comes." Cordy was just beaming.

"Hey, Jon, and hello, handsome." She slipped her arm under Ash's and grabbed his hand and gave it a little squeeze as if to say *hello, I'm home.* She never looked back at Jon, but held Ash's gaze.

"I was looking for you. We need to talk."

"Let's go back to my room. I've got something to tell you, too."

Jon had an angry smirk on his face. "He needs more space. He needs to talk. He is just one of the neediest people I know."

Cordy turned and glared at Jon.

"What, what did I do?" demanded Jon.

"You know what you did, and it's time for you to go to the time-out corner."

"What's a time-out corner?"

Ash laughed and said, "I know this one. It's when a bad boy has to stand in the corner of the room until he's sorry for what he did. What did you do?"

Jon turned and stalked into his room. "That's it. Now Ash is telling me what things mean. That isn't happening. It's just not happening." The door slammed behind him.

Cordy and Ash walked down to her room. Cordy shut the door behind them. "OK, Ash, what did you want to tell me?"

"No, you go first."

"No, Ash. You go first. Mine will take some time."

"OK, while you were sleeping Uriel showed up in the conference room with me."

"What did he want?"

"He wanted to help me answer this question: How did Antar's giants/Nephilim come to be on Earth after the Great Deluge? The answer is unbelievable! He helped me see that all the evil and violent people on Earth were killed in the deluge, but that God saved Antar's seed."

"How is that possible?"

"Antar's DNA was in the eggs of Noah's sons' wives. That means all of their descendants are Antar's descendants. He's been killing his own children! I wonder if he knows that he's been committing filicide?"

Cordy was shocked. "He's not killing them with his own hands but he's using man's worst qualities — ambition, fear, jealousy, and pride — to urge them to kill the Pure of Heart and mankind. He's taken the sick job of quality assurance lab tester."

Cordy fell to the ground and curled into herself, sobbing, "Antar's misguided vengeance killed my parents, the Chief, Sister Agnes, and Linda! If he had understood that all people are his descendants, they wouldn't have had to die!"

Ash picked her up and put her in her bunk. He lay down beside her and held her tight while her sobbing slowly lessened and became occasional hiccups.

After a while Cordy said, "Ash, you're a good man. You are so kind. You're fun, exciting, and full of life. I've become so comfortable with you. You've become my best friend, but there is so much I don't know about you. I have so many unanswered questions, but we haven't had time to talk."

"Well we have time now. Ask away."

"OK, let's see. Where do you see yourself in ten years?"

"In your arms."

"Have you ever been in love?"

"Yes."

"Tell me about that."

"I love my work, but it doesn't compare to the way I love your eyes, the gateway to your soul. I see so much love there."

"I'm touched that you see that. Who do you talk to every day?"

"God."

"If you could wake up tomorrow having gained any one quality or ability, what would it be?"

"Every day I hope to make gains and become stronger in my faith and the ability to love deeper."

"What's your guilty pleasure?"

"Lying down on my back out in the desert looking up at the stars sipping on a bottle of Jack Daniel's."

"What do you value most in a friendship?"

"Truth."

"Complete this sentence: I wish I had someone with whom I could share ..."

"I want to be able to have the one I love to share eternity with me."

"Do you tell your mom everything?"

"I don't have to because of her ability to see into the future so she pretty much knows what's going to happen before it does. It drives me crazy. One time, she punished me for something that hadn't even happened yet."

"How would you feel if your girlfriend made more money than you?"

"Well, you do make more money than I do, and I'm still here, but wait until you see my Christmas list."

"Would you move to another country for your girlfriend in pursuit of her dreams?"

"If she was the woman of my dreams, then my dream already came true."

"Good answer. What do men fear most about commitment?"

"Oh, that would be the unknown. I look at it as an adventure."

"Describe our first kiss.

"I will remember it forever. It was wonderful. The word 'heaven' comes to mind."

"It was like that for me, too. What is your first thought in the morning when you wake up?"

"That I wish that you were next to me."

"Oh, good answer. Do you like to cuddle?"

"You mean like we're doing now?"

"Well, I guess we are. I like it when you hold me tight. It makes me feel safe. Do you dream about me?"

"Every night. You are my dream come true."

"What is your biggest fear?"

"Losing you."

"Why did you stay a virgin for all these years?"

"I felt that a marriage could be greatly fulfilling if the two lovers learned each other's likes and dislikes as they became one."

"Oh, Ash, I feel the same way."

"I thought you were a virgin as well."

"Yes, many have tried, but all have failed."

"What do you mean? How many?"

"No, Ash. I'm asking the questions. I hope we make it through this."

Ash reached over and cradled her face in his hands and kissed her passionately. As they broke apart, Cordy said, "Kiss me again."

"Shush, my love, we have the angels with us. Nothing is going to happen to us. I promise you everything is going to be OK. We survived the icy waters off the coast of Nova Scotia, so bring it on Dark Watchers."

"Don't joke, Ash. You can't even hit anything you aim at." She smiled and started to tickle him.

"Don't do that, Cordy. I am telling you, don't do that. It pushes blood to my extremities. I get aroused, especially when I'm in bed with a beautiful woman I love."

"I think you're going to bust out of those pants."

"See what you started! It's not funny, and it always happens when I get tickled. So, stop it."

"OK, OK, you don't have to get bent out of shape over it. But if your extremities are already engorged then what's the harm if I tickle you more?" She reached over and lightly stroked his side.

"Cordy, please stop. I just want to use this time to get to know one another."

"OK, back to the third degree. When and how did you know you were a Pure of Heart?"

"When I was five years old, I came down with scarlet fever. I remembered one night the fever got so high that they filled the bathtub with ice, but the fever still wouldn't go down. They called the doctor and I remember him checking my lungs and temperature and then he went out in the hallway. It was dark in the room, but the hall light shined in. He told my parents that it was doubtful that I would make it through the night. Then I saw two men sitting at the end of my bed. They both got up, and one came around to the side of the bed and held my hand. I didn't see his mouth move but what I heard was, *it is not your time to come home.* The fever broke immediately.

"I hadn't eaten in days so of course, I yelled out to my parents, 'Can I get something to eat? I'm starving!' They said it was a miracle, but I knew I had been touched by a messenger from God. That is why it was so easy for me to be a drinking buddy with Uriel and to see other angels. What happened to me when I was little gave me a unique understanding of faith. I believe and know that my healing ability comes from my great faith. In the Bible, Mathew 17:20 says: *And Jesus said unto them, Because of your unbelief: for verily I say unto you, if ye have faith as a grain of mustard seed, ye shall say unto this mountain, remove hence to yonder place; and it shall remove; and nothing shall be impossible unto you.*"

"So, you knew when you were just five."

"Yes, and every day I grow stronger in my faith. Now, do I get to ask any questions?"

"Yes, you may, but I don't know if I will answer them." Her eyes sparkled with a playful look. He could see this was going to be a challenge.

"This is a very important question: Do you love me?"

Cordy rolled over on top of him and started to kiss him with great passion. She was barely able to control herself. *If I don't stop soon, I won't be able to.* She had pulled Ash into the burning ring of fire and then in an instant she stopped and sat up on the side of the bed. She was breathing heavy and her heart was racing. "Well, I think that answered that question."

Ash spun himself around and sat up next to her and pulled her into his arms. He gladly returned the kiss with as much intensity as Cordy and may even have pushed her over the edge of no return. "You know in the Old Testament, Abraham took Sarah and she became his wife. I'm thinking I should just take you now, my love."

The intensity was building and Cordy didn't see herself getting off this train. It was a runaway situation. Her body was saying *'take me now'* and, in her head, all she heard was *Yes, Yes, Yes, I am ready*! Suddenly, a knock came from the door.

"Hey Cordy, it's Master Wong. May I come in?"

"No, not right now. I'm getting ready to meet with Ash. I'll be out in a second."

"I'll see you in the conference room in a few minutes," Master Wong said. "Sam told me to give everyone a heads up. A meeting is going to be called."

"Thanks, Master Wong. I'll be there."

Master Wong couldn't resist, "Oh, Ash, that goes for you, too."

The older man chuckled as he headed toward the conference room.

Both looked with shock at each other. How in the world did he know Ash was there too?

Ash looked panicked and felt as if he was having cardiac trauma. *It's not good to be going a thousand miles per hour and then come to a complete stop! It could kill a man.*

Sam's voice rang out over the intercom. "Can I have all of the guests come down to the conference room as soon as possible?" It only took about five minutes for everyone to assemble.

"Well, it isn't good. Brother Michael is no longer with us. The Dark Watchers killed him. Randy just called. He said that Bob and Julia completed the mission and are OK. Ash, the photos of the map have been forwarded to your email."

The room was deathly quiet. Ash looked around the room. Some didn't know Brother Michael, so he decided to say a few words.

"One time when I was on the run with Brother Michael, I told him how dangerous this could all be. He told me that if he was to get killed that it would be his best day because he would be with his Father that day and for me to be happy for him. Jon, break out some of that wine so that we can toast Brother Michael."

When everyone's glasses were full, Ash held up his glass. "Here's to Brother Michael on his happiest of days!" Then Ash had one tear run down his face as he said to himself, *I'll miss you, Brother Michael.*

Cordy grabbed his hand and as she squeezed it, she said, "We have to bring this battle to an end!"

Sam's phone rang. "OK, I'll put you on speaker." It was Ash's dad.

"It's Dad, isn't it?"

"Yes."

"Does he know about Michael?"

"Yes."

CHAPTER 21

Rollin' on the River

Sam put down her cell phone and slid it to the center of the conference table. Ash's father came over the speaker. His voice was broken and strained. "Did they tell you about Brother Michael?"

"Yes."

"You have a picture of the Lost Tribes map of the Mississippi River in your email. Bob said they tried to kill Grey Wolf's puppy Wapek as well. He said you could see where the chain cut into his neck. Brother Michael died saving Wapek."

Cordy's heart was heavy with grief. She wanted to come out of hiding and just start fighting but she knew they were outnumbered by the thousands. "Brother Michael's death won't be in vain." Then Cordy let out a great Mi'kmaq war cry that sent shivers up everyone's spine. On the other end of the phone came a similar Mi'kmaq war cry. "Mary, is that you?"

"Yes, you can't keep a good housekeeper down. I may be old, but I still have the spirit of your great grandfather, the chief, with me always, Star Child. I am trying to take care of Ash's parents. But, I am not sure who is taking care of whom. I am going to miss Brother Michael. He became a close friend."

Then the phone got quiet.

"Dad, I have everyone gathered around. Did you get a chance to look at the map yet?"

"Yes, I did. All I can think of is that we're looking for something that the Templar's brought over from France that had the ability to change earthly things. It was hidden somewhere in the New World. I came across a photo of a stained-glass window down in the St. Louis Cathedral in New Orleans that shows a large box with a Templar flag on it. I noticed they were carrying it with wooden poles just like they used to carry the Ark of the Covenant. I am confident what you are looking for is in the Mississippi Valley.

"The King of France and the Templars had a falling out. As a result, they needed a place to hide all their sacred relics and wealth. The Templars in some cases were the first privateers not beholding to any king or pope. They were constant danger since King Phillip betrayed them and persisted in hunting them down.

"I believe what you are looking for is something that came from Templar treasure or crusaders lost treasures brought back from Jerusalem and the Crusades.

Ash, don't forget the relationship that Napoleon Bonaparte had with the Lafitte family. He ransacked Rome during the war and then, the tombs of the French kings. He may have found something. Jon, are there any records that exist that you know of from back in the 1700s or 1800s?"

"I can check on it. You know when you're young, you never pay attention to what the old people are telling you, and now that I need the information, I wish had paid closer attention."

Sam started to laugh. "Did everyone hear my big brother say he was getting older? That's OK, big brother, I did pay attention to Poppa Jon. I think I can find the records you're talking about."

"Ash, you told me about finding a voodoo witch doctor. Is he there with you?"

"Yes, his name is Chris."

"Chris, I need you to reach out to anyone that would still know some of the old stories from the 1700s. Sometimes local people get involved and they hand down the story and the legends live on. Even if it fills in one piece of the puzzle, it would help."

"I'm on it."

"Well, son, it sounds like you have a great team, but I can't stress enough that I think we are running out of time. I'll call you if I come up with anything else. Be safe."

"I know how to dig a hole and hide if I have to. Be well, Dad."

"Everyone let's get some sleep. It's been a long day."

Sam headed up to the bridge. Everyone but Ash and Cordy headed back to their bunks. Ash fell into one of the conference room chairs and put his hands over his head and sat without saying a word. Cordy sat in a chair across from him, staring at the ceiling.

Cordy looked over at Ash and for the first time noticed how weary he looked both physically and emotionally.

Ash looked up and saw the woman of his dreams sitting just across the table, but it might as well have been a thousand miles. "Cordy, did you notice something funny on the call with my dad?"

"Yes, your mom wasn't on the call with him. Something is wrong."

"I wonder what it is. Maybe it's just the loss of Brother Michael?"

"No, she is having trouble with the pregnancy. I can feel it."

Ash bowed his head. "Oh, dear God, please protect my mother. Oh, Cordy, I just want this to be over. It's draining the life out of me."

"You know back at the mansion Uriel told me to look in the Bible. The sentence he chose said, 'Many are called but few are chosen.' Do you feel like you were chosen?"

"You know I do."

"OK, then you don't have a choice, and you never know when you might have to sacrifice a virgin along the way."

Ash looked at Cordy in disbelief. Then they both started to laugh. Ash wadded up a piece of paper and threw it at her. "Well, enough with having all this fun at my expense, I need to get back to work."

"Is it OK if I stay and help? At least I can listen to you talk out loud."

Ash usually only worked alone but he liked the fact that she wanted to be with him. They both poured over all the information until late into the morning. Then Cordy came over and sat on Ash's lap and asked if he would rub her shoulders. As the tension lessoned, her head leaned into his shoulder. Then she put her head against his. Ash just smiled and held her tight. It only lasted a short time. Sam came bustling in and saw them in their quiet moment.

"Come on, you two, get a room or come to bed with me. One way or another I am crawling into bed." She went into her bedroom, leaving her door wide open. They heard her turn on her shower.

"Ash, let's go before she comes out naked."

Before they could get up, Cordy's cell phone started to ring.

"Hello, Bob. I'm glad you and Julia are OK."

"I don't have to tell you, but it's getting tough out there. Well, to be honest, that's why I'm calling, cupcake. I just got a call on your old cell phone from a little girl named Nancy Huff. She said that she had been kidnapped by some bad men and her best guess was that it happened twelve hours ago. She said to tell Doc Cordy that she thinks her dad is dead because he was lying on the ground, and he wasn't moving. She started to weep hysterically at that point. Nancy said that you would be proud of Sunny because he tried to save her, but they shot him. They drug her pet down the driveway, so she thinks he's dead too. The girl said that Highway Man got away. She also thinks her arm may be broken. I think De Villiers is trying to drag you out of hiding."

"De Villiers is going to pay big-time for this! He is right! I am coming out to fight!"

"Now, hold on, that's not all of it. Nancy said they had about ten to fifteen people in cages. She met another little girl who was in her cage that knew you as well. Her name was Maggie and she showed her how to fold her hands just like Mary Magdalene at the Rock Church. She said if we prayed, everything would be OK."

"They have my girlfriend's daughter, Maggie. Ash, they got my Maggie."

"Bob, what can Cordy and I do?"

"Well, they didn't know she had a phone. It was hidden in a stuffed animal purse. Nancy said it was about to run out of battery. I told her to leave it on, so I could track the signal. It worked. We show they're holding them at a building right next to a museum that looks like a Greek pagan temple. They call it the Parthenon. It holds a large statute of Athena, the Greek goddess of wisdom and justice. The replica of the Parthenon is in Nashville, Tennessee. Cordy, you can't go. That's what they want."

"Bob, what's the plan?" asked Ash.

"Ash, I'm going to send you and Jon in with six of my finest and closest friends."

"I'm going, too," Cordy said.

"You have too much at stake. I can tell you from experience you'll make too many mistakes because of just that. You know I would never hold you back, but you also know that I have the experience and I speak the truth.

"My men will pick you up at the pyramid parking lot and brief you in the air. Master Wong and Chris will be staying with the barge all the way to St. Louis and keep and protect all the artifacts and information that has been accumulated. Cordy, you, Peter, and Sam will be getting off at New Madrid. Sam will get you up to speed and get you to St. Louis. The mission for everyone is to meet up at Peter Woo's house in St. Louis, alive. We have allies there."

"Bob, can you call my dad and ask him to look at any connections between the Nile River and the Mississippi River. I am seeing a pattern, such as there are so many similarities between the rivers and the people who live near them. Water, one of the Keys of Life, was sacred to the Egyptians and to the Native Americans. The water from the river provided a fertile land so the people could grow crops.

"I know that I brought this up before, but the letters and sound of the Egyptian name Isis is in the word Mississippi. Isis carried the ankh which is the Key of Life in ancient Egyptian religion. I've seen Native American symbolism use the ankh on their temple walls, too.

"Memphis, Cairo, and pyramids can be seen along both rivers. Both rivers have sacred buildings along them. Luxor and Karnak are temples along the Nile. The Saint Louis Cathedral in New Orleans is along the Mississippi River. It's not a coincidence."

"I'm on it, Ash. Remember, you all have a price on your head. Everyone is searching for you."

"Ash, don't let anything happen to Maggie or Nancy and the others. You must save them all," pleaded Cordy.

"I show your position about twelve hours out of Memphis. That will put you in just after dark. I will have Sam pull over next to the pyramid and a helicopter will land on the parking lot." Sam was coming into the room dressed in a towel when she overheard Bob's voice on Cordy's phone.

"Bob, this is Sam. I know the place you're talking about. We'll be at the rendezvous point."

"Roger that. You all get some sleep. We've got a big day tomorrow. Be careful, all of you."

The phone clicked off. Sam marched back to her room.

Ash looked over to the door of Sam's bedroom where the gorgeous woman smiled at him. Cordy turned Ash's head back to meet his eyes and shook her head back and forth. Looking into Cordy's eyes, Ash said, "Sam, let's get everyone together one hour before you dock."

"Will do. Now, can I get some sleep?"

CHAPTER 22

Parthenon

Jon and Ash were dressed in black in preparation for their rescue mission. They had already checked the gear that they would need. Now they looked over the map of Nashville one more time.

"It figures that De Villiers would pick this weird offbeat place. He's a historian and into the classics."

"I've seen the magnificent Parthenon in Greece. Have you, Ash?"

"I have, and it's an amazing place. It's one of the greatest architectural feats of mankind." Ash continued, "Athens, Greece, saw its power growing. The Parthenon, was a huge temple to Athena, a Greek goddess known for her great wisdom.

"Athena stood for truth and justice. She helped the Greek heroes such as Heracles and Jason. She would appear to humans and guide them. Plato, the great philosopher, found her greatest wisdom in only fighting for a cause after one tried to use the power of persuasion.

De Villiers must be an admirer and yet he violates everything she represented."

Jon looked at the crystal ball sitting on the table. "We know a beautiful woman who drops in with words of wisdom. You call her the Guardian. I call her 'Diana' after the goddess who fell in love with Orion and had power to control animals. At the Parthenon, you will see sculptures of gods and goddesses. De Villiers knows about the Guardian and how she's played a role in human history."

Ash looked over at the crystal ball, too. He and Jon had put two and two together. He walked closer to the table.

"A huge golden statue of Athena stands in the Parthenon in Nashville, just like in ancient Greece. De Villiers wants the incredible knowledge the Guardian can give him. He thinks she's responsible for the School of Athens."

"Raphael's painting at the Vatican gives tribute to the *School of Athens* where some of the greatest philosophers attended. The teachings of Aristotle, Plato, Socrates, Euclid, and Pythagoras influenced mankind's future."

Ash didn't believe in coincidences and he agreed with Jon. They suspected the Guardian played a major part in man's evolution. He could see how she could have been worshipped as a goddess. He had to ask.

The crystal ball stood on the table, atop the golden triangles and quartz disk which contained the Pure of Heart's library.

"Guardian, I have a question. Did you meet Plato or Pythagoras?"

"Yes, Ash, I did. I helped them as I help you. I dressed differently, though, in those days."

A beautiful woman dressed in a white tunic and gold crown and shield stood before him.

"The Parthenon was inspired by you?"

"Yes, Ash. I've been around a very long time. The Parthenon in Nashville is a replica of the one made for me in Greece. I think it is very symbolic and beautiful, a tribute to Athenian democracy and American democracy. The sculptures within tell the story of the War of Heaven. The names are changed but the stories of the Greeks, Egyptians, and Hebrews are similar. They all have stories of giants and a war for revenge. How many have suffered over time because of the need for revenge?"

"Too many to count, I admit," Jon said. "I wanted revenge for Poppa Jon, but I also know it won't bring him back. Now, I want to save the lives of the Pure of Heart. I am coming out of the darkness and into the light."

"You think De Villiers is close to here?" Ash asked as he pointed to a spot on the map.

"Athena was known for her powers of wisdom and prophecy," the Guardian said. "I can see you're processing the data and your conclusions correctly. Yes, I think he is near there. I would be very careful, Ash. The Dark Watcher wants Cordy's ring. He will kill anybody to get it."

The Guardian disappeared.

CHAPTER 23

Old Dog, New Tricks

Bill, Cordy's grandfather and leader of the Light Watchers, sat at his desk and reflected on all that was happening. He recalled how Chief Saunhac had recruited him as a young man to fulfill this great responsibility. He had promised to protect and save as many children of the Pure of Heart as he could. That promise fell short when he could not protect his own son and daughter-in-law from being killed by Dark Watchers. Now Cordy was in danger. He didn't want to lose her too. He could no longer sit behind a desk. He had to be part of the action. He was going on a mission that could very well be his last. But first, he had to have his businesses in order.

Cordy had shown great wisdom when she chose Bob to be her financial manager and chairman of her corporation. He was a brilliant manager. The work he did was outstanding, and he inspired loyalty. Not only was he shrewd in business and finance, but as a former Navy SEAL, he was exceptional in strategy and covert operations.

Bob's wife, Julia, was an asset, too. However, she didn't start out that way. She had been an instrument of death for the chairman of the Children of the Nephilim. But, Chief Saunhac had known that she was a Pure of Heart and awakened that in her. She rejected her previous murderous way of life and worked with Bob and the others to destroy the Children of the Nephilim organization and the Dark Watchers. Bill was proud of what they had accomplished. They had destroyed the cruelest and deadliest organization in the world.

Light Watchers had been the protectors of mankind and the Pure of Heart since the beginning. Bill had been their leader for a long time. It was time for someone else to take over the reins. Bob would make a great leader when he retired. Bill prepared the necessary documents and recommendations and signed them. He sent them out to the various divisions with the stamp of the all-seeing eye, light beams emanating from the center, informing them of their new leader.

Next, Bill's thoughts turned to Cordy. He was so proud of her. She and her team saved New Orleans and now worked to take down De Villiers. He could no longer let her fight this battle alone. It was now his turn to step up and help.

"Milly, did you send that package to Bob Schaefer special delivery like I wanted?"

"Yes, sir. It should be delivered soon."

"Thanks, Milly. I appreciate everything you've done for me."

"You're so welcome, Bill. I'll make sure Bob gets it."

"You'll have to cancel my appointments for the week. I'm going out of town for a few days. I have to take care of some business."

"Yes, sir. I'll make the calls."

He grabbed his jacket and took one more look at the picture of his beautiful wife, son, and granddaughter on the desk and walked out the door to meet his men for their top secret mission.

CHAPTER 24

Old War Horses

Bill had called in all his old veteran friends to go on a rescue mission. Many of the younger Light Watchers were either on other missions or getting their families prepared. Bill sent out the warning for all the Light Watchers to get ready for the upcoming extinction-level event.

Bill's friends weren't spring chickens, but they still could fight. They had gone on many missions in their early years and had extensive experience in life and death situations. Bill had no reservations they would accomplish their mission and rescue the hostages.

His buddies were saddled up with gear and guns at the airport. Bill rolled out a map showing where the hostages were being held. Bill told them the latest intel from a former Dark Watcher who said that five hostages were being held in a cave in Missouri near Saint Genevieve. The huge limestone cave system was the perfect place for a storage bunker. Bill reported that De Villiers split up the hostages and that another rescue mission was taking place in Tennessee at the same time.

The plan was to sneak up at night and rescue the hostages. It was a very dangerous mission and if anyone wanted to drop out, now was the time to speak up. The five friends of Bill's pulled out a whiskey bottle and passed it around.

Harvey laughed. "You never give us the easy ones, Bill. Remember, when Mark forgot to put on the brake of that jeep in Guatemala and it rolled into the river? I can still see him running and cussing to stop it."

Everybody laughed.

"I guess we old warhorses still have a few battles left in us," Bill said. "I, for one, want to go out in a blaze of glory, not old age. Our main mission is to get the hostages out. I want you all to remember that. Everybody pack up and get on the chopper. Destiny awaits."

They rode laughing and joking into the night as if it were a day at the golf course. With precision they checked their machine guns and grenades.

Bill looked down in the darkness and saw the cave entrance below. "Hell is empty, and all the devils are here."

"You always did love Shakespeare, Bill," Mark, his closest friend, whispered. "The devils are below. Guess we're going to give them a big surprise. Thanks for taking me along, Bill. I know I'm older than most of these guys, but I'll keep up. How's that granddaughter doing?"

Bill smiled. "Best thing that ever happened to me. Let's move out gentlemen."

The helicopter landed, and the group of men dressed in black jumped out and hid behind the trees. The chopper left and flew into the night sky. They were on their own now.

Harvey scanned the area with night googles. "No guards seen. That's weird. Guess they're confident no one is coming. Everybody be on special alert. Something feels wrong."

Mark headed for the cave, covered by his friends, and disappeared into the darkness. All guns pointed on the entrance to the cave. Bill waited with his machine gun ready.

It's too quiet. Where are the guards? Harvey is right. Something's not right.

Mark motioned the all-clear sign and the other men rushed forward.

"It's clear. There's an elevator door. I took out the camera so they're blind. I smeared some black shoe polish on it. They'll think it's bugs."

The cave entrance was hidden with camouflage nets. On the side of the rock stood the steel door of an elevator used by the occupants. The caves in the area could go hundreds of feet below ground.

The men decided to split up. Some would go down to get the hostages while the others would cover them. Bill, Mark, and Harvey would go down and check it out. Radios were all on. The elevator took them to the bottom floor and opened to a huge cave of limestone. The Dark Watchers were using the cave to hide supplies and equipment. The three men quietly snuck down the corridor until they heard voices.

Mark went around the corner and whispered, "We've found them. Three young men and two teenage girls in cells. I found the keys. They told me the jailers are eating in the mess room."

Bill ran to the locks and freed each anxious prisoner. "All of you be quiet. Mark and Harvey, get them out of here and the rest of you, call the 'chopper to pick you up. I'll keep them busy while you get out."

"You got an extra gun?" one of the captives asked. "I promise I won't shoot my foot. I'm ex-military."

Bill nodded to his friend. "Give them guns. We need all the help we can get."

Mark's knowing eyes met Bill's smiling ones. "OK, let's go, everybody. Follow me before they get dessert. Harvey, lead on and I'll cover you. You kids follow Harvey. And Bill, don't be a hero. Just keep them busy and get out of here."

Bill chambered a round in his gun and headed to the mess hall.

"Mark, tell my granddaughter I love her. Now get the hell out of here."

"Understood!" Mark ran as fast as he could to keep up with Harvey and the others.

Bill heard laughter down the hall and saw about twenty men sitting around a long table eating dinner. In the back of Bill's mind, a little voice filled his head. *This is too easy. Sometimes a sacrifice must be made.*

Mark and the others made it to the chopper. They waited in silence for Bill to join them.

Harvey whispered on the radio. "C'mon, Bill, get the hell out of there."

Bill yelled to the Dark Watchers, "Hands up, everybody!"

None of the men moved. They all raised their hands in the air. He noticed some were smiling and the hairs on his arms raised up. His intuition told him something was wrong. A blow came from behind his head and blackness took him.

Mark radioed Bill over and over but there was no answer. "Man down! Let's get out of here! We've got civilians!"

Shots rang out in the distance. Bill's comrades watched their enemy fire at them, but they had escaped into the night because of Bill's sacrifice.

CHAPTER 25

Know Thy Self,
Know Thy Enemy

The barge pulled up to the moorings alongside the pyramid. The crew members pushed out a gangplank. Ash and Jon threw open the hatch, popped out on deck and were already at the end of the gangplank when Ash felt a pulling on the back of his jacket. It was Cordy. She was right behind him.

"Cordy, you know you can't come. It's too dangerous. They're setting a trap for you."

"Shut up, you good looking dirt-digger and kiss me."

Ash pulled her in tight and kissed her with all the passion he had. His hand slid down to her lower back as he pulled her in tighter, the spark becoming a flame.

Jon cleared his throat, "Ahem, we have to get a move on, monsieur and mademoiselle."

Cordy placed a letter in Ash's hand. "Here's some light reading for your helicopter ride."

Cordy turned and ran back to the barge. "You better come back to me!"

"I won't let you down!" Ash ran and caught up with Jon. When they got to the top of the steps Ash looked over and could not believe what he was seeing. The pyramid was a sporting goods store. He had seen it all now. They could hear the incoming choppers and had just enough time to get to the pickup site at the end of the parking lot. Everyone thought it was a promotion for the store. One of the choppers came down and picked up Ash and Jon. Off into the dark night they went, not knowing what dangers were ahead.

Jon started going over all the gear as he kept talking to Ash, but the archaeologist wasn't listening. He was opening the letter Cordy had given him, but it was too dark, and he couldn't see anything. Jon said, "Here are your night vision goggles."

Ash put them on and looked down at the letter. It was the best letter he had ever read, and it only had one word on it. Ash folded the note back up, placed it in its envelope, and then put it into his top pocket. A big smile came to his face. Jon looked over at the smiling man and thought if he didn't start paying attention to what he was saying, he was going to die and soon.

Ash looked over at Jon and asked him if he had a phone.

"You know Sam took our phones just in case we were caught."

"Yes, I know she did, but I also know you. Now can I have the phone?"

Jon reached in his sock and pulled out a miniature phone. "You know we have been together too long. You know me too well." He handed it to Ash, shaking his head.

Ash had trouble putting in the numbers on the tiny phone

with the helicopter bouncing all around. He still managed to call his dad. "Dad, is mom there? Can you put her on?"

"Yes, but she can't talk for long. The pregnancy has taken its toll on her. She's very weak."

"I knew something was up when she didn't get on last time we talked."

"Here she is."

"Mom, I don't have much time, but I wanted you to be the first to know. I asked Cordy if she would marry me, and she said yes. Mom, I am engaged to the most amazing woman in the world."

"Yes, I knew you were going to get engaged. I saw it in a vision when we were on the run back in Egypt. I am so happy for you, son."

Jon was waving for him to get off the phone as the pilot came on the intercom. "Fifteen minutes till touchdown." Jon started to wave more franticly.

"Mom, I love you. Tell Dad I love him, too."

"I'm listening in, son. We love you too. Be safe."

Ash hung up and rubbed his forehead then looked over at Jon with a smug smile. "Well, I guess the best man won. Oh, and why are all my contacts in your phone?" He scrolled down the list and saw Dirty Dottie's number highlighted.

"What's the deal with Dirty Dottie?"

Jon quickly changed the subject. "Oh no, I am not going to concede the best man won. If Cordy would have partaken in some of what the best man had to offer, she would not have picked you. And Bob put all your contacts on the phone with mine. I was going to ask you about Dirty Dottie, but not now. Ash, get your gear on. We only have ten minutes till touchdown, so get a move on. Do you know where we are landing?"

"Randy sent it over, but I didn't have time to work out all the details. The chopper is going to land on the lawn of the Parthenon."

"The Parthenon. That's in Athens, Greece, isn't it? That doesn't make any sense."

Ash explained, "They built a complete replica in Nashville. It has a two-story statue of Athena in it. What we are looking for is in front. It's a granite monolith that is a monument, honoring General Robertson. He was an early companion of the explorer Daniel Boone and cofounded what is now Nashville. He worked with the Cherokees and other tribes along the Mississippi River. In World War II, they named a ship after him."

"Well, thank you, professor, for the history lesson. Where do you come up with this stuff?"

"The Internet," Ash said with a smile. "We are looking for an outside air vent to the right of the monolith. De Villiers has an underground complex there. I hope we'll be going in the back door."

"I don't like this. Pagan temples, goddesses and who is this Daniel Boone man who worked with the tribes?"

Ash broke out in song, and he was by no means a good singer. "Daniel Boone was a man, yes a big man! With an eye like an eagle and as tall as a mountain was he! That's all I can remember; the reruns were on TV when I was a kid. It was in Arabic with English subtitles, and it really helped me learn English."

A voice on the intercom told them to get ready; it was one minute to touchdown. Ash and Jon checked their weapons and chambered a round. The chopper landed and Jon threw open the door. The other chopper was right behind them.

Jon motioned for everyone to join up. "Everyone listen up. Ash and I will go in first and the rest of the team will secure the perimeter. If we're not out in thirty minutes, we're probably dead, so unleash hell and come in using all your fire power." Everyone gave Jon a thumb up.

Ash had located the air shaft to the underground bunker. It was just where he thought it was going to be, to the right of the granite monolith and hidden by some bushes. Using a bolt cutter, Ash snapped the lock like butter. "I'll go first, Jon."

"I don't think so. If you start to lay down cover fire, you'll probably shoot me." Jon pulled himself up on the edge and then jumped in and Ash followed behind him. When he got to the bottom of the air shaft, he saw Jon with his hands above his head, surrounded by three men.

"Well, what happened, Monsieur Superman?"

"It was a trap, just like we thought."

The Dark Watchers ordered them to drop their weapons. One Dark Watcher turned to the other two, saying, "Looks like the bait worked. De Villiers will be pleased with us. We have one of the most notorious Pure of Heart and the famous Dark Watcher traitor, Jon Lafitte. However, he'll be mad because the woman isn't with them. You two take the prisoners to the holding area while I call De Villiers."

They walked Jon and Ash down the hall to an elevator and pushed the down button for the twenty-third floor. When the doors opened, Jon and Ash found themselves in what appeared to be a prison facility. The Dark Watchers frisked them and confiscated the things in their pockets, including Jon's small pocket knife. They placed them on a table at the beginning of the cell row. The two guards looked at the items on the table and picked up and admired Jon's knife.

Jon yelled at the top of his lungs, "You take that knife, and I will rip your head off and cram it down your neck!"

"Tough words, Frenchie, since you'll soon be dead. De Villiers is coming here to kill you personally."

They bound their hands behind their backs, tied their feet, and shoved them into the second cell. Jon continued screaming and swearing obscenities. The guards laughed at the railing traitor and went upstairs to await De Villiers. Jon's rant panicked the young girls and they moved to the far side of their cell.

Ash saw their fear and chastised Jon, "Calm down! You're scaring the two girls next to us."

Jon looked over and saw the girls huddled together. He was embarrassed for his outburst and loss of control. He apologized, "I am sorry, young ladies, for scaring you. That pocket knife is a family heirloom. It has been passed down for many generations. I don't intend to lose it. That man knows who I am, and he knows that if he takes that knife, I will keep my promise. But don't worry. I would never seek my revenge in front of you."

Jon then looked around their surroundings, taking inventory of everyone he saw. In the first cell were the two young girls. In the third cell was a very tall man, about six feet seven with long dark hair. He had the features of a Native American. In the remaining cells were an older man, two women in their early twenties, and three boys and three girls in their early teens. Twelve in all. They would all fit in the rescue chopper.

Jon called out to the captives, "We're here to get you out!"

The tall man in the next cell smirked, "Big words for someone who just got hog-tied and thrown into lockup!"

Noting the differences in the man's speech patterns, Jon asked suspiciously, "Who are you?"

"My name is Remington Madoc. Most just call me Mad Dog. I am chief of an ancient Native American tribe of Welsh Indians. My ancestors landed at Mobile Bay around 1170, three hundred years before Columbus discovered America. They called us giants in the early days, hence my height. The leader at that time was Prince Madoc. His blood was mingled with the Choctaw, Comanche, Navajo, and Cherokee.

"I was a close friend of Chief Saunhac. He visited me many times at DeSoto National Forest where we sat in the five caves and celebrated the memories of our ancestors. We kept in contact with each other through email as well.

"I saw Chief Saunhac not too long before he died. He told me that he had had a vision and that one day I would be called upon to help the Pure of Heart. Guess that day has come."

"So how did a very tall Welsh man end up in a Dark Watcher cell?" asked Jon.

"They tracked Chief's emails back to me. When they captured me, they told me that I wasn't the one they wanted. They were looking to capture Chief Saunhac's great-granddaughter, Cordelia or Star Child, and a Pure of Heart who goes by the name Ash or Little Rabbit."

"I'm Ash."

"I know you're Jon Lafitte," Remington continued. "I've seen your wanted poster. The reward for you is huge. Ash, you're wanted as well, but alive, for even more money. As Chief Saunhac's friend, how can I help?"

"I'm working on it. Ash, do you have any ideas?"

"No, but I bet these two girls are Nancy and Maggie." Neither girl looked up or made a sound.

Realizing the girls were frightened and uncertain of their identities, Ash said, "I would like to introduce myself. My name is Ash and the loud-mouth over there is Jon. Cordy McDermott and I are engaged. Cordy told me that Maggie likes to feed ducks and can't help but talk all the time. She also told me that Nancy is a very brave girl, that she helped bring Highway Man into the world. We are here to rescue you."

With that the two girls jumped up and came running over to the side of the cell. "You have to know Cordy! Only Cordy knows those things about us."

Holding her arm, Nancy said, "I'm Nancy, and she's Maggie. Sorry we didn't talk right away. My dad is a highway patrolman, and he said to never talk to strangers. Plus, that loud-mouth over there is kind of scary."

Rolling his eyes, Jon asked where Ash had put his small phone. It wasn't lying on the table with their other things.

"It started to fall out of my top pocket as we started down the shaft. I put it in my pouch, so I could have both of my hands free."

Jon gave a puzzled look. "Maybe it's my French, but I'm confused. People don't have pouches."

"I have a secret pouch in the front of these pants," Ash explained. "When I travel with small, precious artifacts, I carry them in the pouch. They can't be felt in a pat-down. If I encounter a thief or in this case, armed guards, they don't know that I'm carrying anything special. So, when I needed my hands, I slid the phone into my secret pouch."

"Well, get it out!" ordered Jon.

"Jon, my hands are tied behind my back — just like yours. You're going to have to back up to me and reach into my pants and get the phone out of the pouch. And by the way, I go commando, so please be careful."

Jon looked incredulously at Ash. "You have got to be kidding me! Girls, turn around. You don't want to watch this."

Nancy and Maggie did as he ordered.

Remington's eyes twinkled with amusement as Jon backed up to Ash. As he slid his hands down the front of Ash's pants, Ash inhaled and held his breath, giving Jon as much room as possible. Jon finally reached the phone but given the close quarters and Ash's lack of underwear, he had difficulty grabbing it. He carefully wrapped his hand around the phone, but it slipped away. Cursing in French, Jon tried again but to no avail. In exasperation, Jon said, "There isn't enough room for me to grab it and hold onto it." Jon tried one more time to reach into his pants to get the phone and hit a button. Before he could get the phone freed, it started dialing.

A familiar voice came over the line. To Ash's relief and horror, the phone somehow ended up on speaker. "Hello! How can I do you? This is Dirty Dottie, the Belle of Memphis. Hello? Hello? If this is a prank call, I'm exhausted from all-day rehearsals, so good-bye."

Before Ash could reply, Dirty Dottie had hung up.

"Call her back Jon."

"What do you mean? I didn't intentionally call her. I was just trying to get the phone out and must have hit the dial. You had her on the screen when you turned it off in the chopper."

Jon finally got a firm hand on the phone and tried to yank it out of Ash's pants but couldn't pull it out. He hit redial this time and they were greeted by the message: "This is Dirty Dottie. If this is a prank call, keep the number and we'll start fresh tomorrow."

Ash could tell that it wasn't a recording; it was just Dottie being Dottie. "Talk to her."

"Mademoiselle Dirty Dottie, don't hang up," Jon implored in his strong French accent. "Whatever you do, don't hang up."

Dottie yelled out to her husband, who was in the other room, "Darling, did you arrange for one of those love calls to get me in the mood before we head to bliss?"

Dottie stretched out on her bed and drew the phone closer to her ear. "I'm ready, you dirty Frenchman. You're really turning me on with that French accent. I'm all ears."

"Dottie, this is Ash. Stop talking! We have two young girls here."

The woman smiled when she heard his voice.

"Well, is that my ass man? The last time I saw you, you were on a horse bare-ass naked on national TV. How's it hanging, my ass man? You know that night we had on the ship was so much fun. The next morning, I sat there contemplating for hours as you lay there standing at attention. You reminded me more of a thick and girthy bull than a long and dangly race horse. After having months to think about that, I would say you have the best of both."

"Dottie," Ash pleaded, "Stop talking and just listen. I'm in trouble and need your help. Do you have the phone number of the woman who called you the last time I was in trouble?"

"Yes."

"Can you three-way me in to that number?" asked Ash.

"I don't know how to do that but hold on. I'll ask my husband."

"Honey, Ash wants to know if you could do a three-way."

Dottie's husband scolded, "Now, Dottie, you know I don't do that, no matter how many times you ask me."

"No, no, no. I don't mean that kind of a three-way. I mean the kind with the phone number thing you do."

Her husband came in and pushed the necessary buttons and handed the phone back to Dottie. "Thanks for pushing my buttons, honey." Shaking his head, he kissed her on the top of the head and walked out of the room.

The room could hear the phone ringing and then a voice, "Hello, this is Cordy. Is this Dottie?"

"Yes, ma'am it is. Hold on. Ash wants me to have a three-way with you but remember, he has two young girls with him."

In her excitement upon hearing that the girls had been found, Cordy completely missed Dottie's teasing. "Oh, they found them. Thank God!"

At the same time, the two frustrated men shouted, "Dottie, stop!"

"Cordy, this is Jon. We have the girls and ten other hostages. Call Bob and tell him to call the strike force. Tell him we are twenty-three floors down. Call immediately! We're running out of time!"

"Jon, tell me, are Ash and the girls OK?"

Ash, Nancy, and Maggie called out as one that they were fine.

"It's such a relief to hear your voices," Cordy said tearfully.

"Dry it up, Cordy. We're running out of time. De Villiers and his men will be here any minute. Call Bob now!"

"I'm on it!" Cordy hung up.

Ash took over the conversation. "Dottie, thank you for helping us. You may have saved our lives. Can you stay on the line for a few more minutes, just in case we need you again? And please be quiet. Remember our two young girls."

"I sure will, my ass man. What happens in a few minutes?"

"All hell is going to break loose. While we're on this subject, Jon, you let them capture us!"

"Yes! It was the only way to get De Villiers' men to take us to the hostages. We have to get out of this cell and release the rest of them."

"Hey guys, would this help?" Nancy asked, holding Jon's knife.

Both men shouted "yes!" at the same time. Jon hopped over to the side of the cell, and Nancy cut the rope from his hands. She then handed Jon the knife and he quickly cut the rope from his feet and then the ropes binding Ash.

Jon turned back to the girls and asked, "Nancy, how did you get the knife?"

Holding her injured arm close to her, Nancy showed him. She walked up to the front of the cell, turned sidewise, slid through the bars, and walked over to the table holding the items the guards had taken from Jon and Ash.

Jon laughed and said, "Well that works for me. Please bring me the bolt cutters, and the guns."

"I'm not supposed to touch guns," Nancy indignantly declared.

From the phone, Dirty Dottie said, "Oh, that reminds me of an old Andrews sisters song." She started to sing, "I didn't know the gun was loaded. And I'll never do it again."

With flaming red cheeks, both Ash and Jon shouted, "Dottie, shut up now!"

Nancy shook her head and said, "That lady keeps talking Greek. I really don't understand anything she's saying."

Relieved, Ash responded, "That's a really good thing, Nancy."

Nancy brought the bolt cutters to Jon. As she passed the bolt cutters, Ash gently wrapped his hand around her arm. Her first reaction was to pull away. She looked at Ash and asked, "What are you doing, Mr. Ash?"

"I'm fixing your broken arm. Just close your eyes. This won't take long. It won't hurt."

Nancy closed her eyes and her arm started to tingle. In less than a minute, Ash was finished, and Nancy's arm was healed.

Meanwhile, Jon was trying to cut the bars with the bolt cutters, but he didn't have enough strength to dent the thick metal. Remington stuck his hand through the bars from his adjoining cell.

131

"Hand them over." Jon handed the bolt cutters to him and with great strength, Remington applied pressure on the handles. There was a crunching noise as he continued to exert pressure. Suddenly the bar snapped. He snapped a second bar then pulled them apart and stepped outside of his cell. He wasted no time and snapped and bent the bars to Jon and Ash's cell, so they could escape, too.

Jon and Ash ran and grabbed their guns off the table. Then Jon ran to each cell and picked the locks, freeing the remaining Pure of Hearts.

Nancy and Maggie squeezed through the small opening in their cell and joined them. They ran to Ash and gave him a big hug.

"Can I be your flower girl?" Maggie asked.

"You'll have to talk to Cordy about that, but I don't see why not."

Ash noticed that Nancy had tears running down her cheeks. He got down on his knees and asked, "What's wrong, honey?"

"Everyone I love is dead."

"Cordy loves you. She sent me to save you. I promise you that when we get married you can come live with us." Ash kissed her on the forehead and wiped away a tear.

Nancy broke into a small smile, "How about Highway Man?"

"He can come live with us, too," Ash assured her.

"Ass man, everything OK there?" Ash had forgotten Dottie was still on the line.

"Right now, we're OK. You were a life saver again. Thanks so much. I've got to go now. I have to get this group of Pure of Hearts to Memphis, hide them, and then meet up with Cordy. Again, thank you so much. Au revoir."

"Hold on, Ash. I may still be able to help you. My husband bought me a paddlewheel riverboat, so I could sing and dance in my old age. I can't believe I just said that. Let me rephrase — in my prime-time years. We're in downtown Memphis right now at the base of the river front. Get them here and I can hide them all."

"Dottie, you've saved my ass again."

"Well it is a nice ass to save. Just look for a paddle steamer by the name of *The Belle of The Ball*. See you in a few."

"Everyone get up against the wall by the elevator," Jon yelled. They could hear gunshots being fired on the upper floors. And then the doors opened. It was their second team taking out the Dark Watchers. Their rescuers had arrived. Jon and Ash felt a sigh of relief when they saw them.

The rescue commander told Jon, "All is secured, but we need to go now." They reached the choppers and took off with no casualties. Jon took Nancy and Maggie with him and Ash had the rest of the Pure of Hearts in the other helicopter. The pilot handed Ash the mic from the cockpit. Cordy was on the end of the line.

"Everything went well. No casualties and the girls are on their way back to you with Jon. I'm with the other rescued hostages via Memphis. Dottie is there. She just received a paddlewheel steamer from her husband. She'll hide the rest of the Pure of Hearts on her steamboat. She has plenty of room."

"You be careful, Ash."

"I'm not afraid of any Dark Watchers."

"I'm not talking about Dark Watchers. I'm talking about Dirty Dottie. She's the one I'm worried about."

"Nothing to worry about, my love. I'm an engaged man now. Meet me in St. Louis at Peter's house."

"I can hear the choppers in the distance. I have to go. I love you with all my heart, so much it hurts." Click, and she was gone.

In the doorway of the chopper was a bright light and a man standing with a dark long overcoat. It was Uriel, helping to give safe passage to the Pure of Heart in the dark of night. Ash just nodded his head with a thank you.

Jon's helicopter zoomed along the Mississippi. He continued to scan the area to ensure that the Dark Watchers had not followed them. In the distance he could see the barge, captained by Sam, approaching the New Madrid lock and dam, their rendezvous location.

When the helicopter landed, the barge pulled up to its side. Jon lowered Nancy and Maggie down the hatch into Cordy's waiting arms. She hugged them both with grateful tears streaming down her face. Mouthing a *thank you* to Jon, she prayed that Ash and the others were safe as well.

Chapter 26

Life Upon the Wicked Stage

Ash and the chopper pilot searched for a place to land on the downtown riverfront, but nothing looked safe and all the parking lots looked full. Ash pulled out Jon's phone and called Dottie.

"Hello, this is Dirty Dottie. How may I do you?"

"Cut it out, Dottie. I know you can see it's me on your caller ID."

"Can't get mad at a girl for trying, can you?"

"Dottie, we don't have anywhere to land the chopper. Can you pick us up at the pyramid just upstream?"

"I know the one. Just a second. Precious, do you know if all the customers have returned to the boat? Hold on, my precious is calling the captain."

"Did I hear you right? You called your husband precious?"

"Well, I must admit that he's been able to keep a smile on my face most of the day and for a woman my age, that is precious. Here he comes now. Not literally, of course. He said, we're a go. Everyone came back early so we'll be there in —what's that, precious? — see you in thirty minutes, my ass man."

"Thanks, Dottie."

The chopper swung around and was already coming up on the parking lot of the pyramid. "Remington, there is a sporting goods store inside. Here are some gift cards. Take the Pure of Heart in and have them get what they need. Get them down to the pier in twenty minutes. I'll be just behind you. Don't wait for me; just go." They all hit the parking lot running.

Ash checked the chopper to make sure that they had left nothing behind. Thanking the pilot for his service to the mission of the Pure of Heart, he followed the group to the store.

Once inside he threw some essentials together, one of them being a package of underwear. *I'm not going near Dottie without protection,* he thought.

Then he saw a small jewelry counter and ran over to the clerk, "Please show me the most expensive engagement and wedding ring you have."

"Sir, we really aren't a wedding ring kind of store. This is the most expensive ring we have."

"I'll take it, but I was really looking for something like this young woman is wearing." Ash said, pointing toward a woman in her seventies.

"My husband has been gone for a long time now. I was thinking of trading it in for something like the one you are looking at."

"If I were to buy the ring in the case and give you the rest of the balance of the gift card, could we make a deal?" Ash asked.

"If it will be going to a loving couple, I would be proud to make that deal."

The clerk rang up the ring and gave it to the woman. Seeing the balance on the gift card, the gracious elderly woman let out a sigh, "There is thirty-nine thousand dollars left on the card.

"Young man, tell your fiancée this is a vintage antique ring with a two-and- a-half carat European-cut diamond. The wedding band is from before 1910 and has orange blossoms all around it."

"Thank you. She will love it. Let me assure you, it is going to a loving couple."

Ash was really running behind and didn't expect to see the boat there when he got to the pier. But, it was still waiting for him. Ash spotted a Dark Watcher going into the pyramid, so he decided to make a dash for the river boat.

He could hear Dottie singing an old song in the main dining room. As he ran into the room, he saw Dottie. She was a classic picture of a Southern belle. He had seen some old movies of ladies from the south, but Dottie put them all to shame.

"Dottie, where can I hide? I have a Dark Watcher on my heels. Like two minutes and closing."

"Well, let's go with what worked last time I saved you. Get in under my dress."

"Dottie, I don't have time to put on your dress."

She lifted the back of her hoop skirt. "Get in or get shot."

Ash looked at the door and could hear some commotion with security. It didn't sound like security was winning. *I can't believe I've only been on the boat for just a few minutes, and she already has me where she wants me.* Ash jumped up on stage and slid on his knees under the hoop skirt. At the same time, the Dark Watcher came around the corner.

"How dare you interrupt my rehearsal! Stop immediately and

declare what your mental malfunction is! You never interrupt a woman in the middle of a performance!"

Ash had never heard a woman disarm a man so quickly. When he slid under the skirt he was utterly shocked by what he found, but then again it *was* Dirty Dottie. She was wearing a black thong trimmed in red lace and the only place to hold onto was the front of her thighs. They were firm and pretty spectacular, just as he had remembered from that night in Jerusalem.

"I am sorry, ma'am. I saw a man come in here that just got on the boat. We think he's a terrorist."

"You mean Big Jim Black? I call him Big Daddy."

"I need to talk to the man that came in here just a minute ago."

"Well if you must, go through the side door over there and go down the corridor to Cabin 2. You will find Big Daddy there. I'm warning you the boat will be pulling away from the dock in less than five minutes. Oh, and one more thing, Big Daddy doesn't like to be disturbed."

"Thank you, ma'am. I'll remember that." The Dark Watcher took off running. Dottie pulled her phone out of her corset. She sent a text to her husband warning him of their unwelcome visitor and his intent. She pressed play on the CD player and started the music over again and began to sing. She had the voice of an angel.

"Dottie, is the coast clear?"

"Not yet, my ass man. Hold on a little longer. You're young and should have lots of stamina." It was getting hotter and hotter underneath the hoop skirt, and Ash's hands began to perspire. One slipped off her thigh and went straight to her cheek, and he had to squeeze tight to hold on and keep himself from falling.

"Oh yeah, ass man, what a grip."

The Dark Watcher came upon Cabin 2 with great caution and his gun drawn. He knocked on the door.

"This better be good. Who is it, and what the hell do you want?" The voice was like a roaring lion.

"This is Memphis police. I just need to ask you a few questions, sir."

The door opened and there stood Dottie's husband. "What the hell can I do for you, you little scum bucket? You're lucky I didn't fire a group of six on your scrawny ass."

"Sorry for the interruption, sir, but I was told you just got back to the boat."

"That's correct. I needed to get some cash from the ATM. Is there a law against that?"

"No, sir. The description I have of the terrorist doesn't match you. I'm sorry for disturbing you."

"You're lucky I don't kick your ass. Now get out of here."

The Dark Watcher heard the steam whistle, signaling the ship was getting ready to depart. He ran back across the auditorium where Dottie was and apologized for interrupting her again. He made it just in time to jump and make it to shore. Two other Dark Watchers came running down the dock. The little scum bucket told them the boat was clean.

"The coast is clear, my ass man, but you don't have to let go of my ass. I'm good."

Ash emerged hot and sweaty. "I can't thank you enough, Dottie. You have just saved all of our lives."

"Oh, that's OK, Ash. I'm sure we can work out something. It's late and I'm off to see Big Daddy. And in case you're wondering, that was my husband who helped. He's a great man. Your group is down in Cabins 6,7, and 8. I will see you for breakfast."

CHAPTER 27

Deep Down

After the barge finished making its turn, Sam came over the intercom. "Cordy, please meet me in the conference room in fifteen minutes."

As she was coming down the corridor she could see Jon coming from the other direction. They both reached the doorway at the same time and went in. "Hey, big brother, I just said Cordy. That doesn't include you."

"Something is going down. I can feel it."

"You can stay and listen but don't interrupt."

"Cordy, I think we may have a problem. The Dark Watchers are closing in. Just in the last three hours we've had several helicopters hover just off the starboard side of the bridge of the towboat. They're looking for any sign of the Pure of Heart. Now they're also looking at other towboats the same way. One thing can be sure, it's getting intense. You're no longer safe here."

"So, here's what I'm thinking. We have a secret cave opening that was created by the New Madrid earthquakes that we have been using for smuggling ever since the ground opened in 1811. The earthquake was so bad that the Mississippi ran backward, creating small waterfalls and a great lake by the name of Reelfoot. This particular cave runs all the way from New Madrid to St. Louis. What I want to do is take Peter and you up through the cave and let Jon continue with Master Wong, Chris, Nancy and Maggie on the barge."

It wouldn't hurt to get Peter off the water.

"I heard of there being up to 6,400 caves in the state of Missouri but never knew they could travel so far underground."

"Well, here comes the hard part. We will have to climb a vertical cliff of over a thousand feet. When we reach the cave, it'll take us at least ten hours of nonstop dirt bike riding to get through it. I feel confident that I can get you to Peter's house in St. Louis safely."

"That is, if we don't fall off the cliff or die in the cave. It's not the size of the dog in the fight, it's the size of the fight in the dog, as Mark Twain said. Let's do it, Sam."

"I'm in. I think Peter will be, too."

"Can I speak now, little sister?"

"Yes, Jon, now you may speak. I'm amazed that you kept your mouth closed for so long."

"Did I hear you, right? You're going to leave me here to babysit the two girls? Babysit? The words didn't come out of your mouth, but I can read between the lines."

"Know this, Jon. There isn't anything I wouldn't do for you," Cordy chastised. "I would even save a corporation for you. I know you will get them home safely."

With no other choice, Jon petulantly responded to Cordy, "I wondered how long it was going to take you to bring that up. OK, I'll do it. I'll babysit the two young girls."

"We'll have to go through the lock and dam in New Madrid, and then it'll be ten minutes north of there. It'll be chilly in the cave so dress appropriately and no luggage. I'll see you in two hours."

Cordy went back to explain to Peter the new plan. He was all for it. He couldn't wait to get off the water. Then she had to deal with telling the girls that she was leaving them with the "scary French man."

She came around the door to the room where the girls were staying. Nancy had become a little magnet and as soon as she saw Cordy, she came running.

Maggie watched Nancy race across the room and thought, *I can't imagine what it would be like to be an orphan. It just isn't fair that Nancy has lost everything.* When she got to Cordy, Cordy opened her arms and took her into a bear hug. Maggie smiled to herself, *Nancy doesn't realize it yet. She hasn't lost everything because she still has Cordy.*

"Maggie, come on over here. I need a big hug from you as well, plus we need to talk about what's next in our journey.

"Nancy, remember that day when it was just you and me in the trailer and we saved Highway Man? Remember how brave you were even when you were scared?"

"Yes, I remember."

"Well, I'm going to ask you to be brave just like then. The bad men who are hunting me will stop at nothing. So, it's time for me to separate from the group. I have a favor to ask each of you. You both met my fiancé, Ash. What do you think?"

"He's a hunk!" replied Maggie.

"He's really nice." answered Nancy.

"Well, he doesn't know it yet but we're going to have a big wedding reception, and I really need some help planning the music. We're fortunate to have an international DJ on board."

Chris peeked around the corner. "Hello. It's a big project, but we need to pick out a total of four hours of music, and we have only twelve hours to get it done before we reach St. Louis. Can you help me get it done?"

"Yes," the two girls cheered.

"Meet me down in the mess hall, and we'll get started."

The two girls grabbed some pens and paper, hugged Cordy, and off they went. *Well, that was easier than I thought it was going to be.* She headed down to meet Sam and Peter.

She made her way back to the front of the barge and when she got there she found Sam and Peter and one of the crew at the steering wheel. She jumped in. Sam called the bridge and ordered the barge to come to a full stop.

"Captain Sam, we are a go for launch."

"Everybody hold on." The front opened and the speed boat rocketed forward as if it had been shot from a cannon.

Peter shrieked, "Oh, man!" as he held on to the sides in a white-knuckled grip.

Within minutes they were at the river's cliff. The boat pulled into a small inlet and let the three rock climbers out. Sam went first, then Cordy, and Peter was last. It was going to be very dangerous because it was a free climb, meaning no ropes.

"Try to keep pace with me and follow in my footsteps, if you can."

They were just about to the summit when Sam lost her grip. She fell past Cordy, who was unable to catch her. Peter had more time to react. He wrapped his arm around the root of a tree that was overhanging the cliff as he reached to grab Sam. Her body slammed up against the rock, but she was holding on with everything she had. She couldn't believe Peter was able to hold on. He pulled her up to the tree, so she could get a good grip.

Sam had never felt that caliber of strength in a man before.

Her heart was beating out of her chest, and she wasn't sure if it was because of the fall or Peter.

When they reached the top, there was a small hunting cabin that looked like a hobbit's home. The house was covered with a mound of earth to reduce heat loss. Cordy recognized the ancient mound builder structure. Sam shut the door, went over to the center of the floor, lifted a ring just on the edge of a rug, and opened a trap door to a set of steps. At the bottom of the steps was a room that was 300 feet by 500 feet. It was breathtaking. There were a dozen Honda 70 trail bikes.

"Does everyone know how to ride?"

"Yes, it's like the one I had as a little girl. My dad bought it for me."

"I used to race when I was a young man, but it's been years."

"OK, I'll lead. I'll put Peter in the middle, and, Cordy, you can bring up the rear."

They started the engines and headed deep down into the dark tunnel.

CHAPTER 28

The Quiet before the Storm

Jon walked down the hallways of the barge thinking of ways that everyone could get out of this alive. He kept coming up with the same answer: it wasn't likely.

The girls and Chris were hard at work putting together the music list for the reception. Master Wong was just getting warmed up for his tai chi, so he decided to join him.

"Master Wong, before we get started, why am I not able to focus? I have always been able to focus."

"It's because you don't feel like you're in control anymore. Jon, your sister has taken on the most dangerous part of the mission and you're left with an old man and two little girls, not to mention a voodoo king. You also lost the battle over Cordy."

"Yes, that's it. How can I get my focus back?"

"We only have a few hours before we dock in St. Louis. How are you planning to get us to Peter's house without being detected?"

"I don't know."

"Focus on that and you will start to find your way back to center. Make sure your plan is good enough not to get us killed." They started tai chi and Master Wong could see the wheels start to turn in Jon's head. They weren't very far in to the tai chi routine when Jon apologized for having to leave. He went down to the conference room and called Bob.

"Bob, it's Jon. I need some recon done on Nancy's relatives. Not quite sure where she's going when we get into St. Louis. If Maggie goes back to her mom, then won't the Dark Watchers just go back and kidnap them again?"

"Yes, I think they will. We haven't contacted any of the family members yet. Let me do some digging and I'll get back to you."

Jon looked at how far it was to Peter's house — just seven and a half miles. It might as well have been a thousand with all the Dark Watchers looking for them.

Jon's phone rang. "Hello, Bob. Did you come up with anything?"

"Yes, I did. It seems that Nancy's neighbor is a customer and friend of Cordy's, a Mrs. Johnson. When I called her, she said she had heard about the kidnapping but couldn't get any information on Nancy's father or what happened. No one knows where Tim Huff went after he lost his daughter. I told her that we needed someone to watch Nancy and a friend for a little while. She didn't hesitate to say yes. I told her there could be a risk and that they would need to be picked up down by the river front next to the Arch. You just need to give me a time."

"That's great. I'm estimating we should be at the Gateway Arch on the riverfront in about five hours. She won't be able to miss us. We'll be in a souped-up speed boat."

"Jon, I have to tell you something. De Villiers must be really scared of you. He just raised the bounty on you to three million dollars dead. I can say that you're safe with Mrs. Johnson but outside of her, you're on your own. I'll text you her contact information. Good-bye, my friend, and God speed." *If he makes it out of this alive it will be a miracle.*

A few minutes later Bob's phone started ringing. "Hello, this is Mrs. Johnson. Is this Mr. Bob?"

"Yes, it's Bob. We talked a few minutes ago about Nancy. How can I help you, Mrs. Johnson?"

"I was just thinking about that terrible day, Bob. When they found Nancy's dog, Sunny, he was almost gone. The officer who brought the poor dog to me, Mike White, said that it was hard to kill a good dog and even harder to kill a great highway patrolman. I'm thinking that I'll pay Mike a visit on my way out to get Nancy. He lives just down the highway from here. If anybody knows anything about Tim, his friend Mike would know. Did you have any information on his death?"

"No, he just fell off the grid. No funeral notice, no obituary, but that might be what they want with the kidnapping. Don't play detective, Mrs. Johnson."

After Jon finished the arrangements with Bob, time went quickly as the Mississippi pushed them closer to their destination. Jon packed all of Ash's artifacts and information and moved everyone to a speed boat. It would be a lot easier going out than it had been coming in.

They were only about a mile from the Gateway Arch, their destination. When they got there, Mrs. Johnson would take responsibility for the girls. Jon had to admit that he would miss them. They had proven to be quite brave and resilient. Shaking his head at himself, he reflected, *I must be getting sentimental in my old age.*

They pulled up to a dock along the cobblestone beach. Jon spotted a Suburban SUV with a graphic on the side featuring the name, "Johnson Farms." The white Suburban jumped the curb and bulleted down to the water's edge. The door flung open and a tearful man and a happy dog bounded out of the car. It was Highway Patrolman Tim Huff and Sunny!

A loud cry came from the boat, "Daddy!"

Jon assisted everyone off the speed boat and sent the driver back to the barge. He didn't want them to be seen so he quickly moved his troops into the Suburban. Nancy held on tight to her father with Sunny licking his way in between them.

They proceeded to Peter's house. When he was certain no one was watching them, Jon hurried the group into the house. It was imperative that they not be seen to ensure their safety. Once inside, there was another shout of pleasure. Sitting on the couch in the living room was Maggie's mother. Bob had managed to get her smuggled in earlier that day.

CHAPTER 29

Judas Coins

According to legend, one of the most cursed items in existence is the thirty pieces of silver given to Judas when he sold out his friend to the Jewish chief priests. Later Judas realized the great sin he had committed. With remorse for his actions he returned the silver to the high priests and then hung himself from a tree.

The high priests needed to rid themselves of the coins after Judas' death as they were convinced that evil had attached itself to them due to their treachery. After all, the coins were blood money; they had paid for the death of a Pure of Heart. To empty their coffers of the cursed coins, they purchased a field from a greedy land owner to bury Judas, the poor, and foreigners. Not suspecting their curse, the land owner was happy to accept the coins as payment.

Later, the land owner discovered the truth of the coins — that they were the ones that had been given to Judas. Being a superstitious man, he believed blood money carried evil on its silver lining. He feared for himself and his family. He decided that he would keep the coins separate and in a locked box.

Many terrible incidents started happening to the land owner. His family died in a fire. He contracted leprosy. He was convinced these things happened to him because of the coins. To bring the hardships to an end, he gave the coins to a man as a loan repayment. He warned the money lender that the silver coins had belonged to Judas.

The coins intrigued the money lender as he was a collector of evil. He knew someone would pay handsomely for them. As greed filled his heart, he kept the coins separate from the rest of his collection and waited for someone to purchase them. In time, he sold the coins and the curse continued to anyone who touched them.

Years became centuries. The cursed Judas coins were passed down through time and eventually came into the possession of the Children of the Nephilim. A treasure for them because of the great evil they caused, yet they made sure never to touch them for touching them guaranteed certain doom---madness, incurable disease, bankruptcy, devastation, death, to name a few.

De Villiers' family knew about the coins as early as in the days of the Crusades. They believed in the curse and believed in the evil power of the silver. They wanted nothing to do with the coins.

De Villiers, however, was convinced that he was smarter than his ancestors. He did not believe such superstitious mumbo-jumbo. He saw himself as a sorcerer of the highest order and knew how to deal with evil. He would not succumb to the curse of the coins.

De Villiers trained in the dark arts and hunted down the silver coins. He was convinced that the chairman of the Children of the Nephilim had them in his possession. When the Nephilim headquarters burned to the ground, he searched the ruins finding the coins in their fire proof box among the ashes. Opening the box, De Villiers lustfully lifted the coins with his naked hands. Feeling the power of the coins rush through him, De Villiers desired to become the greatest and most powerful man in the universe. As his power increased, he found himself touching the coins more and more. With the power of the coins came the curse. The evil of the coins seeped into De Villiers' mind and paranoia and madness began.

In his consuming lust for power, De Villiers orchestrated events so that he would become the Grandmaster of the Dark Watchers. He then united the Dark Watchers with the remnants of the Children of the Nephilim creating an evil organization beyond compare. He knew the only challenge to his position as Grandmaster and his plans would be the Lafitte family. To put that to an end, during a Dark Watcher tribunal meeting, De Villiers executed Poppa Jon for disagreeing with his propositions. No one would argue with him now. However, he had made a great enemy in Jon Lafitte, Poppa Jon's grandson.

De Villiers smiled as he admired the painting hanging in his dining hall, the meeting room of the Dark Watcher tribunal. It was a copy of the Caravaggio painting, *The Taking of Christ*. It depicted Judas betraying Jesus for thirty pieces of silver. De Villiers mused aloud, "Some say money is the root of all evil. Bollocks to that! Judas was a fool for killing himself. Money is power! I will destroy the Lafitte empire. I will gather up all the enterprises of the Nephilim — their human trafficking, their drug cartel, their money laundering companies, and increase my wealth and my power!"

De Villiers reclined on a chaise and continued reflecting on the painting. Isis, his beloved cat, jumped into his lap. At times she seemed to be his only friend. He had found her abandoned, sitting on his door step. She had become his constant companion filling the emptiness he often felt as a loner. At times Isis could anger him, but in the end, she was always there for him, no matter his mood. Her loyalty couldn't be bought, unlike that of men such as Judas.

De Villiers closed his eyes and contemplated his next steps. He developed a plan in which he would trap Cordy and her friends. With Cordy as his captive, he would acquire her Solomon's ring, the most powerful treasure in the world. Stroking Isis' soft fur, he whispered to her, "Everything is going to plan, my dear. With the ring I will not only rule Earth, but the entire universe. Antar will bend to me!"

CHAPTER 30

Shake, Rattle, and Roll

Sam slowed down as they entered the cathedral, a huge room in the cave. She dismounted from her bike and aimed her headlamp to shine on a gas generator. Three pulls and the spectacular room lit up. Cordy and Peter were awestruck at the beauty before them. Cordy thought, *calling this room the cathedral is perfect. You really feel like you are in the presence of God here. Isn't it amazing that some of the most dazzling part of God's handiwork never gets seen in the light of day?*

They turned off their bikes and took off their helmets. Sam walked over to some tubs that contained supplies. She pulled out a small cook stove, coffee pot and cups. "I think a break is in order. Would anyone like a cup of coffee, water or juice?"

"Wow, you have all the comforts of home here. I'll take coffee and water," answered Peter.

"Cordy, how about you?"

"I'll just take coffee, thanks."

"Peter, how do you take your coffee?"

Peter whispered, "I like my coffee like I like my women — strong."

Sam ever so slowly turned back to him, smiled and shook her head. Peter had an ear-to-ear grin. "You know, Peter, I could take you down even with your fancy dancing, hack-and-whack karate."

"Be careful. He's really good, Sam."

Sam finished making the coffee and as she handed Peter his cup, she smirked, "Be careful, Peter. This cup might be too hot and strong for you."

She gave out a little chuckle. "How do you like our hideout?"

"A perfect refuge from the law." Peter smiled at her.

"How did you like your coffee?"

Peter looked at her with a mischievous grin and teased, "I found it a little weak and wanting."

"Are you insulting the cook? You're asking for trouble. OK, you caught me on the cliff and saved my life," Sam said, standing up. "You pulled me to safety. But I can still beat you in a physical match anytime and anywhere."

"Now, we'll say three takedowns and the match is won." Peter got up and started to circle Sam. "Cordy, you be the referee."

"You two, cut it out. We need to get back on the road, or trail, as it is."

Sam threw the rest of her coffee out of her cup. "Don't worry, this won't take long."

"OK, go ahead and kill one another. I can't believe you two. Get ready, go!"

Peter grabbed Sam quickly and rolled her over and laid her on the ground with such control she hardly felt it. Peter lay on top of her, looked into her eyes and said, "That's one."

She pushed him off and got up. "That was luck."

Once again Peter circled her and grabbed her upper thigh, twisted, and just before she hit the ground, he caught her and laid her softly beneath him. "That's two."

Now he could see just how miffed she was, so he gave her a little chuckle, just infuriating her further. She jumped up and grabbed his arm as fast as she could and tried to get him off-balance, but he spun like a top and pulled her back once again, putting her ever so softly on the ground. He started to say something but then unexpectedly kissed Sam instead.

She started to push him off but then she kissed him back with more passion than she had ever had for any man. They heard a voice say, "Get a room, you two, but not until we're out of here." Cordy helped lift Sam to her feet

"He is really fast and really good," Sam exclaimed in awe.

"Yes, he is, and I've beaten him many times in competition, so you better watch out when you're around my Ash."

"I get your meaning, sister."

Sam looked at Peter as he was getting up and gave him a smile. "Come on, we have to get a move on." She put away the camping gear and started her motorbike, so they would have light when she turned off the generator. Once she had everything settled, she jumped on her bike and took off. Peter and Cordy followed close behind.

They had been traveling about two hours when suddenly the ground began to shake. Sam yelled, "Hurry, there is a bridge up ahead."

Just as she was approaching a wooden bridge that crossed a deep fissure, the bridge collapsed. Sam laid the Honda on its side to avoid going over the side. Peter slid into her and almost pushed her to her death. Thankfully, Cordy stopped in time.

"Are you two OK?"

"Yes!"

Cordy said, "I'm going back to see if we can get out the way we came in." She turned her bike around and took off. She didn't get far when she had to turn around. The path was blocked by boulders. "We can't go back. The cave has collapsed behind us, and unless we can fly. I don't see us crossing the gorge."

Sam and Peter had gotten up and were looking for a way along the wall that would get them out, but there was no hope. They came back to where Cordy was to assess the situation. "It's definitely not looking good."

Peter drove back to the cave-in and then measured the length back to the edge of the fissure. Then all the ground shook again, absorbing a small after-shock. A few boulders dropped from above. They sat down and just took it all in, wondering how they would escape.

"Do either of you two have a cell phone?" Peter asked.

"We don't have a chance in hell of getting a call out of here."

"I just want it for the calculator." Sam handed him her phone.

He put numbers in, and then nodded his head and said, "It'll work."

"What will work?"

"I can jump the gorge and make it to the other side."

Sam and Cordy looked at him incredulously. He jumped to his feet. "I double-checked my calculations, and everything says I can make the jump."

"Don't do it, please, don't do it. Cordy, make him stop. If you miss, you'll surely drown at the bottom of the gorge. There's a river;

I can hear it." *He was going to risk a death that he feared all his life, what a man!*

"What option do we have? If we don't do anything, we'll certainly die."

Peter started his motorbike and went back to the cave-in to be able to have room to gather as much speed as he could. Then he headed toward the gorge as fast as he could. When he passed the women, he was flying. Over the edge he went. As it seemed that he had miscalculated and was falling to his death, the girls screamed.

Peter leapt from the motorbike and barely grabbed the cable to the now-broken bridge. He slammed into the wall and let out a deep grunt, indicating he had hit hard. Then he slowly pulled himself up to the other side.

"I told you my calculations said I could make it to the other side. Just me, though. Not the bike."

The women looked at one another, and they had blood in their eyes. "Just you wait until I get a hold of you, Mr. Peter."

Peter reached down and grabbed the broken side of the bridge and pulled it level with the other side and wedged a long board over to the other side. Cordy drove over to the other side. Sam followed, pulling Peter in for a passionate kiss when she reached him. "Thank you for saving our lives." Then she punched him in the shoulder as hard as she could. "That's for scaring me."

Cordy slammed into his other shoulder.

The women started their motorbikes just as another aftershock came.

"Let's get out of here. You can ride behind me," Sam said, looking at Peter.

He pulled up close and held onto her hips. She pulled his arms all the way around her. He just leaned in and smiled.

157

It was only another hour until they came to the tunnel that led to the St. Louis catacombs. A city under the city — only a few knew about this world.

"You know, a long time ago, they could load barrels of beer on a conveyer system and it would travel a mile without being touched by a human hand, until it was lifted onto a barge."

They switched out the bikes for a jeep and emerged from under the hill of one of the breweries onto railroad tracks and headed to Peter's house.

When they walked in, Nancy and Maggie came running to hug Cordy. She looked up and saw a very alive Tim Huff holding a happy dog. *Nancy's not an orphan.* She saw Jon in the corner and when to him and embraced him. "Thank you! What about Ash?"

"He hasn't made it in yet."

Peter took off his shirt to examine his wounds. Jon recognized the bruises on his shoulders; he knew where those beauties had come from. *I think I was better off with the little girls.*

CHAPTER 31

Explore, Dream, Discover

Peter's house was bustling with a group of people who were relieved to be in a safe place at last. Everyone knew that the worst was still to come but, for now, they could let down their guard and laugh, tell stories, and even joke.

Cordy sat on the couch, sandwiched between Nancy and Maggie. They were telling her all about anything and everything.

Peter had just finished making sure everyone was taken care of and, coming up behind Sam and Jon, called out to everyone in the room, "Would anyone like to have a guided tour of the house?"

But no one heard him among the light-hearted conversation. He was getting ready to ask again, louder this time, when Sam spun around and said, "I would like to have a special tour."

Jon whipped his head around, and looked at the two of them.

Oh, no, Peter's in trouble. Run, Peter, run! But before he could say anything the two escaped and left him alone.

"Where should we start?" Peter asked. He reached down and gently took Sam's hand in his and led her to a bookcase in his study. He pulled out a book on the top far-right side, and the bookcase slid to the side, revealing an elevator. Peter pushed the down button.

"We house about fifty dragons, all men who have been wronged by Dark Watchers. We have secret offices all around the world, but this is the headquarters."

The doors of the elevator opened, and they entered. Sam noticed that it had only two floors to pick from. Peter pushed B1. When the doors re-opened she could see a bustling communication center. It was higher tech than what the Lafitte organization had.

"Wow, Peter. I had no idea that you were running a worldwide operation."

"Just down the hall is our shipping and receiving."

They entered a room that contained one of the most impressive armories Sam had ever seen.

"You really know how to impress a girl. May I go in and browse through the hardware? Oh cool, you have a whole wall just for Chinese weapons. Let's see, you have swords of all types, knives and a little of everything. Peter, you have weapons from almost every country in the world!"

"Yes, I picked them out myself."

"You've been saving Pure of Hearts all over the world? I wish I could travel but running the U.S. operation has kept me in the States."

"Yes, my first journey was at eleven, but honestly, it was my life that was saved."

"I know. Master Wong told me all about your mother and father and how they saved you from the Nephilim."

"I trained with Master Wong as hard as I could until I was fifteen. Then I took a trip to the Soviet Union and brought back two Pure of Hearts. I took the SKS automatic carbine as a souvenir off the man who was trying to kill them. I have killed many who were evil in nature and wouldn't be reasoned with, but I also have saved many Pure of Heart." *She didn't blink an eye when I told her, she is not afraid of me.*

"I saw on the elevator a B2 button. What's below us?"

"It's the residence quarters for the fifty dragons and a tunnel that goes under the street to the parking garage. We lease the bottom level of the garage, so no one can when we're coming or going out of the residence. It's like having our own bat cave. Come on, I have something special to show you." Peter reached down and took her hand again. It caught her off guard and she looked back at him with surprise.

No guy has ever had any interest in holding my hand, though they've certainly been interested in touching my body. But this guy is different. He's never looked down when he talks to me. He always looks me in my eyes. Peter is different than the rest. He's a gentleman. I think I'll let him hold my hand. After all, he did save my life, not once, but twice.

They entered the elevator and he pushed the button for the main floor. When the door opened, Jon looked over and saw them holding hands and rolled his eyes. Cordy wasn't shocked at all to see the chemistry between the pair. She saw how Peter was flirting with Sam back in the cave. Cordy gave him a thumbs up.

Peter led Sam through the main kitchen and then outside to the backyard. *I thought he wanted to show me something special. Is his bedroom outside? Anytime a man has said he had something special to show me, we ended up in his bedroom and what he had wasn't very special.*

"My garden has been inspired by my world travels. I tend to spend too much time working on it, but I tell everyone it's good therapy. What I wanted to show you is back here in the corner."

As they rounded the corner the pathway opened up to a small courtyard and nestled under two-hundred-year-old oak trees was a shipping container with sliding glass windows on three sides. When they got closer, Sam could see that the one side that didn't have windows was the side that had the original doors and, on the outside, it had a stencil painting of a dragon with a large white X over the dragon.

Sam stopped in her tracks. "Peter, is this the same shipping container that you almost died in?"

"Yes, it is. It took me five years to find it and track down the group of Nephilim that was responsible for my parents' deaths." He was still holding her hand and gave it a little squeeze. "Come on, what I have to show you is inside."

Peter walked on with Sam in tow. He could tell she was hesitant to go in. He kicked off his shoes, and she followed suit.

As they entered, she had a feeling of tranquility and peace come over her. "Peter, let me ask you something. Am I the first person beside yourself to enter this sacred place?"

"Other than Master Wong, yes, you are, Sam." On the left wall without windows hung a white cotton belt looped delicately over a single peg on the wall. Next to it was his fathers' black leather belt that had saved his life, and to the right of that was a cotton black belt symbolizing the tie he had with his father. When Peter was a small boy, his father would teach him and together they would practice their karate and martial arts.

Sam started to cry uncontrollably. She knew that Peter was letting her into his life in a way he hadn't done with anyone else. She felt privileged, honored and scared at the same time. "In some way, you brought me home to meet your parents."

"That's exactly it, Sam. You are so intuitive and smart. I have all of my memories up until the last one of my mother and father sacrificing their lives for me."

Sam's sobs slowly eased, and she gained control. "Do you come here often?"

"If I am in town, I come to pay my respects daily. For some who know the story, they would say that this isn't healthy for me. I have no burial site to go to and this has become my memorial to them both. You would have liked my mother. She was a special woman who was selfless and loving. She sacrificed many of her wants and needs for my wants and needs. My mother worked hard to make sure I was equipped with the knowledge, skills, and abilities to make it in this crazy world we live in. She was always there for me.

"I believe my mother is looking down on me and I still, to this day, feel her unconditional love for me. She made me feel as though I were the most important person in the world. I know that she would be happy and overjoyed knowing that you are in my life. You are in my life, aren't you?"

Sam brushed his hair back out of his face and gave him a soft kiss that seemed to last forever. When they broke apart, they smiled at each other.

"You bet I am!" Then he kissed her back. She looked into his eyes. "Tell me about your father."

"I would have to put his ability to protect at the top of the list. He saved my life. He made life fun in that he had the ability to teach me about so many things in life, and it never seemed as if he was my teacher but rather my friend. He set high standards but showed me through how he lived that they could be met. When my father did get mad at me, I was afraid he would never get over it, but he always did.

"He taught me how to have faith in Christ, God and the Holy Spirit. He treated my mom as if she was a queen, with respect. She was his partner. My early days were filled with learning karate. He was my sensei. I have been training in the martial arts my whole life, so in many ways he has been with me every day. I miss him dearly."

"Would you like something to drink?"

"Yes, I would."

Peter opened a small cabinet at the end of a white futon, revealing a mini refrigerator. He reached in and pulled out two bottles of water. "That's the best I can do out here. I could go back to the house and get you something else."

"No, the water will do just fine." They both sat down on the futon and started to talk. Peter told her about his world travels.

Sam shared. "Someday, I hope to be able to travel, but ever since I was seventeen, I started working in the family business and just never found time to travel. Other than Canada and Mexico, I've never been outside of the United States."

"You know, Sam, when we were in the cave, I jumped to the other side not just to save you and Cordy but to save myself as well. On the boat you gave me a chance to face my fears. That was a wild ride, you must admit. You have given me back my life without fear of water. You let me start to dream of a life outside of the Dragon."

"I do have to say that it was a wild ride and only the second time I had to do that. The first time was much easier in that the barge was standing still." They both started to laugh.

"You know Sam, a popular man once said, 'Twenty years from now you will be more disappointed by the things that you didn't do, than by the ones you did do. So, throw off the bowlines. Sail away from safe harbor. Catch the trade winds in your sails. Explore. Dream. Discover.' I love Mark Twain."

"I know what you're talking about, Peter. I'm already having those kinds of thoughts. They talked for hours and then realized the sun was starting to come up. *I have had the time of my life just sitting and talking to a man who just held my hand.* "We should go to bed."

"I agree."

Peter led her back to the main house and when they got to the living room, no one was there. They had all gone to bed.

Peter walked Sam over to the elevator and pushed the up button. "I believe your room is upstairs." He kissed her. "Goodnight, Sam. Sleep tight."

"You aren't coming up?"

"No, my room is downstairs with the Dragons." Then the elevator door closed.

I think Peter is something special. What a first date!

CHAPTER 32

Enlightenment

Ash didn't sleep a wink. He kept thinking to himself: *Cordy said yes! This amazing woman said yes to my marriage proposal! I am the luckiest guy in the world.*

Remington was sound asleep but as Ash got out of bed, the giant started to stir. "I'm sorry. I didn't mean to wake you. Why don't you sleep in? I'm just headed down for some coffee since I'm not sleeping."

"No, just give me a second."

They headed down to the dining room and as they walked in, a voice rang out. "Well, there is my Ash man." As they walked up to Dottie's table, she batted her eyes and trilled, "Who is this tall drink of manhood?"

"Remington, may I introduce a close dear friend of mine, Dirty Dottie. She has saved my life many times and in some perverted way, I love her dearly."

"So, Dottie, how did you get to be the belle of the Mississippi?"

"Well it's a short story. My husband gave me this magnificent paddle wheel as a retirement present. He thought that I would like to sing and dance but with smaller audiences. He was right, and I do enjoy that part. However, he should've never used the word retirement, so he's in the dog house and probably will be there for the rest of his life."

"It is a pleasure to meet you, Mrs. Dirty Dottie."

"You have a Welsh accent but look like a Native American, and I'm picking up some Cajun. Interesting combination."

"Yes, ma'am, a little Acadian and a little French."

Dottie waved the waiter over and ordered two chicory coffees and some New Orleans beignets. "Well, you young studs, I have to get ready for the first morning show, so I'll leave you to it." She got up and as she walked by Ash, she gave him a little squeeze on the thigh and a big smile.

"Will we see you tonight at dinner, with your husband?"

"Oh no. He left for the east coast last night after you came aboard. It'll be just us three. He just had to get back to the harbor and take care of his boats."

As Dottie walked out of the dining room, Ash moaned, "Oh no, let the games begin."

"Well, she's an interesting person."

"Oh, she's much more than interesting. You have no idea. So, how did you end up getting caught by the Dark Watchers?"

"It's almost too embarrassing to tell. I went out in the morning to let the dog out and bam, just like that, they tased me and down I went. They must've been following the chief for some time because I live way out in the middle of the forest. I think I know why they wanted to take me as hostage — so I couldn't help you. The chief said you'd be looking for an artifact that went way back to Egyptian times. He couldn't see it in his vision but knew it was important."

"Wow, here I am, an archaeologist from Egypt talking to a Welsh Indian looking for something halfway around the world that's Egyptian. The chief was right. I need help."

"No, it makes sense. My family came here in 1170, three hundred years before Christopher Columbus. But what most people don't know is who came before us. My family found all kinds of Egyptian artifacts. In fact, our next stop is Cairo, Illinois. It's known as Little Egypt, and there's a cave not too far from there called Burrows Cave where many Egyptian artifacts were found. There was a cave in the Grand Canyon that had Egyptian artifacts as well. So, my guess is that they came years before my family did. The chief said you would have a map on with you."

"I don't have it with me, but I can get a copy sent to me." Ash pulled out the little cell phone that Jon had and called his father. It went to voice mail. *That's not good.* Ash tried again but still no answer. Ash started to panic. *Something's wrong.* Then all of the sudden, the phone started to ring, and it was his father on the caller ID.

"You scared me when you didn't answer."

"You scared us when the phone rang, and it wasn't from anyone we knew."

"Yeah, what are you doing calling back an unfamiliar number?"

"It's that mother of yours. She said to live on the wild side. She'll never change."

"How's she doing?"

"Not very well, but she's hanging in there. It bothers her that she can't see what is happening with you. She feels if she could, it would help. Anyway, how can I help you?"

"I need to get the picture of the map from the Vatican faxed to me. Remington, hand me that brochure on the Belle, please. The fax number is 367-246-6386."

"Your mother wants to know who Remington is and what is the Belle, and did you know that the fax number, when you spell it out, says 'for a good time'?"

"Remington is a Welsh Indian, the Belle is a river boat, and, no, I didn't know what the fax number spelled out, but I'm not surprised."

"Alright, son, the fax is on its way."

"Tell mom I love her and to behave. I'll see her soon."

Turning to Remington, Ash said, "Let's head down to the office and pick up that fax."

Remington studied the map. "What you have here is a treasure map of artifacts. You're going to be looking for a church that has the name of God on it. See the two wooden rods on the outside?"

"Yes."

"In history, what wooden rod had blooms coming from it?"

"Aaron's rod. You can't be serious. How did it get there? You know that's exactly what we're looking for — something that has the power to control nature."

"I don't think the question is how it got there, but rather who wanted it there and was it for the Pure of Heart?"

"Let's go back to the room and look at the Bible in the drawer."

They got back to the room, and Ash looked for the passage. "I think it's in 1 Kings chapters 8 and 9. Yes, here it is, *there was nothing in the ark except the two tablets of stone, which Moses put there at Horeb, when the Lord made a covenant with the children of Israel, when they came out of the land of Egypt.*"

"So, Remington, how did you know?"

"My family had been smuggling up the river many years before the Lafitte family. I recognized Jon when you came to rescue us. When I was young, I remember hearing a story of a great Templar Master bringing items up the river that came from Solomon's house. One of the items was a blooming stick with no roots."

"That would explain how De Villiers found Solomon's ring. Now he's looking for Aaron's rod." As soon as Ash got the words out, a bright light came from behind him. *It could only be Uriel.*

Remington smiled and nodded his head. "My friend, great warrior Uriel, how are you?"

"I am good, Mad Dog. I see you have met my friend Ash."

"Ash, Mad Dog, take theses sunglasses and put them on. When Mad Dog squints it scares me. Looks like you two figured out what you are looking for. Ash, Cordy will know where the church is. Mad Dog, go back to the Welsh caves and in one of the five caves, you will find the last artifact drawn on the back wall and where to find it. Your family smuggled it up the Mississippi River a long time ago."

The trio could here bells ringing, announcing the next stop of Cairo. In some way it made Ash feel for a brief moment as if he were back in Egypt. Uriel pulled out a plastic Zip-lock bag and gave it to Mad Dog. "Sorry to say, this is for the map. We don't want it to get wet."

"Why would it get wet?"

"We are about to have some Dark Watcher company. I don't see any way off the boat except to swim for it."

"I hope you know how to dog paddle, Remington. It was a pleasure and honor to meet you. We couldn't have done it without you. Everything is connected. Your work is not done yet. Find the Pure of Heart treasures of your ancestors. You know where to look."

"I am a tried and true river rat." Remington walked over to the side rail and lowered himself into the river.

Ash reached out and shook his hand. "Good-bye Mad Dog, Remington, Rat, or just my friend." Then he let go and they watched him swim for shore.

"You better get going, or they will take you back into custody."

"What do you suggest I do?"

"If I were you, I would find Dirty Dottie and assume the position."

Ash took off running and just as the boat was docking he turned into the theater and there was Dottie with her hoop skirt. Dottie smiled and lifted up the back of the hoop and in slid Ash, just like old times.

Dottie had asked the Pure of Hearts who were hiding to join her on stage in costume as part of the show, so they blended in perfectly. Three Dark Watchers went room to room but found no one. They went to the gang plank and headed for their cars.

"Are they gone yet or not? Why do you only wear thongs?"

"It's all about the feel, the touch."

"They're gone, aren't they?"

"Well, yes, but I was just about to ..."

Ash came flying out with sweat dripping from his scarlet face.

"Next stop, St. Louis. Come on, St. Louis!"

CHAPTER 33

In the Arms of the Angels

Ash and the Pure of Heart were only four hours from the Gateway to the West, St. Louis, Missouri. Dottie had just finished her last show of the day and was behaving herself. Ash told the Pure of Heart to get their things packed and be on the deck thirty minutes before docking time. He wanted everyone prepared in case Dark Watchers were waiting for them again and they had to make a run for it. They gave him a thumbs up and he returned the gesture.

Ash strolled along the deck enjoying a few moments of no chaos. As he approached the bow, he saw a familiar bright light. He had no doubt who emanated the light. He turned the corner and there stood Uriel. "Hello, Uriel. What can I do for you?"

"Ash, of all the men I have met through time, you've had one of the most caring and loving hearts. Your faith is strong and your righteousness unwavering. I brought an old friend with me."

"Funny, I don't see anyone with you."

Uriel pulled out a brand-new bottle of Jack Daniel's whiskey.

"Yes, you are a good friend." He pulled off the cap and took a long drink.

What Ash didn't know was that 1,820 miles away, his mother was about to give premature birth to her twins. She had been in labor for more than twelve hours. Nothing she did slowed down the contractions. Like it or not, the twins were going to be born long before their due date. This situation was further complicated by the fact that a terrible storm had blown through, knocking down power lines and trees. Not wanting to further risk the twins' births, Han had called the paramedics to take them to the hospital. But the paramedics' progress was hindered due to the roads being blocked.

Mary, Chief Saunhac's former housekeeper, had become good friends with Ash's mother. She would not let these parents-to-be worry or doubt that these babies would come into the world safely and healthy. When they fretted, she assured them all would be well. After the paramedics became detained due to the road conditions, Mary called the area Mi'kmaq midwife to come and assist them.

The midwife and three paramedics, Michael, Gabriel, and Raphael, arrived at the same time. The midwife assessed Aziza's condition and told her the twins' birth was imminent.

Looking at the three paramedics, the midwife ordered, "Don't just stand there. Get ready!"

She told Aziza to push. With one push, Aziza delivered a tiny boy. The paramedics quickly put monitors on the baby and the readings were alarming. Michael went over and picked up the baby and cuddled him. Miraculously, the monitors started registering normal readings.

Before they could celebrate, Aziza had another contraction and a tiny baby girl was born. She was dusky in appearance and non-responsive. It didn't look like she was going to survive, but Gabriel went over and picked her up and she took a deep breath, her color restoring to a healthy pink.

There was no time to rejoice because Aziza's monitors started screaming. The mother started having a seizure. She was crashing! She flat-lined before they could administer any medical treatment. Han was beside himself in grief. Aziza was the love of his life! How would he raise these twins by himself?

Raphael walked over to Aziza. Tenderly, he slid his arm behind her back and cradled her. Instantly, her pulse and blood pressure returned, and the monitor showed a normal heart rhythm. Aziza opened her eyes to see tears running down Han's face.

Han thought, *these three men are a gift from heaven. They saved my Aziza and my two newborn babies.*

Michael and Gabriel brought the babies to Aziza. She reached out and stroked their tiny hands. They were sleeping peacefully. Aziza sighed with relief and thanks.

"Thank you everyone for everything you've done to bring my children safely into this world." She closed her eyes and remarkably her ability to see things in the outside world immediately returned. She could see Ash leaning up against a wall with Uriel drinking a bottle of Jack Daniels. She frowned and thought, *I will have to talk to him about that drinking!*

Uriel took another big swig of Jack and handed the bottle back to Ash.

"You know, Ash, all those years you've been praying, you never asked for anything personal until the other day. When you were with Cordy in the conference room, you bowed your head in prayer and petitioned. 'Oh, dear God, protect my mother.' Never underestimate the power of prayer."

"I never have, Uriel."

"I know, Ash. Do you still have that little phone? Did you wash it off?"

"Yes, very funny."

"Call your father."

He pulled out the phone and called immediately. "Dad, is that you?"

"Yes, my oldest son. Your little brother, sister and mother are all here. They are doing very well. Uriel's buddies came by to help — Michael, Gabriel and Raphael. It's a miracle, but I don't have to tell you that. I've got to go. There are a lot of things happening. I love you, son."

Tears ran down Ash's face and he fell to his knees to give thanks. He looked over at Uriel, who simply tipped his hat and smiled.

"Uriel, will you do me a favor? Take Cordy's wedding ring so that it's not taken from me if I am caught. I couldn't bear to lose it."

"Sure, no problem."

As he turned and walked around the corner, a tear came to Ash's eye, and the light was gone. *God works in mysterious ways.*

What seemed like minutes took hours and the Belle was pulling up in front of the St. Louis Arch. Ash went in and grabbed his bag before he heard it one more time.

"Is that my Ash man? I have something for you. You weren't going to leave without saying good-bye, were you?"

"Of course, not. How's my Dirty Dottie doing?"

"Well, I'm doing just fine. Come here and I'll give it to you. I'll give it to you really good."

Ash walked closer and Dottie reached down and grabbed his left butt cheek. Then he surprised her. He wrapped his arms around her, pulled her in close, and kissed her hard and long, a romantic kiss she'd never forget. When he broke the kiss, Dottie started to lose her footing. "Thank you for saving my life many times over DD." *Only her close friends called her DD.*

"You can't leave me now."

"Yes, I can. I got a girl waiting for me."

"No, I really have something for you, but what just happened was really good, too." She ran into her office and came back out. "It's a fax — a picture." She handed it to him. His father had sent a picture of the new family.

"DD, how will I ever repay you? You've saved my life and now you've given me this precious gift. Thank you! Thank you!"

The steam whistle blew, and Ash returned to the deck. As the boat docked Ash could see three highway patrol cars seemingly waiting for them. Cautiously, Ash approached the side and a uniformed man called out, "I'm Tim Huff, Nancy's father. You're safe. We're here to take you and the rest of your group to Peter's house. We need to hurry to keep your arrival a secret."

Ash looked back at DD and he could see her blowing kisses. *She is a pretty remarkable woman!*

CHAPTER 34

Nile of the West

Peter Woo owned a century-old brick mansion near Forest Park. He had renovated the mansion to be his home and to serve as the Dragons' headquarters for their world-wide organization. Master Wong held the highest position as Head Dragon and resided with him. The Dragons worldwide vowed to protect the Pure of Heart and their treasures with their lives. For that reason, Peter and Master Wong provided refuge to Cordy and Ash and all the other Pure of Hearts.

The mansion housed massive technologically advanced computers and communications networks in the basement. Ash was talking with his father on a computer about the map of the Lost Tribes. Han had examined it and were amazed at the detail. Ash and Han both knew the legends of the Lost Tribes of Israel, but they saw the story as symbolic. The academics saw things differently. The New World, though harsh, was filled with promise and hope. What better place for the Pure of Heart to place a prized and powerful relic out of the hands of the Children of the Nephilim? They had no doubt the Native Americans had guarded the treasure for centuries.

They focused on the budding rod on the map. Han summarized up the legend of Aaron's rod. He explained that some scholars believed the rod, blessed with incredible power, hailed back to Adam and could only be wielded by one with a pure heart. These scholars suggested that the rod was passed down to Noah and then to Joseph, who lived in Egypt. Moses acquired it from his father-in-law Jethro. Both Moses and Aaron wielded the rod in an attempt to convince the pharaoh to release the Israelites from Egyptian slavery. The rod, later to be called Aaron's rod, was eventually stored in the Ark of the Covenant and traveled with the Israelites. Over time the Ark of the Covenant and its contents were lost. Legends and myths formed on where the holy relics were buried.

Another story that circulated academic secret societies was that the Lost Tribes of Israel went West. Some early European explorers believed the tribes of the New World could have been the Lost Tribes. It seemed the best possibility to explain the Native American presence in America.

After reviewing journals of early North American explorers, many scholars described the Mississippi River as the Nile of the West due to the similarities between the two rivers. In 1541, De Soto came to the Mississippi River and recorded his observations of the Emerald Mound of the Natchez tribe. The mound served as their ceremonial center and was headed by their chief, the Great Sun, similar to the pyramids in Egypt and Ra, the Sun God.

Louis Joliet and Jacque Marquette ventured down the Mississippi to discover a Mississippian culture that had constructed mounds along the river. The mounds were scattered over the land and considered sacred. Another mound they noted was so large that it rivaled the pyramids in Egypt.

Like the Egyptians and their Nile River, the Mississippians developed an expansive trading network, using the Mississippi River as their transportation system. New Orleans became a trading post where many tribes came to barter their wares. As the Nile did in Egypt, the Mississippi River became integral to the Mississippian way of life.

Han placed the Lost Tribe map over an old map of early Saint Louis. The emblem of the rod of Aaron was on a spot near the Mississippi River and a log cabin. Ash placed a map of Saint Louis over it.

"Well, I'll be. I think I know where it is. Dad, you did great work."

Han smiled, "It may not be enough to have the rod. You may need sacred words to release its power."

"Where would I find them?"

"It seems by coincidence that you have the sarcophagus of the mummy of Henut-Wedjebu located near you," Han said. "I believe the sacred words are written on the inside of her coffin. It's at the Saint Louis Art Museum. They found it at Ancient Memphis. Rameses II, who was the pharaoh supposedly during Moses' time, used those same words to try to save his first-born son from death. I believe the problem with him was his heart. Anyway, the one who holds the rod must be pure of heart. Pride and arrogance caused Rameses' downfall, and his young son paid the price. Let's remember these objects came from Egypt. The words may not activate the rod, but they may be necessary to empower the other artifacts that you possess. Your friend is still there at the museum. All you need to do is get a look at the sarcophagus."

Ash laughed. "You make it sound so simple. I'll get over there and make a surprise visit to an old friend."

CHAPTER 35

Mystery Woman

After everybody fell asleep that night, Jon opened his bedroom window and climbed down the limb of a huge, old oak tree that stood outside his room. He walked past mansions and the well-known Forest Park. The darkness was perfect cover as he walked down the street to the Plaza Hotel, built in 1922 and the epitome of luxury with its marble floors and regal columns. The Frenchman made sure he wasn't followed. No one could know where he was going — not even Sam, who he trusted with his life. If his sister knew he was out, she'd want to come, too, but Jon needed to keep his secret hidden.

Jon took the back stairs and anxiously knocked on the hotel door. He had known the guest for a long time but wasn't certain what to expect as they had a tumultuous history. The door opened and before him was a sexy woman adorned in black lace lingerie. Extending a drink to him, she purred, "Entrez."

She's even more beautiful than when I last saw her, Jon thought. Don't fall under her spell.

"You let me down." His anger vibrated across the room causing her to cringe.

"I know Jon, I'm sorry. I tried. You must believe me, I tried." Her misty eyes begged him to understand.

Jon's angry eyes stared into hers, searching for honesty. *Is she hiding anything from me?* They were long-time lovers and he found it hard to believe she would betray him.

She fixed herself a cocktail and stood before him. They clinked their glasses and tossed back their drinks, the fire of the liquor coursing through them. She lightly stroked his cheek, and then gently kissed his lips. The gentleness that she intended to calm him only inflamed his anger. He pulled her to him and returned her kiss with urgency. She understood his heart, his need and she let his passion carry them. They hungrily tore at each other's clothes. Clinging to each other, they kissed passionately, not uttering any words. At the culmination of their love-making, Jon's anger cooled, and a warmth filled his heart.

Jon held her in his arms. "It's been a long time, but that doesn't seem to be a problem for us."

"No, we are always able to pick up where we left off.

"I'm glad you came. I thought you were going to die in New Orleans during the hurricane. You scared the hell out of me. I need to know you're in control."

"Of course I'm in control. I'm Jon Lafitte! On another subject, I may have to ask you to do some things for me. Can I count on you?"

"Jon, you know I'll do anything for you. You really can trust me." He looked intently into her eyes. She never wavered as she returned his piercing stare. What he saw was love and truth. Relief flooded his heart.

Time was running out and this could be their last night together for a while. The lovers fell into each other arms, languorously kissing each other intensely. This time Jon was gentler, for he knew he could trust her with his life.

The woman wanted to ask Jon if he loved her. But it really didn't matter whether he did. The dark-haired Frenchman was the only man who'd ever touched her heart. She would die for him, and now he believed it.

Jon put on his clothes and kissed the sensuous woman still in bed. Her thick hair fell down her back as she watched him get ready to leave.

"You have to leave so soon?"

He looked over at the tempting eyes of the siren pleading him to stay.

Jon sat on the bed and kissed her luscious lips one more time.

"Yes, I don't want them to miss me and get suspicious. We will meet again. You must be careful, too."

"Oui, I'll be careful, but, Jon, I must warn you I can't guarantee..." Jon put his finger to her lips.

"I know. Just do your best, and I forgive you. Do you forgive me?"

"I love you, Jon, no matter what happens. There is nothing to forgive. Everything I do is for you."

Jon winked at her and left the room. He ran out of the Plaza Hotel's back door into the night. The cool air felt good against his face and his heart felt light again. *Women are like fine wine. Cordy is one flavor and my secret mistress is another. It seems as if I love them both, but one expects more of me than the other.*

Cordy is sweet, but stubborn. I owe her a great deal for saving my family. But time has changed us both.

My sexy vixen knows me well and understands me. After all this time, I thought she'd find another man, but she hasn't. She loves me!

Love finds strange bedfellows. I am the wealthiest man in the world for I've loved and have been loved.

At the mansion Jon climbed up the tree and crawled back through the open window. The Frenchman fell into bed and slept soundly dreaming of a ménage a trois with the women he loved. Why choose? Enjoy them both! Frenchmen have more fun, it's true.

CHAPTER 36

Leaked Report

Great minds gathered together to discuss worldwide data regarding Earth's atmosphere, meteorology, and geology. One of the participants was Pierre, Jon Lafitte's good friend. Pierre and Jon had met in college. Thanks to their love for the stars, they studied together and worked on several projects, each using his expertise. One of those projects was Jon's thesis on the cause of the Pioneer anomaly. Jon completed the research and Pierre provided the data and mathematics.

Mathematicians, astronomers, physicists and geologists sat in the room reviewing the latest results from all over the world. Data poured in from a space station revolving around Earth. Satellite reports downloaded to their computers. What they saw truly terrified them. The anxiety increased when representatives from the United Nations, representatives from the National Security

Agency, and generals from all over the world joined their meeting.

The head of the United Nations started off with their report. The magnetic field of Earth was weakening at a rapid pace. Compasses were constantly being adjusted.

A pole shift or pole reversal could be imminent. The last pole reversal occurred several hundred thousand years ago, but the data was suggesting that it could happen again.

The Earth's magnetosphere protects the planet form solar winds and radiation. Would it be affected? Meteorologists placed their results on the screen showing increased violent weather patterns. They predicted that a weakened Earth magnetosphere could cause atmospheric winds to increase.

The geologists submitted their report. They observed disturbances in Earth's inner molten core causing increased volcanic eruptions.

When all reports were presented, and the data compiled and analyzed, the scientists and world leaders shared their dire conclusions. It appeared that Earth's atmosphere was on course to be destroyed by the harmful cosmic radiation of space. Most life on Earth would die. A hush fell over the room at the horrific news.

After the data was shared, questions were allowed from the audience. Pierre stood up and asked the most compelling question of the day, "Knowing the great danger ahead, can mankind survive if we work to together to protect as many as we can?"

The answers given alarmed him. One group of scientists agreed that the general population shouldn't be told of the impending doom because they weren't one hundred percent certain of their conclusions. They didn't want to cause unnecessary panic or a stock market collapse in the event they had misinterpreted the data. Another group of scientists totally disagreed with the findings and felt it was all nonsense and left the room in a huff. Military from the different countries refused to work with each other due to their mistrust.

Pierre shook his head and thought, *civilization as we know it might be at risk and all they offer is the opportunity to hide our heads in the sand. Mankind is being tested and it is failing.*

Pierre looked at the data again and shuddered. He wanted to believe it was wrong but as a scientist he couldn't deny it. Prophets for the past hundred years had warned of a major extinction-level event. Here the data showed it might happen. The reports showed hurricanes with tremendous strength, severe earthquakes occurring all over the world, and floods devastating crops and killing thousands in the next year. If mankind didn't do anything, those thousands of deaths would change to millions. Regardless of what the leaders said, action had to be taken if there was any hope for mankind's survival.

Pierre recalled an earlier extinction level event — Noah and the Great Flood. *How did mankind survive?* Noah placed the Keys of Life in an ark for the survival of life on Earth. The old story rang with a grain of truth. What Noah, his family and mankind to come needed to survive was contained on the ark. *Could there be a modern day ark?*

What would mankind need to survive this current situation? Pierre remembered an article he had read. A team of scientists and psychologists made a list of essentials for what mankind needed to survive a cataclysmic event. They suggested that there would be a need for seed banks, energy production, clean water production, and tools. Why couldn't these things be put in special containers and dispersed all over the world — like mini-Noah's arks? Something could be done to save mankind!

Pierre called Jon, "Jon, I have just come out of a distressing meeting. This information isn't supposed to be released to the public, but I think you need to be aware of it. I've sent a copy of the report to your email, but I'll summarize what it says.

"The magnetosphere is weakening, and the poles may shift at any time. They can't stop the deterioration. We're looking at an extinction-level event and if mankind survives it will knock us back to the Stone Age. The powers-to-be don't want this information shared with the public. They are making no plans to save the people.

"I think we need to take a lesson from Noah and his ark. I have an idea on how we could set up mini-arks around the world, if I could get anyone to listen to me. I feel like I'm on the Titanic, and I should grab my violin."

"Thank you for sending me the report," Jon said. "I've known for a while that things were bad. Don't give up hope, my friend. Mankind, even in its darkest moments is resilient and hopeful.

"I'll give your report to my friends in New York. They're already working on an idea like your mini-arks. They have immense means. We can try to save as many as we can.

"I have to admit that I'm disappointed in the fact that the countries won't coordinate their aid to others. Am I surprised? No, not in the least. Unfortunately, the regular people will be the last to know."

Pierre sighed, "The report is in your email, but I remind you, it's very scary. If I hear any more news, I'll call you."

"Merci, Pierre. Au revoir!"

CHAPTER 37

Washington's Sword

Bob and Julia brought Wapek home with them. Bob made a trip to the pet store, practically buying out the place. Julia laughed. "Geez, Bob, you bought him three beds with better mattresses than our own. I figured he would sleep with us."

Her husband pulled out toys and a bag of gourmet dog food. "Wapek gets only the finest."

The dog wagged his tail and barked. Bob poured the dog food into a bowl with Wapek's name on it and set it on the kitchen floor.

The dog's ears went up and he started growling. Bob and Julia looked at each other and pulled out their guns. Someone knocked at their door and a voice called out. "Special delivery!"

Wapek growled when he heard the stranger's voice.

"Hush, Wapek, and stay," Bob ordered.

Julia positioned herself to the side of the door to cover Bob. She wasn't taking any chances.

Bob looked through the peep hole in the door. A delivery man stood holding a package.

"Are you expecting any sexy lingerie?" Bob whispered.

Julia gave him a cocky smile. "I don't need any sexy lingerie to get you turned on, Bob."

Bob prepared to open the door, his military instincts on high alert. "Point taken."

He opened the door and pointed his gun at the head of a delivery man chewing gum. "Hands in the air!"

The delivery man dropped his package along with his gum.

Julia saw through the crack in the door that they had the intruder where they wanted him.

"Don't shoot! I'm here to deliver a package to Bob from Bill McDermott. I need you to sign for it. You don't have to tip me."

"I'll sign for it, and then get the hell out of here!" Bob picked up the package and signed the papers. The scared man ran from the door and leaped into his van. His wheels screeched as he drove away. He screamed out the window. "You people are crazy!"

Bob closed the door and opened the box with care. "What the hell did Bill send me?"

Bob and Julia looked inside the box. They couldn't believe what they saw. Lying inside was a beautiful sword with a delicate engraving on it. A letter of authenticity accompanied it. George Washington held this sword at Valley Forge. It was given to him by Marquis de Lafayette.

Bob couldn't believe he was holding George Washington's sword. Julia sighed. "How am I ever going to top this birthday gift? Hey, read the note inside." She handed it to him.

"Cordy picked the perfect man to help her in her quest. You've done a fantastic job and are like a son to me. When I took charge of the Light Watchers I was given this Washington sword. I've decided to hand the sword to you. The Light Watchers treasure this sword. It has special powers in the hands of a true fighter. Washington said, 'Real men despise battle but never run from it.' Use the sword wisely, protect it, follow your destiny.

"Happy Birthday, Bob, from Bill."

Bob kissed Julia and smiled. "This is awesome. Washington is one of my favorite generals of all time."

He picked up the sword and it started to vibrate and sparkle.

"I've read all about Washington's life and even though he was a military man most of his life, he hated war. He said, 'My first wish is to see the plague of mankind, war, banished from the earth.' Cordy and I believe we can change the world and so did Washington and Lafayette. The sword is the symbol of the crusader who dedicates his life in aiding mankind. One thing I've learned through this whole journey is that what we do today affects tomorrow. The Pure of Heart and Light Watchers knew their sacrifices would give mankind hope for a better future. We are part of that quest. Bill's an inspiration to me. We both won and lost, but we still keep fighting."

"He mailed you this package a couple days ago," Julia said, with worry in her voice. "He gave you the Light Watchers' most prized treasure. He's passing the leadership of the Light Watchers to you. You need to call Bill right away. Something's wrong Bob."

The Washington's sword lit up while in Bob's hand. "Well damn, Bill, what the hell did you do?"

CHAPTER 38

Lafayette's Gift

The American Continental Army camped at Valley Forge during Christmas in 1777. George Washington watched as his
troops died of cold, starvation, and disease.

He looked out over a collection of log huts and his troops. He
was so proud of his rag-tag army. But, he worried as well. Many
men had no shoes to wear in the snow. Their clothes were falling
apart. Many were sick. Thankfully, women supported their efforts
and volunteered to tend the sick. Even Martha, his wife, was aiding
his men. She planned to gather some city women together to sew
garments and mend ragged clothes for his troops.

Tears filled his eyes. *What an army to command! They are so
loyal and dedicated, but if we don't get help soon, they will lose hope
and the army will disband. That'll be the end of dreams of freedom
for the colonists.*

Marquis de Lafayette, a young handsome Frenchman, approached George. With him was an Oneida tribeswoman, Polly Cooper. Lafayette had made a pact with the Oneida tribe and at Lafayette's encouragement, they became allies with the Continental Army. One way the Oneida tribe contributed to their new alliance was providing maize to the troops to eat. Maize was different from the corn the colonists were accustomed to, so Polly had taught them how to prepare it.

George shook Lafayette's cold hand and hugged a surprised Polly. "Lafayette, thank you, and thank you so much, Miss Cooper, for helping to feed my men and teaching them how to cook your corn. I've heard only good things about your cooking. It's a blessing you came."

Polly humbly bowed. "The Oneida people are with you. We hope to see a free country for all our people. If you excuse me, General, I must get back to the kitchens."

George nodded. "Yes, by all means. I just wanted to express my gratitude to you."

Polly bowed again and headed to the kitchen hut where a line of starving men waited outside for their rations.

Lafayette's French accent added to his charm. "We have angels watching over us, George. The Light Watchers and the Pure of Heart have united and feel the dream of a republic is possible. I have a present to give you. General, follow me."

George followed Lafayette to his log cabin, where a fire was burning in the fireplace. "Polly Cooper is an angel. I hope your gift is more food and weapons for my men. I don't know what I would do without you, my friend."

Lafayette smiled. "I will give you something better. I give you hope in these dreary times." He pointed to a cloth-draped box sitting on his table.

"I will pour us something warm, a sherry I brought with me from France."

He handed George a glass filled with the amber liquid.

"I dreamt last night of an angel with red hair. He told me to give you this family treasure."

George looked at Lafayette with surprise. "I, too, had a dream of a red-haired angel with a sword in his hand. He told me that what we do here will change the world and give hope to mankind. The Pure of Heart will give democracy to the world. What did he say to you?"

"The angel and I traveled through time," Lafayette recounted. "I stood next to my ancestor, Gilbert de Motier Lafayette III, in the siege of Orleans. Joan of Arc carried the Sword of Heaven and raised it into the air right next to me.

"She said, 'Lafayettes, your fight for freedom will change history forever. You are right to remind George that slavery is wrong. You will achieve freedom and in the years, to come, slavery will be abolished. All men will be equal. Your legacy will be remembered.'

"The angel then took me back to the Crusades where Richard the Lionheart carried the Sword of Earth. I saw him waving it in battle. My ancestor, dressed in white robes with a red cross, showed me a sword found at the Dome of the Rock in Jerusalem. He said it was Enoch's sword. Enoch was an ancestor of Noah's, who was guardian of all the treasures of heaven. The angel said, 'Give this sword to George, for it will help win his war and save mankind. They must have hope for the future.'"

Lafayette removed the cloth. In the box lay a glimmering sword. "A general who fights for freedom must have a sword worthy of him. My family would be honored if you would carry this into battle with you."

George smiled and raised his glass with Lafayette. "We can't lose with angels and Joan of Arc on our side."

CHAPTER 39

Hidden Words

The morning brought disturbing news. Television reports all over the world showed that volcanoes were erupting amid earthquakes and storms. The general public was beginning to panic although announcers attempted to minimize the seriousness of the situation.

After reading Pierre's report, Jon contacted some of his former astrophysicist colleagues. They confirmed Earth's magnetosphere weakness. Their data showed incoming cosmic radiation and an increase in solar activity. They further verified that the shifting of the poles was becoming a greater concern. Earth's shield, which protected all life on the planet from death by cosmic radiation, was deteriorating, and deteriorating quickly. Once the shield was gone, all life — humans, animals, plants — would die and the seas would be destroyed.

Jon re-read the reports and thought, *this is an ominous warning to the Pure of Heart. Time is running out! Mankind faced extinction before and survived. Thankfully, the ancient ones left the tools necessary to survive for their children. We just have to find them all.*

He looked over to the dining room table. Ash, Cordy, and a few of the Dragons were finalizing their plan to walk to the art museum to view the sarcophagus of the mummy of Henut-Wedjebu. She was a long-dead priestess who might hold the secret to operating one of the Keys of Life. He decided to join them on this adventure. A little more security never hurt.

As they walked to the art museum, Ash shared some information about the mummy in the sarcophagus and other ancient Egypt tidbits.

"The sarcophagus belongs to an Egyptian priestess, Henut-Wedjebu. She lived in the Old Kingdom in ancient Memphis. She probably protected the Keys of Life. She was a beautiful vocalist for the temple of Amun. Her husband was an overseer for the temple of Aten.

"Ramses II built Abu Simbel. He knew Moses and Aaron, according to some archaeologists. My friend and teacher, Richard Brown, is the administrator of the museum and is going to let me get a look inside the sarcophagus."

"Do you trust him?" Jon asked.

"I have no reason not to," Ash said.

Jon winced. "You don't know, so that means everyone, be on alert for Dark Watchers. We should split up and keep in touch with these walkie-talkies."

Jon pulled out a pair of devices from his back pack. "Anybody see anything unusual, notify us, and then head back to Peter's house."

"If you notice anybody following you, try to lose them in Forest Park. Use the map I gave you. The park is filled with hiding places. Keep us informed of your location," added Cordy.

Outside of the Saint Louis Art Museum stood a huge statue of Saint Louis, the crusader king, carrying a sword aimed at heaven as he sat on a huge horse.

"The sword symbolizes the Sword of Heaven!" Jon said. "I think we're in the right place."

Ash and Cordy went to Richard Brown's office while the others split up and walked around the museum.

A middle-aged man in a gray suit greeted them. "Ash, what a wonderful surprise. I couldn't believe it when I got your text message. I'm so glad to see you. And who is this lovely lady?"

Ash shook hands and introduced Cordy. "Cordy, this is one of my professors, Richard Brown. He doesn't dig in the sand anymore. Richard, meet Cordy."

Richard laughed. "It's my bad back, Ash, or else I'd be with you in Egypt sweating. At least, that's my excuse, Cordy. Well, enough small talk. Let me show you the sarcophagus. I know Ash is anxious to see her."

Richard led them downstairs into the Egyptian antiquities room. He pulled out a key and opened a case which held a coffin of black and gold. The coffin featured a woman's face. Her eyes were lapis lazuli colored. There were three black crosses on a field of gold with a female angel whose gold wings were spread out. She had a smile on her face as if she were waiting for them.

Ash gasped when he saw her. "Oh, Richard, she's in amazing condition. Can I see the inside of the coffin?"

"Of course, but what are you looking for Ash? Maybe I can help?"

"I'm looking for an inscription," Ash said. "Did you discover any?"

Richard asked. "How on the earth did you know, Ash? No one knows the inscription is there. Please, look and read it. It's there."

Ash looked inside the sarcophagus. "It's written in hieroglyphs. Thanks to Napoleon, we may never have found the Rosetta stone to decipher this message."

"Napoleon was fascinated with Egypt," Richard said. "He believed Western civilization began there. He knew Egypt contained treasures and he believed an emperor needed them if he was to succeed. I think Napoleon believed in magic or the power of these ancient relics from an ancient civilization long ago. Some say the technology came from the heavens, and that the lady angel carries the message."

Cordy watched Ash's excitement in opening such a beautiful artifact. His eyes started to tear up when he saw the inscription written on the inside of the coffin. Richard grinned at his surprised face.

"Beautiful, isn't it? Please share it with your delightful friend."

Ash's voice trembled slightly. "I am a Child of the Nile. All are born free and equal. They are blessed with reason and knowledge of good and evil. Treat one another as your brother. The Keys of Life are to save all lives."

Cordy's eyes misted up. "She's a wise woman."

Richard closed the lid of the mummy's coffin and locked the glass case. "It's been a secret. I'm so surprised you know about it. How in the world did you suspect it, Ash?"

Ash patted his former teacher on the shoulder. "It was just a hunch. I read something similar in Abu Simbal and wondered if another priestess knew it. I see the two caskets of priestesses with the Egyptian Book of the Dead carved in gold on their tops reside in your display room. Have a look, Cordy. This is Isis, the Egyptian goddess."

Cordy saw a woman with black hair kneeling with her wings apart. "She looks like an angel. Isis is on all three of the coffins."

"Isis was a favorite of the downtrodden," Richard explained. "She carries the ankh, the symbol of the key of life, and a staff for royalty. Her hieroglyph is a sitting woman, a throne, and a bread loaf. She's the symbol for fertility of the land. The Egyptians knew the Nile was the bread basket for the world. The priestesses here served her temple.

"Some people say the Ark of the Covenant had the same symbolism of the winged angel. They were considered the messengers to heaven. Cultures over time mix and use the same symbolism."

"I'm so happy to see you, Ash, but I have an important meeting in a few minutes with one of our donors. Perhaps we could get dinner later? Please feel free to roam around. It was a pleasure to meet you, Cordy."

"Thank you so much, Richard. I'll call you."

Cordy nodded. "Thank you, Professor Brown."

After Richard left them, Ash and Cordy relayed to everyone that the mission was a success, and they should head back to Peter's house.

CHAPTER 40

Rendezvous

Jon left the art museum as soon as Cordy and Ash had achieved their mission. He knew this might be his last chance to see her. The Frenchman headed to the World's Fair Pavilion in Forest Park. It was located near Peter Woo's home. The pavilion was built on a hill that overlooked a huge fountain. The green grass and flowers provided for a beautiful scenic view. He found her standing in the shadows of one of the archways wearing sunglasses and a black dress that hugged her curvaceous figure.

She smiled. "You made it. No one spotted you, did they?"

He shook his head. "No, I snuck out. I checked that nobody followed me. Sam doesn't suspect anything. Do you have everything set up? I don't want any more casualties like last time."

Her voice quivered slightly. "I'm so sorry, Jon. I didn't know. You must believe me. I loved him, too. Forgive me!"

Jon pulled her into his arms. "I forgive you. No matter what happens, I want you to know that. "

She kissed him and placed her head on his chest. "I love you. I won't let you down."

"We may not make it, but we must try to help save the world," Jon whispered. "The reports coming out of NASA and the military are devastating for the planet. I've seen how powerful these devices are and what they can do. The Pure of Heart are really the world's only hope."

She handed him a dossier. "I've copied as much information as I could, just in case I'm discovered."

Jon kissed her again. "Thank you so much for doing this for me and the world. I don't know how to repay you for what you've done. Be very careful."

She smiled and gazed into his passionate brown eyes. His thick brown hair tussled in the wind and she brushed a curl from his forehead. "I told you when I left you that night that I would die for you. I have no regrets. Don't weep for me if I do. As far as repayment, I have a few amorous ideas."

"I bet you do, ma cherie," Jon laughed. "I'll keep you posted on any new information."

She nodded and whispered, "I'll keep you informed as usual, and I'll protect the package.

"Jon, the earthquakes, volcanoes, and rising seas have everyone on high alert. Do you really think these technologies can stop the pole shift?"

"Yes, I do," he said. "If they don't, we still need to try to save as many as we can. Cordy is working on that aspect, too."

She noticed his voice softened when he said Cordy's name. "Do you love her, Jon?"

"I find her a fascinating woman, but I don't believe I'm her kind of man."

"You didn't answer my question."

"I don't know, to be honest. She saved my family. I owe her a great debt."

She knew Jon was attracted to Cordy and his heart was in turmoil.

"Jon Lafitte, this is the first time I've seen you so confused. You're the smartest man I've ever known, and two women have you bewildered." She laughed. "I'm not jealous. You know that, don't you?"

Jon teased. "Are you sure you're not a little?"

"No, I'm not. You've not gone to bed with her either. I can tell. "

The Frenchman knew he couldn't hide anything from her. They'd known each other too long.

She looked at her watch and looked out over the park. "I must go. You should go, too, before they miss you. Adieu, my love."

Jon wrapped his arms around her and gave her a passionate kiss, so they could remember this moment for the rest of their lives. Her heart pounded, and she sighed. He whispered, "Adieu, ma cherie."

He waited for her to leave and then he walked over the grass and through a grove of trees toward Peter's house.

Arriving at his destination, he saw Master Wong, Peter, Chris, and Sam standing in the back yard.

Sam turned and saw Jon approaching. With concern in her eyes, she said, "You didn't come back with the others. Where were you? What took you so long?"

Not meeting her eyes, Jon explained, "I had to make sure no Dark Watchers followed me, so I took a longer route."

Sam knew her brother and knew when he was evading the truth. Just as she was going to press the issue, Jon interrupted her and demanded, "Where are Cordy and Ash?"

"We don't know!" Peter answered worriedly. "As we were leaving the museum, Cordy and Ash spotted Dark Watchers. They told us to take the side exits rather than the front door. That's the last we've heard from them. We've tried to reach them through the walkie-talkies, but there has been no response."

"I don't like this! Something's wrong!" Jon insisted.

"Calm down, Jon. Cordy and Ash can take care of themselves. You know Cordy is well trained in martial arts," assured Master Wong.

Just as he finished his statement their radios started squealing. Cordy's voice could be heard whispering in the background.

CHAPTER 41

Nice Kitty Kitty

As Ash and Cordy left Richard's office and headed down the stairs, Cordy noticed two men dressed in black by the entrance doors. She relayed the news to everyone.

"Everyone get out as quick as you can. We've spotted two possible Dark Watchers at the front door. Try the side exit doors."

Cordy instructed Ash to go down the stairs to the lower level. She knew from her many excursions to the museum that an exit to the side parking lot existed there.

The lower level of the museum was filled with rooms depicting early colonial American furniture. The exhibit consisted of rooms decorated with priceless pieces. They passed a dining room ready for its early American dinner guests. Ash grabbed Cordy and climbed over the red velvet rope into the colonial bedroom exhibit.

Ash said softly, "Cordy, it's time we take the next step and go to bed together."

"OK, but do you think this is the best time?" Cordy smiled at him mischievously.

From the mirror in the room they could see a Dark Watcher checking the display next to them. Ash pointed to the early American bed dressed in colonial quilts.

"Yes, I do. Now get under the bed." He crawled under the bed, and she slithered under with him. Ash held her tightly against him since the bed was very narrow. Cordy loved every minute of it. Her face gazed into his loving eyes and his lips gently touched hers. She pulled him closer and kissed him back. Their bodies fit together perfectly. Cordy felt her arms roam all over Ash's back. The moment broke when the lovers heard footsteps approaching. They saw the shoes of the Dark Watcher stop by the bedroom display. They held their breaths, fearful they would be discovered.

"All clear down here," the Dark Watcher announced on his radio, walking away.

They let out quiet sighs of relief. Ash couldn't resist brushing his lips against her forehead. Cordy smiled up at him and snuggled a little closer. But reality came crashing back. As much as she would have liked to continue this interlude in their little cocoon, Cordy regretfully rolled away from Ash and peeked under the bedspread.

"Coast is clear. Follow me."

"I'm right behind you."

Cordy smiled. "We need to find a way out of here before we get caught."

They scrambled out from under the bed and headed back toward the exit door. They were moving down the hill when they saw more Dark Watchers following after them.

"Uh oh! We've been spotted. I'm going to try to lose them in the zoo."

Cordy had the advantage. She knew Forest Park well. She had frequently visited the large park in the middle of St. Louis. She grabbed Ash's hand and rushed toward the bushes to the path that led to the main gate of the Saint Louis Zoo.

They ran in at a very busy time. They both smiled when they saw the crowds. Hundreds of visitors walked through the zoo. Cordy hoped they could get lost in the crowd. She saw the Red Rock Country sign and knew where they could hide.

The two Dark Watchers ran into the zoo and saw a glimpse of them running through the crowd of strollers and families. Cordy headed for the Cat House. Red Rocks inhabitants included wild lions, leopards, and other varieties. She had worked at the zoo as a veterinarian, so she knew the security codes to get into the cages.

Ash saw a huge orange and black striped tiger lying in his forest habitat as Cordy plugged in the codes to open the habitat door. The lions and tigers roamed around in a forest-like habitat similar to the jungle from which they originated. The trees provided shade and cover for the predators.

"Don't tell me we're going in there. I think we have a better chance with the Dark Watchers."

"Trust me, Ash. It's our only chance to get out of here alive."

As soon as they entered the forest, the huge Bengal tiger licked his lips and his yellow eyes followed them with great interest. He seemed friendly at first, then the tiger shifted his stance to an alert position.

Nervously, Ash whispered, "Nice kitty, kitty."

Cordy smacked his head. "Knock it off, Ash! This is a Bengal tiger, not anything close to a 'kitty.' His name is Max. The zoo called me when Max became ill with a severe infection. I treated him, but it was touch and go for a while. I stayed with him until he was out of danger. Since then, Max and I have had a special bond."

As if understanding her words, Max sauntered over and nuzzled his head against Cordy's thigh. She affectionately petted his head.

Max's instincts kicked in. He sensed Cordy needed protecting. He led Cordy and Ash deeper into the rocks and bushes to further hide them.

In a hushed voice, Cordy explained to Ash, "Tigers are expert hunters. Their hearing and quick reaction time allows them to kill from the side or from behind their prey. They attack at the prey's throat, and then drag it into the bushes. I've seen a tiger take down a water buffalo with ease. If the Dark Watchers follow us into this area, they're going to be in for a big surprise."

The Dark Watchers entered the Cat House by breaking a window in the service shed where supplies were stored. They pulled out their guns and broke down the door, giving them access to the cat habitat. Sensing strangers in their habitat, the feline carnivores raised an alarm with their growls and roars and gathered the cubs together.

The Dark Watchers walked quietly around the rocks and bushes looking for Cordy and Ash. The men walked further into the habitat. Since the jungle was filled with tropical palm trees and bushes to make it feel like the tigers' home, the Watchers didn't realize they had invaded a den of six-hundred-pound carnivores guarding their cubs.

One of them yelled out, "Let's get this over with! Surrender now! If you don't, then it's going to get ugly! You're trapped!"

Meanwhile Max had been stalking the unaware Dark Watchers. He crouched down in the bushes, emitting a low rumble from his throat. Cordy closed her eyes and whispered the chief's mantra, which had a special effect on the animals around her. The assailants heard her soft chanting. They aimed their guns to shoot.

One of the Watchers called out, "Enough, you two! Game time is over. Come out with your hands up, or I shoot you both right here and now!"

Max came out of his hiding place with his rumble increasing to a growl. The other Watcher aimed his gun at him and said, "Zoo kitty cat, you better shut up or I'll put a bullet in your brain. I'd like to kill me a tiger and add you to my trophy list. Yes, maybe I'll just do that."

Max's growl increased to a roar. He showed his fangs, and just as he was ready to pounce, two female tigers that had been hiding on the opposite side sprang out and attacked both men from behind.

Now who was the predator and who was the prey? The sheer size of the tigers knocked the men to the ground. Their swift attack stunned the men. One of the men attempted to shoot at the tigers but his shot went wild. Max joined the fray, clamping down on the shooter's arm and tearing it from his body. The screams of the men filled the air.

From behind the bushes, Cordy and Ash observed the gruesome scene. It was horrendous to watch, but the tigers had saved their lives.

Ash and Cordy ran out of the Cat House still hearing the men's blood-curdling screams.

"I'll never look at a tiger the same ever again, and I definitely will never call it a kitty cat."

"You've learned your lesson." They heard screams and police sirens in the distance.

"I don't see anybody following us. Let's get out of here."

Cordy and Ash ran toward another exit out of the zoo and headed toward Peter's home. Crowds were leaving the zoo in a rush of fear. The remaining Dark Watchers lost them in the crowd.

Ash started to babble. He still was shocked by the gruesome attack. The tiger had been sitting next to them! "What a day! We go to bed together and watch tigers eat Dark Watchers. How romantic!"

Cordy grabbed ahold of Ash and kissed him, pressing his body close to her.

"You're OK, Ash. We're OK. I need you to snap out of it. You're kinda losing it."

Ash hugged her close. "You can kiss me anytime, but I have to talk about it."

Cordy soothed, "Go on and talk, but keep walking."

"You're right. I don't know what I was thinking. I've never been up close and personal with a tiger like I was with Max. My mouth just started babbling. I know he isn't a kitty cat. I know he's one of the most dangerous predators in the jungle. I'll never forget that visit to the zoo. We were going to die. He and his lady friends saved our lives back there. We owe them a special treat. I'll put Bob on it. What do you get a tiger when it saves your life? The Dark Watchers underestimated them. How stupid! I'm so glad you're Max's friend. Cordy, you just amaze me at how courageous you were walking into the lions' den like that."

Cordy kept moving and let him talk. She realized in that moment that Ash didn't like to kill or see others killed. It was probably the reason he was a poor shot; subconsciously, he didn't want to kill. Some people would see that as a weakness, but she saw it as one of his strengths.

She said, "They're wild and unpredictable, especially if you threaten them. I saved Max's life awhile back and now we're even. The chief knew I had the gift. He taught me how to connect with animals and communicate with them. I've spent my whole life saving animals' lives and I think they know it.

"Tigers have been on this earth for over two million years and now you can see why. The thing is they're endangered now and may go extinct. Who knows, man may be next on the endangered list? It's so sad."

"Peter's house isn't very far. We're almost there."

They made a run for it when they saw the houses and went through the back alley so they wouldn't be spotted. Ash and Cordy opened Peter's back door and found everyone had made it.

"Mission accomplished!"

CHAPTER 42

Sacred Ground

Master Wong decided to take the Pure of Heart to the Saint Louis Basilica to give them the history of Saint Louis and the role it played in the Pure of Heart. Sister Agnes had told him the stories of the Pure of Heart underground. The New World and the Old World were connected by a dedicated and trustworthy group who protected the sacred relics and treasures. He pointed out that the street not only had the Basilica on it but the Scottish Rite temple, Moolah Temple, and Saint Francis Xavier's Jesuit College Church.

If one believed in powerful ley lines, this church was built on one. Ley lines are paths believed to reflect earth's spiritual "power lines." Ancient sites like Knowth and Stonehenge, as well as Native American sacred grounds are examples of monuments placed in honor of these powerful places on Earth.

The group left in the dark of night and entered through a back door which was open to the priests at the seminary for late prayers.

Ash, Jon, Sam, Peter, and Chris looked around at the beautiful glistening of color. The church was filled with amazing mosaics.

"Wow!" Chris said.

Jon marveled, "It's breath-taking."

"The Basilica has the most mosaics in the West and one of the largest in the world," Master Wong explained. "Look up above your head and you will see the angels of the Seraphim. It is one of the few mosaics in the world that have them all, including Uriel the Archangel. That's the angel whom Pope Zachary decided to remove from veneration in 745 AD. He carries a flaming sword. He's in the Book of Enoch and the Book of Esdras. Many of you have had connections with him over the weeks we've been together. Why has he shown up? It's because we're in a war that began at the time of Enoch. The children of Earth could face an extinction-level event like the Great Flood of Noah.

"The Pure of Heart have hidden these treasures for millennia. Ash found the Keys of Life in Egypt at the temple of Abu Simbel. Lafitte's family protected the Swords of Fire, Water, Heaven, Earth, and Orion to help us for this time.

"Up above your head is one of the Pure of Heart named Sister Duchesne. She lived in France during the French Revolution, a time when churches were destroyed and burned to the ground. It became a dangerous place for clergy to stay. As a result, she escaped France and moved to America and settled in the St. Louis area.

"Sister Duchesne settled here to teach the Native Americans. She developed a trust with them. Hearing of her kind heart and good works, many tribes traveled to Saint Louis to hear her message and to be baptized.

"Cordy, there is a reason you settled here. You're the next generation to protect the children of Earth.

"But Cordy, you are not in this alone. All of you have made sacrifices to get here. We will need to continue to be strong and support one another if Earth is going to survive."

"Master Wong, the Lost Tribes map has a little log cabin on the Mississippi River," Ash said. "Do you think this is the place?"

Master Wong shook his head. "No, this church was built in the 1900s, but if you're looking for the oldest church here in Saint Louis, it would be the Old Saint Louis Cathedral. It's down by the Saint Louis Arch. I think we need to look there for Aaron's rod. It's very powerful."

"We need to leave early in the morning to see if we can find it," Ash proclaimed.

"The cathedral is located on the same spot as the log cabin," Master Wong continued. "It's right next to the river. The foundation from the old log cabin may still exist."

"We need to take the Guardian," Jon said. "She may be able to help us find it. We may need the Keys of Life, too."

"I've been watching the news. Catastrophes are increasing," Chris said. "The scientists are worried about the magnetosphere and the sun. They think the volcanoes eruptions are increasing. Even Yellowstone is recording a few earthquakes. If that blows, it's over. Time is running out."

"I've seen the reports coming from the astronomers at NASA that a mysterious large object at the edge of our galaxy is causing major gravitational and increased cosmic energy waves," Jon said. "The Earth poles are shifting more and more. Something big is going to happen. I don't think the swords can do it alone."

Cordy sighed. "Well, I guess we need to find Aaron's rod before it's too late."

Peter's determined voice filled the air. "We have to find it. Let's do it for Brother Michael."

With respect, Jon said, "We should light a candle in his honor." The group went to where candles were lit, and they each lit a candle in honor of their brother.

With the angels of the Seraphim looking down on them, they bent their heads and closed their eyes. Jon recited the familiar wisdom of Shakespeare for all to hear:

"From this day to the ending of the world,

But we in it shall be remembered-

We few, we happy few, we band of brothers;

For he to-day that sheds his blood with me

Shall be my brother."

As one, they responded, "Amen."

CHAPTER 43

The Underground

Master Wong explained the Saint Louis connection as they headed back to Peter's house.

"French immigrants settled in Acadia, in the area we now call Nova Scotia. Their numbers grew, and the British became fearful that the Acadians would support the French in the French and Indian War. Thus, in 1755, Britain deported the Acadians from the area. A group of them settled in the New Orleans area and established Acadiana. They later were called Cajuns. Henry Wadsworth Longfellow wrote about their plight in his story about Evangeline.

"After a time, some of the Acadians decided to take boats up the Mississippi River and settle in the area known as Missouri. They established settlements in Saint Louis, Bellefontaine, and Saint Genevieve — all cities along the Mississippi. They developed an underground network to bring much needed supplies to their Acadian families as well as transport the treasures of the Pure of Heart when necessary. The Pure of Heart underground network remains a secret to this day. It has been passed down from generation to generation.

"In 1792, French King Louis XVI was arrested, and the reign of terror began. Churches and sacred ground were ransacked. The Pure of Heart believed some of their precious treasures needed to be moved to the New World for safekeeping. The notorious Jean Lafitte played a role in the underground network, as we know, but he had trusted helpers. He had promised Sister McDermott, who he loved, to help safely transfer the precious items up the river.

"Saint Louis was a city with a rich heritage and started out as a French fur outpost. It later was part of the Louisiana Purchase. Thomas Jefferson sent Lewis and Clark to explore the West. Jefferson asked Lewis to watch for the Madoc Welsh Indians, apparently descending from a Welsh prince who according to legend, came to America in the 1100s. All along the Mississippi were mounds where the symbols of the birdman and sun cross were spotted. The Native American sun cross resembled the Celtic cross of the Welsh and Irish in the Middle Ages. In Mississippian culture, the birdman was a sacred motif used to depict the warrior class and its relationship with the morning star of heaven. The French explorers saw the connections. The underground used them as markers for those on the journey to protect the treasures of their ancestors. Trust was essential.

"The New Madrid earthquakes in 1811 and 1812 were some of the most powerful earthquakes recorded in the Midwest. More than one thousand earthquakes occurred during that time. Some were even felt on the East Coast.

"The New Madrid Fault has been quiet over the years. Scientists say it's overdue for activity. Some prophets predict that when an event occurs it will be catastrophic for the United States. Saint Louis, as well as the entire New Madrid fault zone, could be affected. Some say the Mississippi River will cut the nation in two and the Great Lakes will empty, causing a massive flood. Civilizations will die, and chaos will reign. Animals will suffer, and many will become extinct. The United States as we know it today would be irreparably changed. Some believe the great mass destruction is already beginning. The fault could be the reason we've been lead here.

"It isn't a coincidence that we're all here in Saint Louis. The Pure of Heart underground network went through here. It's why I settled here with Peter, and plus, Cordy lives here. If the signs are right, something major is going to happen in this area.

"The Earth is connected to the great universe. We are only a small planet among many stars. Yet our oceans and the life of our home is precious in a galaxy of desolate lands. As the Guardian says, 'Earth is our home, and we need to protect it with the Keys of Life'. Let's get back and get some rest. Tomorrow is going to be a big day."

"No pressure!" joked Peter. The tension surrounding the group lessened as everyone laughed.

"You all sure know how to show a guy a good time," chuckled Chris.

"You're a child of Queen Marie Laveau of New Orleans. You're here for a reason, Chris," Master Wong pointed out.

"Whatever we have to do to save mankind, I'm hoping to keep my clothes on this time." Ash crossed his fingers and grinned.

CHAPTER 44

Saint Louis
Old Cathedral

Before the sunrise, they were off to the riverfront with the copy of the Lost Tribes map. They watched for any signs of danger. They had brought the Guardian and the Keys of Life just in case they needed them. Both cars had the speaker phones on, and everybody listened on the way.

Jon pulled out a dossier with the information his family had on the Saint Louis Old Cathedral.

"It seems the Lafitte family knew this was an important location to the Pure of Heart, too. The Saint Louis Old Cathedral was built on the same site as the log cabin on the Lost Tribes map in 1770 by Pierre Laclede and Auguste Choteau. They named it after the crusader king Saint Louis IX. He was son of Blanche Castile and grandson to Queen Eleanor of Aquitaine. Richard the Lionheart was his uncle. It stands on some of the most important real estate in early colonial America. The structure was reinforced with stone by Bishop Dubourg from New Orleans in 1818.

"Bishop Dubourg's history is interesting in that he was trained at the Sulpician seminary. He escaped to America to flee from the French terror, when revolutionaries were killing priests and nuns. He brought some of his books with him and was an academic at Georgetown University. He knew George Washington and dined with him. The bishop probably knew my ancestor Jean Lafitte since he lived in New Orleans at the Ursuline Convent. Dubourg recruited Sister Duchesne, too, and brought her here from France. The Vincentians and Dubourg were connected and it was him who started a school at the Miraculous Medal Shrine in Perryville. I can see the connection. Can you, Cordy?"

"Yes, my family farm is near Perryville," Cordy answered. "My parents are buried at the shrine. I found the quartz disk in the grotto there. It makes sense."

"Sister Agnes told me that four Native American chiefs from the Nez Perce tribe were baptized in the church," Master Wong added. "We're on sacred ground."

"William Clark's children were baptized here and Sacagawea's son, too," Peter said. "A Native American woman, Sacagawea is another example of a true Pure of Heart. She joined Lewis and Clark as a guide and interpreter, the only woman who was with the famous explorers. She did a lot for someone who died at an early age of twenty-five."

"We will be looking for a crypt or a basement. The stones used in the foundation of the early church may have been used."

The Saint Louis Old Cathedral had the Hebrew words for the Tetragrammaton, or Yahweh, inscribed on the front surrounded by a triangle.

Ash noticed the Hebrew letters. "The Tetragrammaton is important to Moses and Aaron. The Hebrew name has been found in the Torah and Bible many times. I think we're in the right place. Let's take the Guardian down into the crypt and see what she says."

The team found the crypt in the back and opened the wrought iron gate revealing steps leading underground. A room filled with stone and two marble sarcophagi stood in the chamber. Ash and Cordy placed the two golden triangles together and set the crystal ball on top of them. The Guardian's holographic figure stood before them.

"Good morning, Pure of Heart. What is it you desire?"

The beauty of the Guardian never failed to awe them. She pointed to a marble rectangular box in the corner.

"What you seek is within, and remember the words."

Jon and Peter pushed the heavy lid off the box with the name Aaron Rodkey. Inside was a simple wooden rod and another golden ankh.

The Guardian expounded, "Enoch was the first to have the rod. Its wood comes from a branch from the Garden of Eden. He received the rod and the seeds to help aid the Pure of Heart in saving Earth's children in case of an extinction level event. The rod later came to Moses and Aaron and they used its power to persuade the Egyptian pharaoh to release the Israelites. Use it wisely. Replenish the Earth, like Noah before you."

Jon reached for the rod, but as he got ready to touch it, a bolt of electricity zapped his hand.

"Merde!"

Chris laughed. "I don't need a translation to know that hurt like hell. OK, who's next?"

Everyone took a step back except Ash. He looked at Jon. "You're not a Child of the Nile, but I am."

"Say the words," the Guardian repeated.

Ash whispered the words as he gently wrapped his hand around the rod. "I am a Child of the Nile. All are born free and equal. They are blessed with reason and knowledge of good and evil. Treat one another as your brother. The Keys of Life is to save all lives." The rod lit up as he touched it. The earth began to shake all around them.

"Does anybody know how to shut it off?" Peter yelled.

"Command it to stop," Master Wong ordered.

Ash said the first thing that popped into his mind. "Whoa, big fella, be silent."

The Guardian laughed. "It's going to take some time for you to meld together. The ankh has the Keys of Life, so you have found another seed depository like manna from heaven. You need to look over the Lost Tribes map. You may find another hidden treasure there."

With that, she disappeared.

CHAPTER 45

Land of Giants
and Dragons

They left the crypt just the way they found it and headed back to their cars with the rod of Aaron and the golden ankh.

Ash and Jon looked over the Lost Tribes map. It was Jon who saw the symbol of a sword-wielding giant fighting a dragon. At first glance, it looked like a cross.

"It's France's symbol for Michael the Archangel killing the dragon," Jon said. "I'm surprised it's on a map of Native American tribes. The French explorers must have noticed the similarities in the symbolism."

Sam examined the map since she knew the Mississippi and its locals better than anyone there. "Sacre bleu!"

Everyone looked at Sam's excited face. "I know where this is! We need to go to the cave of the Piasa in Alton. According to legend, a giant, named Chief Ouatoga, killed a man-eating dragon there. The Cahokia tribe painted a huge mural in its honor. It's still there today. The European explorers, Nicolas De Finiels and Father Marquette, saw the mural and reported it back to Versailles. We have to get to Alton. Follow me!"

"Don't we have a casino in Alton?" asked Jon.

"Oui, and Lafitte, our ancestor, is part of a legend that says the family buried treasure there," Sam affirmed.

It dawned on Jon which legend she was talking about. "Mon dieu!"

Their eyes met when she looked at him in the rearview mirror.

Cordy chimed in, "I remember a story about the Alton giant, Robert Pershing Wadlow. He was close to nine feet tall. What a coincidence! We're in the land of giants and dragons."

"I never knew America had dragons. In Haiti, there is a huge stone rock that juts into the sea called Dragon's Cove. His dragon breath is the waves crashing against it. It's a special place because an unusual energy can be felt by those who stand near it. It's a dragon of water. Somehow, I get the feeling this Piasa dragon will be one of fire."

Sam pulled off the Great River Road which wound alongside the Mississippi River onto a gravel road.

"Grab the artifacts. We'll have to hike from here. Everybody, keep an eye out for snakes. The woods and caves are loaded with them," warned Sam.

Jon whispered to Cordy, "I'm sticking with you. "

Cordy whispered back, "I bet you will after what happened in New Orleans."

"What happened in New Orleans?" Ash asked.

Jon smiled wickedly, "What happens in New Orleans stays in New Orleans."

Ash gave him a jealous stare.

Sam decided to play, too. "I agree. What happens in New Orleans stays in New Orleans. Right, Ash and Chris?" They all smiled.

Cordy gave her a jealous stare. "The Lafittes are always up to mischief."

Jon and Sam laughed. "Oui!"

Master Wong redirected the conversation. "Tell me more about your ancestor's wife and her treasure."

Jon's tone got serious. "After the American Navy came to Galveston, our long- ago relative was given an ultimatum. He could give up his piracy and live where he chose or continue the piracy and rot in a jail cell. He decided to shut down the operations in Galveston. He moved up the river to Alton where he married a young bride. He changed his name and died leaving her a great treasure. She lived a life of luxury and told her few friends that her husband was the renowned pirate Jean Lafitte. What better place to hide a treasure than guarded by a terrible dragon. Treasure hunters beware. I don't know what we'll find."

Master Wong said, "Goliath, the giant of old, had a sword designed to match his size. Barely able to pick up the sword due to its weight, David miraculously wielded it to behead Goliath. Goliath's size suggests that he carried Nephilim DNA that was passed through his descendants after the Great Flood.

"It seems we are looking for another ancient Nephilim treasure on the order of the Wishing Cup. Lafitte must have stolen it and hid it. We must be careful. We all know the Nephilim's treasure must be handled with care. I know one thing, only a Pure of Heart can handle it without dying."

Sam took them along a winding path far into the forest. "Despite its danger, this cave is popular to hikers. Lucky for us it's not hiking season, so we shouldn't run into anyone. Besides, I know a back way in. Be careful, the roof of the cave is unstable."

Jon referred to the box he carried, "We have the Sword of Earth. It will protect us and maybe help us find a hidden chamber." As he finished speaking the pummels of the sword began to emit a faint light through the cracks in the box.

The group hiked farther into the forest when Sam finally stopped them, "There it is!"

Chris saw the entrance to the cave. "Wow, that's bigger than I thought. Its huge!"

Ash walked in a few feet. "I can hear water. It sounds like a waterfall and a spring might be to the right. We're going to need some serious light to guide us."

John exclaimed, "No worries. Master Wong, Sam, Ash, and Cordy, come and get your swords." Each picked up the sword they had wielded in the battle at New Orleans.

They walked into the pitch-black cave carrying the Sword of Earth, the Sword of Heaven, the Sword of Fire, the Sword of Water, and the Sword of Orion. The faint glow that the swords had been emitting increased to a brilliance, lighting their way.

Suddenly, the Sword of Earth, carried by Sam began to shake. She felt compelled to point the sword toward the cave wall. When she did, a huge mural of the Piasa dragon — a mixture of bird wings, fish tail, deer antlers, and tiger eyes — was illuminated. Before they could totally process the mural before them, the wall began to move, revealing a secret stone door to a hidden chamber. The cave door automatically opened, beckoning them to come in.

"Sacrebleu!"

CHAPTER 46

Piasa Dragon

Peter carried the crystal ball into the carved rock chamber. It began to vibrate and projected a holographic image of a painted dragon on a wall. Beside the painting stood the Guardian.

"Greetings, my children! Before you is an image of the original painting of the Piasa Dragon, a mystical creature of Earth. The painting was here before the time of the Crusades and is now long faded. Pierre Marquette saw this painting when he explored these lands. He sent back reports to the King of France regarding the painting of this mysterious creature.

"The Cahokia people recount stories of great bird men and dragons who fought in these lands. Legend has it that the tribe's brave warriors fought and finally killed the Piasa Dragon. Be brave, oh warriors, for they killed only the father."

"Who would have thought there were dragons in North America?"

Cordy commented. "But, now that I think about it, the legends of dragons are found all over the world."

The swords gleamed brighter as they moved deeper into the cave. When they reached the center, they stopped short. Before them was a nest of branches with a Piasa dragon in a hibernating deep sleep coiled around a large white egg.

Next to the nest, a glowing sword was plunged into the ground. It was twice as big as any of the swords they carried. Only a giant could have wielded it.

The Guardian appeared again, "Well done, Pure of Heart. You've found Goliath's Sword. It is the Children of the Nephilim's most valued treasure. You know the story of how David used Goliath's own sword to behead him. Like David, one of you must wield Goliath's sword.

"The dragon protects the sword. The one who wields the Sword of Goliath controls the Dragon of Piasa. Choose wisely or die."

Ash threw up his hands. "I hate when she does that...appears and then disappears!"

"We have wielders for all the other swords," Master Wong said. "Peter and Chris remain. Who should we choose?"

Chris' shaky voice filled the room. "I volunteer Peter go first."

"If I remember correctly, dragon's blood is supposed to give one good luck in voodoo," countered Peter. "You're a child of Queen Marie, the voodoo queen. I volunteer Chris go first."

"Peter may be right. My ancestry may suggest that I am the wielder of that mammoth sword. Ethiopian Jews believe they are from the tribe of Dan of which I am a descendant. My parents told me that voodoo was a long tradition of the tribe and that the symbol of the tribe was a coiled serpent. What we have before us is a coiled dragon.

"OK, OK! I'll go first!

"Wait a minute! Am I crazy, or are those a pile of human bones in the corner?"

Ash went over to look. "Yes, they're human. I can't believe this." He picked up the largest skull from the collection of dusty bones.

"These aren't bones from the dragon's latest snack. These bones are very old. This is a Neanderthal skull like the one we saw in the crypt outside Notre Dame. It's like a trademark for the Children of the Nephilim.

"Isn't it interesting that the Dark Watchers use the skull and cross bones as their trademark? It's also the pirates' logo."

Keeping a close eye on the sleeping dragon, Chris inched toward the glowing sword. He prayed that he was the correct wielder. Reaching his destination, the child of Queen Marie embraced the hilt of the sword. Upon his touch, a small tremor shook the ground. Rocks started falling from the walls and ceiling.

"We need to get out of here! It's too dangerous! The walls may cave in! Everyone, get a move on and head for the entrance!" boomed Jon. "Chris, get that sword out of the ground and make a run for it! We'll be waiting for you!"

"Jon, we can't leave Chris!" insisted Ash.

Chris shouted above the crashing of the rocks, "Jon's right — it's too dangerous. Get out everyone! I'll be right behind you! I promise Ash! Now, get going!"

Reluctantly, they all turned around and rushed to the entrance of the cave.

Knowing his friends were on their way to safety, Chris grabbed a hold of the hilt and shifted the sword back and forth. As the sword began to loosen from the ground, Chris began to pull it up. All of a sudden, the sword broke loose, knocking Chris to the ground with its sudden release. He wrapped both hands around the sword and struggled to lift it because of its weight. Finally, he hoisted it and prepared to leave.

Out of the corner of his eye, he saw Queen Marie standing by the wall. She was pointing at something behind him. As he turned around, a rumbling sound surrounded him, and a red eye of an awakened dragon glared at him.

"Oh shit!" He saw the tail move and then the dragon's mouth open. The dragon let out a stream of fire aimed straight for the Pure of Heart. Hoisting the sword on his shoulder, Chris bolted for the cave entrance.

The others stood at the outside of the cave opening. Their worry was increasing by the moment.

Cordy demanded, "What's taking so long? We should have never left him alone!"

Before she finished her tirade, Chris, carrying Goliath's sword, rocketed out of the opening, followed by a stream of fire. The back of his coat was on fire. Ash snuffed the flames and pulled it off him.

"What the hell happened in there, Chris?" asked Ash.

A growl came from inside the cave and struck fear in their hearts.

Peter whispered in wonder, "No, it can't be. It's impossible."

Another stream of fire shot out of the cave forcing them to step farther back. The Piasa dragon stepped out of the cave carrying the white egg in one of her claws. She looked around and gently set the egg on the ground.

"She's protecting the egg," Cordy said. "Nobody make any threatening moves."

"How do we know she's a she? Maybe he's trying to cook his breakfast," suggested Sam.

Jon whispered, "This is not the time to be funny, sister. It's a female. I'm a Frenchman and know a grumpy woman when I see one."

The earth shook again, and the white egg began to crack. Cordy started softly singing Saunhac's Mi'kmaq chant as she approached the dragon. With wariness, the creature's red eyes followed her every move.

The egg cracked open and a small dragon head peeked out. It pulled itself from the shell and squeaked at Cordy. Cordy bowed to the mother dragon and soothingly said, "We won't hurt you or your baby." The mother dragon bowed her head in return as if to say she understood.

The baby dragon waddled over to Chris and bowed to him as he stood holding the glowing Goliath's Sword. With that the mother dragon lovingly licked her baby, and gingerly lifted the baby onto her back with her teeth. The Piasa dragon flapped her wings and took flight above their heads. They watched in awe as the dragons flew toward the river bluffs.

Chris moved forward still holding Goliath's Sword and announced, "I'm the wielder of Goliath's Sword! I could really use a drink right now!"

The crystal ball in Peter's hands lit up and they could hear the Guardian's voice, "I see you are alive, child of Dan. Good job."

CHAPTER 47

Cahokia

S am pulled out a bottle of tequila from her backpack and took a gulp. "I've seen many animals and strange things in my life, but this takes the cake."

She handed the bottle to Jon.

"I thought Chris was barbecued for sure," joked Jon. "But seriously, it's astonishing. The historians got it all wrong. I don't care what any-body says. That was not a bird! I saw a grumpy fire-breathing dragon!"

He took another gulp from the bottle and handed it to Master Wong.

"Dragons are a prominent feature in Chinese folklore. They are associated with the control of weather and water. They are said to guard the heavens with the constellation Draco shining in the night sky. The guardian of the dragons uses a flaming pearl ball, like a crystal ball, to communicate with the dragons.

"I'm honored to have seen a dragon in my lifetime." He raised the bottle to the heavens, drank and then passed it to Peter.

"I was born in the year of the dragon. All my life I've dreamed of seeing one, and now I have. I wonder how long the mother dragon had been hibernating? I think we should name the mother Ying and the baby Yang." With that Peter drank and handed the bottle to Chris.

Taking a swig, Chris declared, "I hope I'm never chased by a fire-breathing dragon ever again." Cordy was the next recipient of the bottle.

"I promised I'd never drink tequila again but what the hell." She sipped slowly at first and then took a big gulp.

Ash grabbed the bottle from her. "Let me save you. I think we need to take a look at the Lost Tribes map again. All of this is leading to a specific location." He took a gulp and pulled out the map as they gathered round. "I saw it downstream. It looks like a huge pyramid." He pointed to it on the map. "There is a circle, too, right next to the river."

Cordy saw the location and suddenly, it dawned on her. "I know where that is. It's a pyramid in Cahokia called Monks Mound. It's one of the largest pyramids in the United States. It's not like an Egyptian pyramid built out of stone. Instead, it's made from dirt. The circle is the woodhenge. It's like Stonehenge or the mounds in Ireland but made with wooden posts. What the hell! Do you guys feel that?"

The ground started to shake, and trees began to fall.

"It's an earthquake!" Chris yelled. "Take cover!"

Although the earthquake only lasted fifteen seconds, their cell phones were all sounding emergency alerts. The text announced that a 6.5 earthquake from the New Madrid fault had occurred. It was further reported that it had been over two hundred years since the last major earthquake. Scientists warned that the current earthquake could be a sign that a major earthquake could be in the near future.

"We're running out of time," Ash said. "Let's go to Cahokia. We better hurry."

They dashed to their cars and followed the Great River Road down to Collinsville, Illinois. All along the road damage from the aftershocks could be seen — cracked streets, overturned cars and fallen buildings. People were stumbling around in a daze.

"Monks Mound is huge. The base of the pyramid is the same size as the Giza Pyramid in Egypt, and it's larger than the Pyramid of the Sun," Cordy said. "You can see we have pyramids all over the planet. They could possibly be a linked network, something the swords and Aaron's rod could activate."

"It makes sense that the structures were made to help protect the planet from what our ancestors knew would threaten us today," Ash said. "It's happened in the past; all the civilizations built the structures on pressure points. We're going to need the Guardian to align everything to keep Earth's balance."

Master Wong pointed out, "Mankind and the planet have been here before. The great flood stories of Noah and Mi'kmaq tell of how all land was destroyed. There are also tales of how mankind survived galactic disruptions. It's believed that an asteroid took out the dinosaurs long ago.

"These stories were told to warn us of this day and to help us prepare. We will have to hope the swords can ward off any major disaster. If Earth is experiencing gravity shifts, that means so are other satellites and planets, too. What we need is a shield to protect us, especially if the magnetosphere weakens. We don't want to end up like the dinosaurs."

"There it is! Look over to the right! That is one big mound! Whoa baby!" Chris yelled.

Monks Mound was a huge multilevel mound with a walkway leading to the top.

"I see the woodhenge, down on the right, too." Peter pointed. "You can see the circle of wood poles."

As they sped down the road to get to the parking lot, Jon passed the tequila bottle around one more time.

CHAPTER 48

Monks Mound

The Cahokia Museum was closed because of the earthquake. Structural damage from the tremors spread out over the region causing government officials to issue warnings for people to stay at home.

The Pure of Heart hefted their swords and treasures and began their ascent up the concrete stairs leading to the top of the large mound pyramid. As they climbed the stairs, Ash related what he had found in his research.

"I can't get over the similarities of this pyramid with the Egyptians and Celts. The Celts had their mounds such as New Grange. The Egyptians had a 'Bird Man' called Horus who carried the Keys of Life. The Native Americans used the symbol of the spiral like the Celts, too. Pretty amazing coincidences."

"The spiral is the force that runs our galaxy and the universe. Black holes spiral and even light can't escape its grip," Jon said.

"The eternal circle of life spirals from spring to winter and then repeats. The Pure of Heart have fought the battle of survival through time. Generation after generation protected Earth. Something is causing an imbalance and we have to correct it."

They climbed to the top of the pyramid and the flat surface of green grass allowed them an amazing view. Very few ancient history books discussed the ancient city, which was larger than London in the 1200s. It was a lost civilization just like the Lost Tribes. A large population lost, and no one knew what happened to them.

Ash pointed to the Mississippi River in the distance. "The similarities to Ancient Egypt are amazing. Like a city built near the Nile, we are standing on a city that was a major agricultural society providing huge amounts of food. The seeds here are different. I'm now wondering if maize and legumes were gifts from the Keys of Life after the Great Flood. Look at the woodhenge on the right — it's a clock to tell them when to plant, just like Stonehenge. It predicts the solstices and equinoxes. The whole compound is based on the sun and moon with the stars as aids to guide them on their travels. In the excavation of the mound, they found a body of a man with a falcon-headed deity. The Egyptian god Horus had a falcon head. Abu Simbel has a solar alignment just like here."

"We need to arrange the swords like we did in New Orleans but the Sword of Orion needs to be between the Sword of Heaven and the Sword of Fire," Jon said. "We need to place the Sword of Goliath between the Sword of Earth and the Sword of Water. Aaron's rod needs to be in the center. We're going to need the Guardian to guide their energy.

"I suspect all the pyramids around the world will produce a network or energy grid to help correct the magnetosphere and inner core of the mantle. The balance will return. I've researched the astrophysics side of things, and this is an incredible chance we're taking. I have a feeling a line of electromagnetic energy is going to be focused into space, too. If any objects out there in our galaxy are causing this, then the Guardian is going to have to calculate a better alignment. It won't take a big push, just a small one to get us back aligned."

Cordy looked at everyone. "Let's do this."

The swords were aligned, with Master Wong plunging the Sword of Fire into the ground, followed by Jon thrusting the Sword of Heaven, and with Ash pushing the Sword of Orion in between them. Sam took the Sword of Earth, placed it in the earth and Cordy forced the Sword of Water in her piece of ground. Chris carried the heavy Sword of Goliath but when he tried to dig it into the earth, the weight of the sword nearly knocked him down.

Chris grunted. "I need a little help over here."

Peter came to his rescue and helped hold up Goliath's Sword while Chris jumped up and down pushing on it. "Why do the swords need to be in the ground? In New Orleans, we held them in the air."

"We must connect to the molten iron core of Earth to stop the imbalance," Jon explained. "The earthquakes are a sign of the tectonic plates shifting. I believe we'll be testing Tesla's theory."

Chris stopped and looked at Jon. "The famous scientist Tesla who worked with electricity and wanted mankind to have free energy? That one?"

Jon nodded. "Yes, that scientist talked about cosmic energy. The sun is going to provide us with the energy to start up the cosmic motor. The energy produced will align Earth and push the Wanderer back out of our galaxy. Aaron's Rod is going to be an accelerator and a switch."

Chris realized they could all die if they miscalculated. Even Earth could be destroyed.

"Peter is going to have to stand by the Sword of Orion if I have the Rod of Aaron in the center," Ash said. "A Child of the Nile must connect with the rod. I'll hold the Guardian as well.

"I believe we are all star children like Chief Saunhac told Cordy. We're going to harness the power of the stars to save us."

"We need to ask the Guardian if we are aligned correctly," Jon said.

Peter handed Ash the crystal ball and Ash asked, "Guardian, is everything lined up correctly?" The hologram of the guardian stood before them.

"I am so proud of you Pure of Heart. Well done. Yes, all is aligned for this critical moment. You've proven that your hearts are filled with love for Earth and her children. Goliath's Sword will search out the bloodline of the giants and connect with them. I feel they are near."

Cordy's phone began to ring in her pocket. "What the hell? Who could be calling now? Hello?"

She had her speakerphone on so everyone could hear.

Cordy heard a familiar arrogant voice. "I have your Grandfather Bill. If you want him to live, we need to talk. You have something I want. How about a trade?"

She felt a stab of cold fear in her heart and begged him, "Don't hurt him, please."

She knew De Villiers would do anything to get Solomon's ring.

Jon and Sam pulled out their guns out but Cordy shook her head. "Don't do it, Jon. They'll kill my grandfather. He wants to make a trade. I know it's a trap, but I have to try and save my grandfather."

A group of twenty armed men dressed in black ran out of the Cahokia Museum doors, which lay at the foot of the pyramid steps.

A group of seven huge muscular men in army fatigues with guns followed them. De Villiers marched out the door holding his cat Isis in his arms while Mindy pushed a bruised and battered Bill up the stairs of Monks Mound. He ordered the men in black to stay at the bottom and guard any escape they had. The other seven armed men followed De Villiers and Mindy. Everyone at the top pulled out their weapons and aimed at each other. The Guardian watched the stalemate before her.

Jon pointed his gun at De Villiers' head. "Who's going to blink first?"

Cordy pleaded with the Guardian. "Do something. Please take me but save my grandfather."

The Guardian gazed down at her. "A sacrifice must be made. You're on Monks Mound, a place of sacrifice. Many have died here. I don't choose who lives or dies. Mankind must decide good versus evil."

Ash argued, "Brother Michael sacrificed his life to get to the Rod of Aaron. It's enough."

"Noted, but this war has gone on for a very, very long time," the Guardian said. "I can't interfere in your destiny. There is more at stake here than you can imagine."

Jon implored her, "I know men can do evil deeds, Guardian, but please help us. Earth may die."

De Villiers stood looking at the Pure of Heart with a smirk on his face and set Isis down. Mindy pushed Bill toward Cordy. The other men with their guns blocked any escape. They were trapped.

De Villiers sneered, "I see you're surprised to see me. Thank you for gathering all the treasures of the Pure of Heart. You made my job so much easier.

"You want to save the world. Ha! What a short-sighted plan! These treasures you've found can do so much more, and I plan to use them to their fullest potential to fulfill my greatest desire.

"Look before you. I'm sure you notice my Neanderthal army. Yes, thanks to the Children of the Nephilim and their cloning program, the resurrection of the Neanderthal is now my success.

"You're probably wondering why the Sword of Goliath is dormant. It's waiting for Goliath's offspring."

With that statement, the Sword of Goliath lit up and a beam of light exploded from it, connecting it with the Sword of Heaven and the Sword of Fire. The Sword of Fire emitted a beam that connected them to the Sword of Earth, the Sword of Orion and the Sword of Water. A laser force field encircled them. The Neanderthal stood behind it, unable to interfere.

Isis crouched in fear near her master.

Ash stood in the center of it all wondering what they could do to stop this madman who had already killed so many.

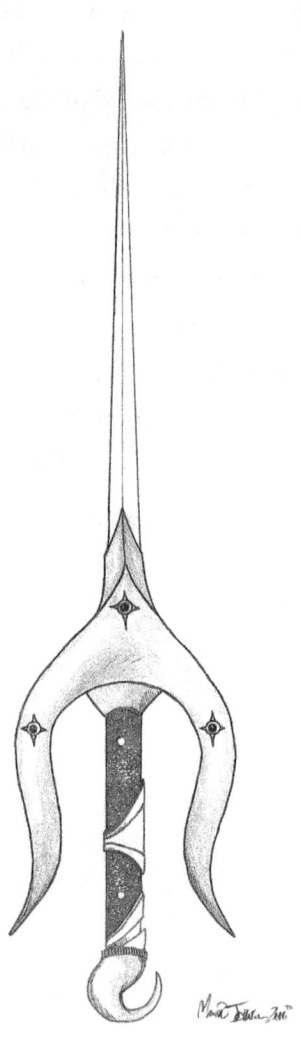

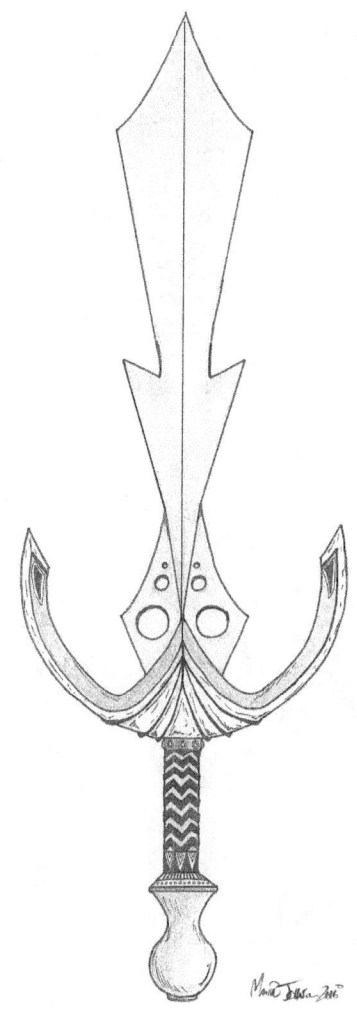

CHAPTER 49

Atonement

All the swords had lit up and static electricity filled the area. Aaron's Rod, held by Ash, was anchored to the ground. Each sword had standing by its side the angels Michael, Gabriel, Raphael, Uriel and Antar. Winds picked up from all the energy from the swords. The leader of the Neanderthals walked outside the perimeter to stand near the Sword of Goliath. He recognized the familiar markings and symbols of his ancestors. Goliath's sword had connected with the DNA within the Neanderthal clone and the memories of the ancient past flooded the mind of their leader.

De Villiers chided, "Well, well, well, I see the gang's all here for the big showdown. Antar got his wish to see his offspring emerge and be my slave. He even got to see the sword he created for his famous headless Goliath. Yes, Antar gave it as a gift to his ill-fated offspring. It has to irk him that David, and now a son of Dan, wields it."

Antar's anxious voice answered De Villiers, "For millennia, I've taken the role of tempting Adam's children to assist in killing the Pure of Heart. I admit I wanted vengeance for the death of my children but over time I've learned the lesson that violence only begets violence. The Pure of Heart have touched my heart. I want to get off this deceiving wheel of revenge and take the path of peace. We need to use compromise and persuasion over violence against each other. De Villiers, I beg you, don't go down this path. You're poisoned. I'm trying to save you from being a tool of evil."

De Villiers looked at Chris standing near the Sword of Goliath. "I see your foot is better. I recognize you. Queen Marie can't save you now."

Chris growled. "We are even now, De Villiers. I refuse to go down the dark path of revenge. Help us save the world."

"Save it? I want to destroy it! You're looking at the new king of the universe. What do I need Earth for? But all of you don't know what I'm talking about — you've got limited imaginations. The bigger they are, the harder they fall, right?

"How surprised Antar was that some of Adam's children's DNA contain the blood of the Nephilim. I wonder how many thousands of years did it take for him to figure it out? Antar's children weren't annihilated, as you can see. Weren't you surprised, Antar, at how attracted you were to the Pure of Heart? Some of them were Neanderthal human hybrids. Who would have guessed you're related? Or did you know all along? It's going to be hard to see your children obeying me, isn't it?"

Antar's eyes burned with anger. "You will regret this."

De Villiers replied with arrogance, "You were just a tool. I'm going to give your master a big surprise."

Cordy begged the Dark Watcher Grandmaster. "Let my grandfather go. You can have all the swords. Just don't kill him."

"You can't deal with him," Jon yelled at Cordy. "He's poisoned by the evil of Judas' coins. De Villiers is a madman. We can't let him take the treasures of the Pure of Heart. Everyone will be doomed."

"Shoot Grandpa Bill if she doesn't give me the ring," De Villiers ordered Mindy.

"Cordy, bring me Solomon's ring now. Make no mistake, she'll kill him. Mindy infiltrated the Children of the Nephilim's headquarters. She did it all on my orders. I've waited for this day for a long time."

"I protected you from the Children of the Nephilim with your aunt because I saw on your star chart your destiny to bear the ring. It's too bad Julia isn't here to watch this, too. Bring me the ring now before I get impatient."

Cordy walked toward De Villiers with tears in her eyes as she took the necklace with the ring off her neck. Grandpa Bill looked lovingly at his granddaughter.

"I love you Cordy. I loved my son and your mother. Don't be afraid, and don't blame yourself. It's not your fault," Grandpa Bill whispered. "Don't give him the ring, honey. All will be lost."

Cordy saw out of the corner of her eye a vision of Chief Saunhac in a Templar robe with the Mi'kmaq symbol of the red cross with the moon and star on it standing near Goliath's Sword.

She heard him whisper. "Don't be afraid, Star Child. I am with you."

De Villiers' eyes filled with excitement as she handed him the ring. He held it up, the silver necklace with a gold ring dangling on it, in front of his eyes. He did it. All the planning and his lifelong ambition to possess Solomon's ring had come to fruition. He held the ultimate power of the heavens. All his dreams had come true in this moment. He didn't care about the swords. Fools — none of them realized that the prize was the ring. With the ring, De Villiers ruled not only Earth but the universe.

"Thank you, my dear," the Dark Watcher Master said. "Now I want all the angels to kneel before their master. The gateway will open for their new ruler."

Michael, Gabriel, Raphael, and Uriel knelt, but Antar was reluctant. Their eyes met each other. All of them had to obey the ring as ordered since the time of Solomon. The swords and rod opened a swirling spiral of energy and the winds around them increased. The gateway was opening using the cosmic power of the swords.

De Villiers voice demanded, "Come closer and kneel before me, Antar! I am the Master of the Universe. All will bow to me and kneel before me."

The angel Antar gave a knowing look to his fellow comrades. They knew this man had to be stopped at all costs. The angels' problem was that they were bonded to obey the holder of the ring. They needed to buy some time. The rebellious leader and father of the Nephilim knelt before De Villiers' feet with head bowed.

Increasing madness fell over De Villiers as the great power of the ring ran through him. He laughed hysterically. "That's so much better, isn't it, Antar? I told you that I would be your master someday."

"Oh, I forgot one thing. Mindy, shoot Bill now."

Two shots hit Grandpa Bill in the chest and he fell to the ground. His eyes closed, and his hands covered the bullet holes in his chest. Cordy screamed in agony. "No, no, I gave you the ring! Why?"

De Villiers laughed at her as the ring dangled from his hand. "Because, my dear, I have the power over life and death. If only my late wife could see me now, and how my father would be smiling at me.

"You fools have played right into my hands." Isis jumped into the air and grabbed the necklace with the ring from De Villiers' hand

and jumped into the arms of Cordy. Surprised, Cordy grabbed the ring and yelled out, "Stop him, Antar! Michael, Gabriel, Uriel, and Raphael, help us! Help save Earth and protect us."

Antar stood up and grabbed De Villiers around the neck and lifted him off the ground.

De Villiers screamed, "Kill them, Kill them all!"

The Neanderthals raised their weapons and aimed. The men at the foot of the pyramid prepared to shoot.

Up in the sky, they heard two screeching cries and the Piasa mother and baby flew down, spraying a large plume of fire at the Dark Watchers' army below. The dragon swooped down and landed near Cordy, staring at the Neanderthal leader. Antar still held a squirming, choking De Villiers, and he ordered the Neanderthal to lay down their weapons. He was their father from long ago. He assured them the Piasa dragon would not harm them.

The cloned Neanderthals surrendered their weapons and Jon grabbed Mindy's gun.

"Well done! I was a little worried, ma cherie," Jon said. "Your acting skills are impressive."

Mindy winked at Jon. "Bill should get some credit, too. He died well."

Grandpa Bill opened one eye, "Is it all clear?"

Holding Isis, Cordy screamed with joy when she saw that he was still alive. He opened his shirt to show everyone the bullet proof vest that was under it.

"Mindy here is a young woman with quite a story to tell. While putting the vest on me when no one was looking, she revealed her true identity and told me her story. De Villiers had no clue of her trickery."

"Jon, I think you have some explaining to do."

"You're right, Bill. Mindy and I do have a past and a present. Mindy and I are former Interpol agents. We worked together in undercover operations for years.

"When the Dark Watchers' power and evil actions began to increase, I knew that the Dark Watchers had to be infiltrated. Mindy volunteered to go undercover and work for De Villiers to spy on him. We agreed that to gain De Villiers' complete trust that she would need to infiltrate the Children of the Nephilim as well, posing as De Villiers' spy."

With Jon's arm around her shoulder, Mindy tearfully said, "But, Jon, I couldn't prevent Poppa Jon's death."

"Ah, ma cherie. You are not to blame. That is De Villiers' fault alone. We will not dwell on what you could not prevent." Jon kissed the top of her head.

Mindy turned into Jon and hugged him. "We did it, didn't we!!"

"Oui, we did!"

While Jon explained Mindy and his plot, Antar immobilized De Villiers with a choke hold. He debated what to do with him, his first choice being to squeeze the life from him. As he tightened his hold, the other angels whispered, "Our orders are to wait." Antar nodded to them in acknowledgment and loosened his hold.

Cordy smiled at Antar, "Thank you!"

Antar returned her smile and said, "You're welcome, Star Child. I enjoyed seeing the surprise on De Villiers' face.

"We have one more task to do as you ordered — save Earth! We'll need all of your help."

Isis purred in Cordy's arm and made eye contact with her. As they stared into each other's eyes they remembered their first meeting at De Villiers' studio in St. Louis. Isis recalled how Cordy had treated her injured paw and removed the pain. Cordy recalled how Isis had given her a gift in return. They both remembered how De Villiers had tested Cordy to see if she was a Pure of Heart.

Cordy snuggled the cat's furry neck and whispered, "Thank you, Isis. Now let's get this show on the road. We have Earth to save."

With that, everyone started moving. The angels stood at their positions. Ash stood in the center holding Aaron's Rod. Cordy stood next to him.

Planet Earth began wobbling on its axis as the poles began to shift. Ocean waves created huge tsunamis heading for cities. Volcanoes erupted with lava, and earthquakes caused tremors around the world.

Uriel yelled to Ash and Cordy, "Say the words and remember the sign!"

Ash called out, "I am a Child of the Nile. All are born free and equal. They are blessed with reason and knowledge of good and evil. Treat one another as your brother. The Keys of Life are to save all lives."

Cordy thought, *what is the sign?* She realized it had been there the whole time. It was the symbol of the Pure of Heart. She folded her hands just like the Magdalene statue, just as Caravaggio's Christ, and just as Cortona's Mary in the Deposition.

In that instant, a blinding light filled the sky knocking the valiant warriors to the ground. The swords increased Earth's magnetosphere shield, resetting Earth's poles and stopping the wobble. The cosmic energy of the sun filled the atomic particles, and the cosmic motor made by the swords pushed a stream of energy out into the galaxy. The Sword of Orion and Sword of Heaven focused the energy to push any dangerous asteroids or planets into deep space. Earth's inner core stabilized, and the poles returned to where they started years ago. The Sword of Water calmed the seas.

The Sword of Fire quieted the volcanoes. The Sword of Earth silenced the earthquakes. In the sky a six-pointed Star of David was formed from the projected light of the swords. The symbol on Solomon's ring had created a golden triangular gateway. A silence came over Earth, and in the distance a rainbow filled the sky.

CHAPTER 50

The Council of Heaven

The swirling circle of energy of the golden triangle engulfed the group in the center. They were blinded by a brilliant illumination and transported to another dimension. Ash, holding Aaron's Rod, and Cordy, holding Isis, found themselves standing with Michael, Uriel, Gabriel, Raphael, and Antar in a room with a raised bench with a marble chess set on top. Sitting at the bench were men and women dressed in shimmery silver clothing.

Gabriel snapped his fingers at the surprised couple. "You must be properly dressed before you speak at the meeting." In an instant, all of them were dressed in the skin-tight silver attire. Ash's muscles and Cordy's curvaceous figure made them appear as perfect human specimens from Earth. De Villiers' clothes, however, remained unchanged.

Uriel passed out sunglasses to everyone from Earth. "You'll need these, even Isis. The light is very bright here." He placed tiny sunglasses on the cat.

Ash looked at Uriel in bewilderment and asked, "Where are we?"

Uriel explained, "You are amidst the Council of Heaven. It is called different names in different cultures. In the Hebrew and Christian bibles, it is called the Lord of Hosts. In Greek mythology, it is Mt. Olympus, where all the gods resided and decided mankind's fate. Norse, Egyptian, Celts, Sumerians, and Chinese call it the Divine Council. Regardless of the name or culture, the Council is a group of highly talented and powerful individuals residing in the heavens fighting the eternal War of Heaven.

"The Council has watched mankind suffer many disasters over time. Civilizations have fallen, and many have died. The Egyptian pyramids, the Maya and Aztec pyramids, Cahokia mounds, and the Parthenon in Greece stand in remembrance of mankind's great power. Yet these civilizations fell from great catastrophes.

"The Keys of Life were gifts from the Council of Heaven to prevent extinction of all life on the planet. They were given with great trepidation knowing mankind's greed and jealousy for power. The angels were ordered to ensure that these treasures did not fall into the wrong hands. The story is repeated over and over again through time to remind men of their past, and yet they forget previously learned lessons and repeat the same errors to pursue their arrogant ways.

"You've journeyed through the golden triangle gateway to appear before the Council. Only a few humans have ever done so, Enoch being one. The Pure of Heart have proven worthy of our trust. We are proud of you. You give us hope for Earth's future."

A sudden burst of light came from the center of the room with a voice booming out of it. "Antar, put De Villiers down and kneel before the Council!"

Antar released the Dark Watcher. De Villiers dropped to the floor and fell on his face. Antar knelt before the Council and bowed his head, saying, "Lord, forgive me for all my transgressions against the Pure of Heart. I have been a participant in many deaths. I repent and ask for mercy and forgiveness. Please look on me with compassion for I realize my sins. You gave me this opportunity. I give you my great thanks."

The glowing light shimmered, and a thousand tiny stars swirled in a whirlwind-like motion as the Lord of Hosts spoke. "You came to us with a penitent heart. You were forgiven before you spoke. Live in my love and share it with the world. Time is the wisest of all for it reveals the truth, does it not?"

Tearfully, Antar responded, "It does. You foresaw this day. Thank you all for giving me hope. At one time, I hated the job given to me as punishment for my pride but over time, I saw your wisdom. I know now how weak evil truly is and yet it corrupts so many.

A silver-haired man came forward. "I am Enoch. You've served us well by testing the hearts of mankind. A tedious job, yes, but one that must be done. How does one learn unless tempted? You were ignorant, and now you are wise."

Enoch looked to the rest of the group. "I am the guardian of heavenly treasures. Antar, who brings us the ring?"

Antar stood up and pointed to Cordy, who was still holding Isis. "A Pure of Heart brings it back home. Cordy and Isis prevented it from remaining in the hands of De Villiers, who is infected with the evil darkness from the cursed coins of Judas."

Enoch smiled at Cordy. "You and Isis have saved the day. The power of Solomon's ring is too great for mankind to bear. If De Villiers had maintained possession of the ring, he would have caused great chaos, especially in the state that he is in. It is time for the ring to be returned."

Out of thin air, a lovely young woman appeared with a white table. Standing in the center of the room she ordered Cordy and Isis to come forward while she stepped aside.

From the great light, the Lord of Hosts spoke again. "Pure of Heart, place Solomon's ring on the table. It has fulfilled its purpose. Earth is saved for now. De Villiers wanted to enter where he was forbidden. His intent was to command the angels and become the most powerful being in the universe. You and Isis saved the ring and now he is brought to us on his knees for judgment.

"Thank you, Cordy and Isis, for all you've done.

"Ash, come forward with Aaron's Rod. We thank you for your service to the Council of Heaven. Your knowledge of the past has aided you in protecting mankind's future. You have touched many hearts."

A curtain raised and Cordy and Ash stood in awe as they gazed at the hundreds of witnesses in a gallery before them. Tears streamed down their faces when they saw Cordy's mother and father, Chief Saunhac, Sister Agnes, Linda, Poppa Jon, and Brother Michael. To their surprise, Highway Man's mother and other animals that Cordy had treated as a veterinarian were in the crowd. Georgette, Isis' dearest friend was there too. All of them, both human and animal, had been restored to the prime of their life.

"You can't touch them since they're not of your world, but of ours. But know they love you, Pure of Heart, and their sacrifices were not in vain. We thank you for your service to the Children of Earth and to the Council of Heaven."

All the angels knelt in honor of the fearless warriors Ash, Cordy, and Isis.

The Lord of Hosts spoke again. "We are not finished here. Ash and Cordy, I see that both of you share the capacity to love one another with complete devotion. Uriel, come forth with the other rings."

Uriel handed Ash Cordy's engagement and wedding rings.

Ash started to stutter, "How did you know? Never mind, stupid question."

Uriel stepped back with a proud smile on his face.

From the light, the Lord of Hosts continued, "One of the Keys of Life is love and compassion for one another. We can read your mind and your heart, Ash. Let me assure you, she loves you as much as you love her. Two virgins such as yourselves, who love each other as you do, should be married. What better place but in front of the Council of Heaven?"

Ash and Cordy, two people who had been dedicated to their professions, who never found love until this crazy journey, looked into each other's eyes and saw a lifetime of promise. With tears in her eyes, Cordy extended her left hand, and Ash slipped the rings on her finger.

"I pronounce you husband and wife," the Lord of Hosts said. "Go now and multiply." Everyone clapped for the couple and Isis gave out a celebratory meow.

Uncertainty clouded Cordy's joy as she asked, "What happened to Earth? Did we do it? Did we stop the poles from shifting? Did we save it?"

"Yes, you did it," Uriel answered. "There was some destruction but nothing as if the poles had shifted."

"The Pure of Heart have, over time, proven mankind is worthy. The supernatural chess game continues, and the war between the darkness and light has not ended."

"What about De Villiers?" Ash asked.

The Council looked down with sadness upon the kneeling De Villiers. Not unlike many others, this child of Adam wanted to control the angels and become dictator of the universe. His judgment awaited.

De Villiers spoke venomous words at the Council of Heaven. "I would have shown you what real power can do with mankind and the universe. You hold us back to enslave us. I will be no slave to you!"

One of the Council members said, "Antar, take De Villiers to quarantine. He must be cleansed of the poison from the Judas coins. The evil consumes him."

"Is this justice?" De Villiers spat out. "I demand a trial!"

"Who will speak in your defense, De Villiers?" asked another member.

"I will speak for myself!"

"You are infected and not able. Is anyone here able to give us one good reason why we should allow him a trial?"

A white chair rose from the floor with a monitor attached to it. Ash and Cordy remained silent while Isis jumped onto the chair.

"It appears that Isis wishes to bear witness and give testimony," Uriel said.

The Lord of Hosts smiled. "You may proceed, Isis."

De Villiers cried out, "She betrayed me! She is not a fair witness!"

"Silence! She is trying to save you!" the Lord of Hosts boomed.

Isis began to testify before the Council in a sweet female voice produced by the monitor.

"First, thank you for allowing me to see my old friend Georgette one more time. How happy she is here.

"Now, as for my master. I was a starving kitten out in the rain with no home. I was afraid, alone, cold, and wet when Georgette, a sweet elderly cat with great wisdom pulled me out of the gutter and set me on the doorstep of a lovely house. She saved my life.

"I was sitting on the doorstep when De Villiers found me. I gazed into his eyes looking and hoping for kindness. What I saw was loneliness. My master picked me up and dried me off. He fed me and in time I could see that he loved me. He became my dearest friend.

"He took me everywhere. I was his closest companion. And then, he obtained the Judas coins. Their terrible evil seeped into his heart replacing his warmth and love for anger and hate. I love him dearly still and want him to be saved.

"De Villiers, my dearest friend, I love you, but you are possessed. You must endure this cleansing.

"Save him, please."

"We owe you a great favor, Isis," the Lord of Host responded. "Your heroic deed saved the world and the Council from disaster. Your testimony holds great weight here. His one act of kindness holds great importance and is on record. Thank you. Do you wish to stay with your master in quarantine or return with Cordy?"

Isis jumped down from the chair and into Cordy's arms.

"She's made her decision," the Lord of Hosts said.

The Council of Heaven whispered to one another.

"The Council must discuss the serious crimes of De Villiers. Unfortunately, he represents many who are greedy for power. We will be watching to see if humanity will progress in their evolution or slide into corruption. We worry they will be like Atlantis, in which their technology caused their civilization to self-destruct. Through the Tree of Life, man knows good and evil just like us. Dangerous experiment without precaution can cause great harm. We've despaired for mankind and their future, but the Pure of Heart give us hope.

"The Council of Heaven protects life in the universe. The Keys of Life are there to aid the Pure of Heart in that goal. You must guard them well. Do not let corrupted men take them.

"Mankind must also remember to have compassion for one another, or it will be doomed. Earth is too valuable a planet to let it be destroyed. The Guardian is programmed to protect it at all costs. She has done well over the generations.

"Antar will take care of De Villiers' decontamination. Maybe someday he will get that trial. One way or the other, justice will be served. De Villiers has fallen but we do not give up hope for his redemption.

"Ash, Cordy, and Isis, go now and rejoice!"

CHAPTER 51

Quarantine

Antar snapped his fingers and in the next second, darkness engulfed the kneeling De Villiers.

"You must be cleansed because you're unclean due to your contact with the Judas coins. A negative energy has contaminated you."

He beckoned, "Keeper, cleanse the prisoner." A small robot walked in and a disinfecting scanner roamed the prisoner's entire body. De Villiers screamed with pain as a dark cloud oozed out of him.

Antar took out his sword. "Keeper, imprison the darkness." A door opened from the bottom of the rock floor and the keeper, with the help of Antar, pulled the dark cloud into the containment unit. De Villiers felt weakened and groggy. "What have you done to me?"

"You've been poisoned by the darkness. It consumes any life force and feeds on anger, jealousy, and hatred. You were filled with it. We need to make sure none remains. You'll be here until the Council decides your fate."

De Villiers laughed hysterically. "You've always looked down on Adam's children, Antar, but how did it feel to kneel before one of them who, for a moment, became the most powerful being in the universe? You're weak, Antar. The Council used you as a pawn and played you. We could have joined forces and beat them."

"You were the weak one. I willingly took the job to be the tester of mankind. I'd whisper in their ears, urging them to do what they desired against their brothers. I couldn't turn the Pure of Heart, but you were easy. Your arrogance and lust for power made you an easy target. You served your purpose."

"How long will it take for them to decide?"

"Time has no meaning here, De Villiers. You must wait until you're summoned. I should thank you for giving me the opportunity to redeem myself in their eyes. I was like you, arrogant and wanting to be the most powerful being in the universe. I almost succumbed to that evil. Your resourcefulness impressed me. The puppet master pulling the strings. But I wondered who was pulling your strings?

"Enjoy your time here and contemplate your choices. The keeper will watch over you. Oh, and one more thing — you may hear some screams every now and then. It happens often here."

Antar disappeared.

De Villiers viewed his cold dark surroundings. It was a room of stone, not unlike a cave. A rock table, rock carved recliner chair, stone bed, a stone television set and a rock carved toilet filled his room.

The keeper placed a small tray on the table. "Lunch is ready, De Villiers."

The angry man stood up and started to attack the small robot. An electric taser shot out of the arm of the keeper and hit De Villiers, making him scream in pain as his whole body filled with fire. The man lost consciousness.

He woke up in a dark room and noticed the television playing a black and white movie. Every bone in his body ached as he pulled himself into the stone recliner. A little boy with his back turned entered the halls of a prep school. Something seemed familiar about the boy and the school. The child cried and cried. He didn't want to go to school as he watched his parents leave him. De Villiers felt in his heart the abandonment of the five-year-old child and tears rolled down his cheeks. The boy turned to face the screen, and to De Villiers' shock, the little boy was him.

Somehow the Council had placed the memories of his life in a film and made a television series out of it. One part of him wanted to close his eyes and ignore it, but he found the television never shut off. The man realized there was no lying or trying to conceal the truth from his jailers. Somehow, they had tapped into his memories and produced this surreal show. His life played on before him.

He sat watching his sad life unfold on the television and every moment felt as real as the moment it occurred. His heart filled with loneliness. Would anyone miss him? He thought of Isis and even though he hated her, there was a part of him that could never stop loving the cat who betrayed him. In many ways, she reminded him of his late wife. The show continued as he saw how he hurt them both without regret or remorse.

The keeper brought in his tasteless meals every day, and De Villiers watched his life story play over and over. Other jail mates would scream in terror every now and then. He wondered at first why they were screaming and weeping.

"Keeper, why do they cry and scream?" he asked. "Do you torture them?"

"Time moves slowly here, and their demons awaken and torment them," the keeper answered. "The mind is a powerful and yet fragile thing. Decontamination is a slow process and a painful one. You've been infected with one of the worst entities. I will scan you every day to see when the parasite is completely gone."

The robot left him, and De Villiers sat watching the television, afraid to fall asleep. The nightmares increased when he drifted into slumber. The Carravagio painting he so adored, *The Taking of Christ,* played out in his dreams except there, he was Judas. He felt anger at his friend for wasting money from Mary's anointing him with precious oils. He felt the lust for revenge against a master who didn't listen to him. And he felt the moment of greed when he sold out the one he loved. Guilt and depression flooded him as he threw the coins away and tied the rope around his neck. He often woke up choking and screaming in fear. Day after day continued in the same way.

De Villiers lived in fear that the Council of the Heavens would forget his existence and leave him there for eternity.

CHAPTER 52

Rainbow

Jon and the others picked themselves off the ground. A brilliant rainbow shined in the sky. It was Master Wong who noticed first and pointed to it.

"Cordy, where are you?" Grandpa Bill yelled, worry in his voice.

Mindy scanned the area. "I don't see De Villiers either."

The Piasa mother and baby had killed all of De Villiers' men but the Neanderthal clones placed their weapons before the dragon and knelt before the Pure of Heart. They followed Goliath's sword and its wielder.

Master Wong approached their commander, "The Piasa recognizes you."

The commander answered, "We recognize the power of Goliath's Sword. The Pure of Heart wield it and we obey you. The Piasa dragon knows we mean her no harm."

Master Wong bowed and said, "Arise, free men, and welcome." All the Neanderthal clones rose and shook the elderly man's hand.

"Guardian, where are Ash and Cordy?" Jon asked. "Are they alive?"

"They are alive," the Guardian answered. "They are in the presence of the Council of Heavens."

Sam looked at Jon, "Who are they?"

The Guardian smiled. "My employers and the protectors of the universe."

Chris walked over. "They took Ash and Cordy for what reason?"

Peter Woo brushed off his clothes. "Cordy had Solomon's ring. I have a feeling the owner wanted it back."

It was in that moment a light flashed in the center of Monks Mound. Ash and Cordy, who carried Isis in her arms, stood before them.

Grandpa Bill smiled. "Cordy, you're all right. What happened?"

Ash trumpeted, "We got married by the Lord of Hosts. The Council of Heaven told us to go and multiply."

Cordy kissed Ash and whispered, "I hope you like cats." Isis looked up at Ash with her adoring cat eyes.

Ash petted the cat. "I love this cat. She saved the day."

Grandpa Bill shook Ash's hand. "Welcome to the family, Ash." He hugged his granddaughter.

Jon walked over with his arm around Mindy. "Congratulations, both of you."

Cordy hugged her and whispered, "Thank you so much for saving my grandfather's life. I won't forget what you've done."

Mindy kissed Jon's cheek. "I did it for him. He saved my life when I was younger and trained me to fight evil men like the chairman and De Villiers. I love him and would die before I would ever hurt him. What happened to De Villiers? Did you kill him, I hope?"

The Guardian heard her and answered from the crystal ball. "The Council will take care of him. He's in quarantine so he can harm no one else. The Council has found revenge only brings great sadness and leads in a destructive cycle. Violence begets violence, and the Council discourages it as much as possible. I assure you he will go through a very unpleasant experience in quarantine and hopefully get rid of the darkness that possesses him.

"I want to congratulate you, Ash and Cordy, on your marriage. And to all the Pure of Heart, thank you for saving Earth's children from this great disaster. You have made your ancestors proud."

Sam watched her brother's admiring eyes follow Mindy. His heart was not broken at the news of Cordy's marriage. Jon would miss the challenge of the beautiful Cordy, but he definitely was fond of Mindy. He didn't have to change for Mindy. Jon would always be Jon and Mindy loved him for the man he was. Her brother was happy.

Sam searched her heart and knew Ash would never settle down with a wild woman like her. Peter put his arm around her waist. Mischief sparkled in her eyes. "I think you and I should celebrate tonight."

Peter's loving eyes met hers. "I agree. I'll show you some karate moves."

"I have a few different positions to show you, but they aren't karate moves."

Chris ran over and slapped Ash's back. "You're a brave man, Ash, getting married, but I can see why. Cordy is the best."

Master Wong smiled at Cordy. "I'm so proud of my student. Her life journey has brought hardship and joy. A rich life is one of our greatest accomplishments. I wish you both the best."

The rainbow continued to shine over the green fields.

CHAPTER 53

A New Beginning

Before leaving New Orleans, Cordy handed Randy an envelope with directions to give to Bob. Amid rescuing the Pure of Heart from the Dark Watchers' underground bunker, and arranging their safe haven, there had been no time for Bob to open it. At the moment, all was calm, so Bob took advantage of the moment and opened the envelope. Inside was a folder containing legal documents.

Bob's eyes teared up as he read the legal document stating that not only was he the administrator for Cordy's trust, he was now the head of the company and owner of all the company shares. The amazing woman had donated her entire fortune to the company designed to create a better world and put Bob in charge of it.

"She thinks she isn't going to make it."

Julia kissed his cheek to soothe him. "No, where she is going, money is the one thing she doesn't need to burden her. She's free don't you see? She's making the sacrifice to save the world both in action and deed. She knows that with her funds, you are the best man to continue her quest."

"Well, I'll be damned, cupcake! You surprised me! I promise, I will not let you down!"

If the Pure of Heart were successful in their mission of stopping the pole shift, the little arks and bunkers would remain for the next disaster. The other essentials would be used to help avoid famine and starvation. Linda's words before her death would come true. She would be proud of what they did.

Wapek barked when he heard the knock on the door.

Randy rushed into the office. "I've got them on satellite. They're in Cahokia at Monks Mound. I'm sending the satellite stream to the Dragons headquarters as well."

Bob and Julia ran to the communications center. On the screen they saw the swords arranged in a circle. An angel stood beside each sword and Ash stood in the center holding Aaron's rod.

As they anticipated a spectacular victory like that in New Orleans, they saw De Villiers, accompanied by Neanderthal men climb the stairs. Armed Dark Watchers stormed the base. They observed De Villiers demanding Solomon's ring and Cordy giving it to him. In horror they watched as Mindy assassinated Bill.

Julia screamed, "I know her. That's Mindy. She replaced me as the Chairman's assistant. She unwittingly killed the Chairman with my secret Bloody Mary recipe."

Bob corrected her, "No, I killed the bastard."

"Yes, you finished him off, but she was the one who poisoned him with the Bloody Marys. Now she's killed Bill. I can't believe she's working for De Villiers!"

All the while they discussed Mindy, their eyes never left the screen. Isis leaped and snatched the ring from De Villiers. Antar lunged and grabbed De Villiers around the neck.

"Get outta here!" Randy exclaimed. "Is that a fire-breathing dragon that just cooked the Dark Watchers? When did we get a dragon?"

"Yep, and it looks like it prefers well-done Dark Watchers," Bob commented nonchalantly.

To their utter amazement they watched as Bill stood to his feet revealing a Kevlar vest underneath his shirt.

The angels moved back to the swords. Cordy joined Ash in the center. Things began to shake on the screen and in the communications center. Bob and Julia looked around as their building swayed back and forth, glass windows broke, and ceiling tiles fell around them. Miraculously they didn't lose power.

Back on the screen, Ash could be seen reciting words, and Cordy positioning her hands in the same manner as the Mary Magdalene statue. A blinding light burst before them. The shaking stopped. A hush filled the room as they watched Ash and Cordy disappear.

They watched as the remaining warriors celebrated their victory of saving the world and defeating De Villiers. And, just as suddenly as Ash and Cordy had disappeared, they reappeared.

Ash and Cordy were jubilant as they rejoined their friends. Cordy could be seen flashing wedding rings and Ash beaming brightly at his new bride.

Bob asked incredulously, "When in the hell did they get married?"

"I told you, Bob. Ash and Cordy love each other. I love happy endings."

CHAPTER 54

Hang on Dottie

The showboat left the dock and sailed down the muddy Mississippi to pick up passengers for the riverboat cruise. Dottie sat at her dressing table putting on her make up. The past few days had produced more excitement than she wanted for a lifetime. The suspense was killing her as she wondered what Ash and that naughty Frenchman were up to. They'd received a message from New York that something important was going to happen.

"Come quick, Dottie," her husband call. "We've got satellite feed from the headquarters in New York."

Dirty Dottie rolled her eyes. "Come quick, he says, where have I heard that one before? I'm on my way." Dottie was dressed in her Southern Belle costume for the show that day. She and her husband stared at the computer watching the drama at Cahokia play before them.

"I thought I'd seen it all, but is that dragons?"

"No, honey, you're not going senile. I see them, too."

"Oh, look at those big guys, Dottie. They have to be over seven feet tall."

"I assure you, there's an old wives' tale about the taller the man, the bigger he is." Dottie's husband never understood how she could have a one-track mind, even during a global catastrophe.

"I was thinking of the old saying, the bigger they are, the harder they fall."

The couple was shocked when the swords and rod activated the flashing light connecting to the poles and magnetosphere. The boat rocked furiously at the same time. The satellite signal faded in and out. The earth quaked, and the river quickly rose.

Dottie fell into her husband's lap and the rolling chair shifted from one side of the room to the other. The two of them screamed in fear. They banged against the wall and propelled to the other side.

"Oh, oh, I feel it!" Dottie shouted. "It's an earthquake."

She grabbed for the one body part she loved to grab on her lover. He grabbed for his favorite Dottie part, using both hands.

She decided if they were going to die she was going out in a blaze of glory. Her husband agreed. Kissing each other they enflamed their desire. Just as they were reaching the height of their passion, the shaking stopped. The river became still. A disheveled couple turned around to see the television reveal that the day was saved.

Dottie watched as Ash and Cordy kissed each other. "I knew it. They love each other. Look, he gave her a ring. Another good-looking hunk bites the dust. It's such a shame."

A frown formed on her face, and her husband spotted it.

"What's wrong, honey? The world is saved, and love triumphed. What more could you ask for?"

"Well, frankly, I'm a little disappointed."

"I hope it wasn't me, Dottie. I tried my best."

"No, darling, your performance was magnificent as usual."

Her husband put his arms around her to comfort her. He knew he was making a mistake, but he had to ask her.

"What more could you ask for?"

She smiled. "I was hoping I could see Ash's naked ass one more time for old time's sake."

He laughed. "Get up close to that screen and let me blow up that picture for you. I got a surprise for you." Her husband zoomed in on Ash and Cordy wearing their skin-tight futuristic silver body suits. Every bulging muscle was revealed to the lucky beholder's eyes.

"Oh, that's so much better. Oh my, oh my, you can see everything."

The elderly man got closer, too. "He's one lucky guy. She's damn hot."

Dottie grinned. "I love it when you talk dirty."

CHAPTER 55

Ying and Yang

W hat are we going to do with the dragons?" Chris asked. "Momma and baby need a home, and I don't think the world is ready to know the truth about them."

"The Sword of Goliath communicates and commands the dragons. Anyone who touches the sword can telepathically talk to the dragon," the Guardian said. "Try it, Chris."

Chris touched the sword. "I like Peter's idea for names. We will call you Ying and you, Yang. Thank you for helping us against the Dark Watchers."

The mother's eyes glowed red and she opened her mouth, showing her teeth. Chris thought she was getting ready to eat him but then realized she was simply smiling. He bowed to her and all the Pure of Heart bowed as well. Chris could hear her voice in his mind, "Thank you, Pure of Heart."

Master Wong touched the sword. "You honor us, old one. I have the perfect home for you and your baby. If you allow me to ride you, I will show you a land where you can live with abundant food and shelter."

"Wise one, you do not need to touch the sword to communicate with us. You are a dragon also. As dragons, our minds are connected telepathically. Yang and I welcome the safe haven you offer. Climb aboard and direct us to this new place."

"You're going to ride her. No way, man." Chris laughed.

Ying bowed her head and Master Wong climbed aboard. "The Dragon Society has a hideout deep in the Ozarks. The cave is part of the Meramec Caverns system. They will have a huge forest to hunt in and many rivers and lakes to find fish. I've dreamed all my life of living with the dragons."

"They deserve a chance to live free. Ying and Yang, go with Master Wong and obey him," Chris said.

The baby, Yang, walked over to Cordy and put its head close for her to pet. She smiled and stroked its scaly lizard-like head. She was the only one who could communicate without using the sword. Her gift served her well with animals and dragons.

"Thank you both for saving us," Cordy said.

Master Wong waved good-bye and told Ying the directions to the cave. As they ascended, he let out a whoop of exhilaration. He giggled and called down to his friends, "I'll call you when we get there." Yang followed closely after its mother.

Watching Master Wong and the dragons fade into the distance, Cordy wistfully whispered, "Be safe, old friend! Be safe!"

Master Wong kept the dragons close to the ground to avoid radar detection, small planes, and electrical lines. They entered the dense Ozark woods and headed to a large cave, their new home.

The cave was no ordinary cave. Master Wong had discovered this cave long ago. Due to its size and remoteness, he determined it was a perfect place for the Dragon Society to retreat for meditation and for additional combat training or, in the case of threat, it could serve as an emergency bunker. Being a forward thinker, he had it outfitted with electricity, running water, and plenty of food. When Master Wong established the cave as a retreat center/bunker, it was with the intent of providing safety and training to future human dragons. Never in his imagination did he think he would be training real life dragons as well.

The entrance area of the cave was wide. Master Wong deemed that it provided plenty of room for Ying and Yang to sleep. He had a private room deeper in the cave.

Although meditating, tai chi, and combat training had always been priorities to Master Wong, he now felt that he had an additional duty to guide the Piasa. Perhaps this was what he had been training for all his life.

Master Wong sent text messages and updates to his friends regarding the dragons' assimilation to the Ozark Woods. They were night hunters, eating catfish, bass, trout, and deer. If by chance they were spotted by a hiker or a farmer, their tales were attributed to poor eye sight or a UFO report. Some thought they were seeing a huge bald eagle.

A great love grew between Ying, Yang, and Master Wong. In the evenings, after the dragons' nightly hunt, Ying and Master Wong spent long hours telepathically sharing stories of their past. Ying loved hearing about Master Wong and the Dragons' crusade to aid the Pure of Heart. Master Wong never tired of hearing of Ying's tales of dealing with man over the centuries. A contentment spread over Master Wong as he reflected on how wonderful and rich his life had become.

Who knew the future? The Dragon Society would help protect the precious dragons of the past. One never knew how long they would be with them. Hibernation could occur again. Master Wong knew the dragons had awakened and were there for a reason. Perhaps the Pure of Heart would be called on to save the world again. The cave would be a great hiding place for some of the Pure of Heart treasures, and the dragons would be there to assist them once again.

CHAPTER 56

Wild Bill

I texted your buddies. I believe they'll be here in a few minutes," Mindy whispered to Bill.

A chopper could be heard coming toward them from a distance. It landed on top of Monks Mound and out jumped Bill's friends with machine guns, ready for a fight.

Mark yelled out, "Are you OK, Bill?"

"I'm fine, Mark. Put down your guns and meet my grand-daughter."

Harvey and the others came over and hugged Bill. "We thought we lost you, Bill. Damn, I'm glad you made it."

"We flew in from the air force base over yonder. It looks from your shirt you've been shot," Mark said.

Bill winced. "Luckily, I wore a bullet proof vest given to me by a friend."

"You may need to be checked out in case you broke a rib," Mark said. "They have a hospital nearby. Need a lift?"

Bill nodded as he held his side. "Good idea."

Harvey ran up to Cordy. "Howdy doodie! I'm Harvey, been a friend of Bill's since basic training. We're old war buddies. I knew your grandmother. You're just as pretty as she was."

The rest of the smiling crew shook hands with Cordy and Ash.

"Did you guys get the hostages back to their families?" Bill asked.

They all saluted and answered together, "Yes, sir. Mission accomplished!"

"Well, boys, this is cause for a celebration. I'm buying. But first, take me to the hospital."

Harvey and Mark grabbed ahold of Bill's arm and walked him to the waiting helicopter.

The medic saw he was bruised and scratched up, but everything checked out. Harvey passed him some whiskey for medicinal use.

"You're a lucky son of a gun, Bill. We thought we lost you back there."

"Don't I know it, Harvey. A man who has wonderful friends is a rich man."

"You got a pretty granddaughter. I can see she has a young buck. What's he do?"

"He's an archaeologist."

"A nerd, what a shame. He's a lucky guy! She's a real doll."

"You good old boys need to know that Bill is going into retirement after all this," Bill said. "I handed over the General's sword to Bob. He's a great guy. I feel the Light Watchers are in good hands. I'm getting too old to be doing this. Bob's going to help run the company for me."

They all laughed. "Every week from here on out will be six Saturdays and a Sunday. Fishing, golfing, and having lots of fun sounds good to us. You should have heard us huffing and puffing that last mission, trying to get to the chopper. We thought we were going to die of a heart attack. Yes, it's time, Wild Bill."

"I remember when we young nitwits bragged about how many women we kissed. Now we can brag about how big our fish are," Mark said.

Bill saw trees knocked down below them. "Look down there. What a mess."

They looked below at the ground, where damage from just a few seconds worth of earthquakes could be seen. And it could have been worse if it hadn't been for the treasures of the Pure of Heart working together. He remembered the powerful energy emitted by them. He couldn't believe what he saw but he knew he witnessed a moment in man's history where an apocalypse was postponed. Billions were saved. Tears of joy filled his eyes.

"Harvey, give me another shot of whiskey. Cheers, boys."

They started singing "There Once Was a Man from Nantucket."

CHAPTER 57

Ménage à Trois

After saying good-bye to Master Wong and Grandpa Bill, the rest of the weary warriors sat down on the top of the mound to regroup. Mindy, Cordy, and Sam were sitting next to each other. Cordy said, "You and Jon seem well-suited."

"We are. Thankfully, he's finally figuring that out. We've had a complicated relationship.

"When I was young, I fled an abusive home and became a prostitute on the streets of Paris where the children of Nephilim ran drugs and sex-trafficking operations. I was arrested for murdering one of my clients, a sadistic drug lord who was looking for a good time but found the wrong girl. For some reason, Jon was at the prison and heard my story. Seeing the warrior and chameleon within me, he recruited me and groomed me to be an Interpol undercover agent. He became my commander.

"We had incredible chemistry from the very beginning of our relationship. It was as if we could read each other's mind, which made us very good partners because we were so in tune with each other.

"One night in Paris, while undercover, our smoldering passion erupted to the surface when we were fighting over a plan. I kissed Jon to shut him up but all that did was unleash his desire. That night we made love for hours. I had known for a long time that I loved Jon, but that thought had never crossed his mind, until that night. The dynamics of our relationship changed. Jon became overly protective.

"Our emotional bond had become too strong between us. It had become a liability that could have gotten either one of us killed, so Jon urged Interpol to assign us each a new partner. However, we remained lovers.

"Jon shared with me his growing concern regarding De Villiers and the Dark Watcher organization. He feared that the Lafitte family was going to be targeted by him. We weren't sure how to proceed with those concerns when an opportunity arose.

"I was working an undercover mission when De Villiers approached me. He knew of my past and connections with the Children of the Nephilim and thought those connections and experiences would be an asset to him. He offered me a job as his assistant.

"I saw this as a way to get inside and find out what De Villiers' plans were. Jon didn't want me to take this undercover job, but he knew it was the best way to get information and that I had the skill to do whatever the job required."

Tears were streaming down her face, "But, to be absolutely convincing, I had to play the role as De Villiers' lover as well as his assistant. I hated that, but it was necessary.

"I didn't gain De Villiers' complete trust until I infiltrated the Children of the Nephilim. Then I was spying on De Villiers and the Chairman, playing them against each other.

"De Villiers remained fairly predictable until he came into contact with the Judas coins. As his madness increased, his threats against Jon and his family increased. I feared that he would kill Jon if we didn't stop him once and for all.

"I never broke my cover until saving your grandfather."

"And again, I thank you for that," Cordy replied.

Mindy's phone pinged with a text message. "Jon, there is a group text circulating among the Dark Watchers' families. You and I are included on it.

"The Dark Watchers are in need of a new Grandmaster. They are describing their hatred for De Villiers. They were beginning to lose faith in him as he became more dictatorial. Then when he murdered Poppa Jon right before their eyes, they knew he was out of control, but they were too frightened to confront him and remove him from power. Now, that he is 'retired', they are discussing his replacement.

"They've taken a vote and they want you to take the position as Dark Watcher Grandmaster and have recommended Sam and I as your seconds in command."

"Whoa, whoa, whoa! Wait a minute! That is not going to happen!" Jon exclaimed adamantly. "I have to make a phone call."

Walking away from the group, Jon called a familiar number.

Recognizing the number, Bob answered, "Hello, Frenchie! What can I do for you?"

"I have a request to make. Cordy tells me that you're head of the Light Watchers now."

"Yes, Bill turned over the reins to me when he retired."

"I'd like to come on board with you. I want to be known as an official Light Watcher. When the Lafitte family joined the battle with the Pure of Heart, it was to honor a long-ago pledge. There wasn't any ideology behind it, just maintaining the family honor. But, as time went on, my feelings changed from a sense of duty to believing in the Pure of Heart cause. I want to continue being a part of that cause. It's time for the Lafitte family to step out of the dark of the Dark Watchers and into the light of the Light Watchers. Will you have me and my family?"

"Well, Jon, after all we've been through, I thought you were a Light Watcher. Never questioned it for a moment. But, if official is what you need, then official you shall have. Welcome aboard!"

"Thank you, Bob! We'll get together soon and share a bottle of wine. Tell Julia hello." With that, Jon ended the connection and returned to the group.

"Mindy and Sam, after all that we have been through with the Pure of Heart, I don't believe that our family can return to the gray and black morals of the Dark Watchers. Those questionable morals cost Poppa Jon his life. We were on the front lines and saw the effects of the fight of good and evil, right and wrong, and love and hate. We can't go back to the dark. If we do, what we fought for, the lives we saved, and the love we've found will have been in vain. We have to stay in the light to help maintain and carry on the Pure of Heart cause.

"I will be replying to the group text declining the position as Dark Watcher Grandmaster and sever the Lafitte family association with the organization.

I'm going to encourage that the Dark Watcher organization disband.

"Bob has officially accepted our family as Light Watchers. I hope the two of you are in agreement and support my decision."

Mindy responded, "After my dealings with the Dark Watchers and the Children of the Nephilim, I've been questioning how we could be part of that world again. I don't want to see the likes of them ever re-establish their power. I stand with you in the light."

"Brother, brother, you are one hundred percent correct. After what they allowed to happen to Poppa Jon and their pursuit to kill us on De Villiers' orders, and their questionable morals, how could we ever trust them to respect and follow our leadership? After waging this war with the Pure of Heart, I believe the Lafitte family is firm in their convictions and will never compromise those as leading the Dark Watchers would require. I, too, brother, brother, stand with you in the light!"

"Alright, we're united then." Jon sent his text message and said, "Done! Only time will tell whether or not the Dark Watchers see the error of their ways and terminate their organization. Whatever their decision, the Lafitte family is in the light!"

Jon, Mindy, Sam, Peter, Cordy, and Ash packed their treasures and went their separate ways, waving to Chris as they departed.

After driving a short way, Jon pulled over onto a viewing deck of the Mississippi River. He turned to Mindy and asked, "Did you mean it when you said that you would go anywhere with me?"

"Yes, of course I did. I'm here now, aren't I? I don't care where we're headed as long as we're together."

"How does Houston sound? Pierre has some work at NASA for me. I hope the Guardian can help us with our research."

Mindy laughed, "Oh, Jon, I think you just want another beautiful and desirable woman to talk about the stars with. You're under her spell, admit it."

They had placed the crystal ball on the dashboard. As it began to glow, an image of the dazzling Guardian emerged.

"I believe I heard my name being discussed," said the Guardian.

"That you did, Guardian, or as I like to call you, Diana. Let me introduce you to my lady friend, Mindy."

"Hello, Mindy. I think we share a love for this man. You are perfect for him for I see that your heart is true and fights for justice. You and I will get along just fine."

Jon's eyes lit up with mischief. "I've always wanted to be in a *ménage à trois* with two exquisite ladies. Today, fate is smiling on me. I get my wish. Merci."

CHAPTER 58

Honeymoon Escape

As they drove away, Cordy looked over at Ash and was dazzled at the reality that he was now her husband. And even more dazzling was the fact that they had been married by the Lord of Hosts!

"Ash, this is all real, right? We did defeat De Villiers, didn't we? We saved mankind, didn't we? We really are married, right? I didn't dream all of this."

"No, my love, it's all true. Look at your left ring finger. I put those rings there myself."

Admiring her rings, she said, "You know it's customary after the wedding that the couple goes on a honeymoon. Since this is all so spur of the moment, I don't have a clue where to go. Look at us, we're still wearing the silver clothes from our visit with the Council of Heaven. This isn't exactly how I envisioned my honeymoon."

"That's OK, my darling. While you were saying good-by to your grandfather, I made a call. I have everything arranged. Close your eyes and rest up. It'll be twenty-five minutes or so before we get to our destination."

"Oh, Ash, you are always thinking! Wherever we go, I know I'll love it."

"How do you know that?"

"Because any time we're together, I am the happiest person in the world."

He beamed back at her, "The same goes for me."

Cordy yawned and said, "I didn't sleep at all last night in anticipation of the battle we fought today. There was so much at stake. Now, I can hardly keep my eyes open. I think everything is catching up with me."

"Rest now, sweetheart. We'll be there soon." He squeezed her hand. When she didn't return his squeeze, he gave her a quick glance to see that she had fallen asleep.

Ash checked his GPS and continued to follow the directions to their destination. Bringing the car to a stop, he lightly pushed her hair back from her forehead and gently kissed her. "Wake up, sleepy head, we're here."

Rubbing her eyes, Cordy sat up and looked around. She couldn't believe what was before her. Ash had taken her to her home in St. Louis. She hadn't been there since she went to Montreal to meet her grandfather and started the quest of the Pure of Heart.

Her eyes welled up with tears. "Oh Ash, you couldn't have made this day more precious to me. Isis, we're home, baby." She reached over and pulled Ash in for a kiss. "I can't wait to show you my, I mean, our, home."

Being ever the gentleman, Ash went around to open the door for Cordy, but she had already bounded out of the car and was running to the door in glee. She stopped short and went into an attack stance when she saw a strange man standing at her front door.

"Cordy, hold on! Wait! Stop! Let me explain! He's one of ours!"

Cordy looked at Ash skeptically, "Are you sure? We've been chased for what seems like forever by Dark Watchers. This isn't how I want to start my honeymoon."

"Really, he's one of ours. Randy wanted to make sure that we weren't interrupted by anything or anyone, so he positioned a guard at your front and back door."

"OK," she said, and to the relief of the guard, she resumed a normal stance.

Ash continued, "Randy also contacted your friend, Kay. She let the guys in to air out the place. She also went grocery shopping for us, so we have everything we need to stay put for a week, if not longer."

"Oh, honey, this is going to be a long honeymoon." Cordy leaned into Ash and passionately kissed him, igniting his desire. She crooked her finger at him and purred, "Follow me."

Cordy led Ash to her bedroom. To her surprise the room was showered in candle light. "You've thought of everything."

They lay down on the bed stroking and nipping at each other. It felt good to be home and in the arms of the man she loved and respected. Cordy looked deeply into Ash's eyes and said, "I have a confession to make. Remember when we were in that hotel room when we were in Ireland? I think I was already in love with you. It was the first time in my life that I didn't want to be in control, I didn't want to be alone. You made me feel so safe. I think subconsciously, I knew you were my soulmate. I wanted you then. I struggled with following my heart and maintaining my convictions. But, it was worth the wait. I love you, Ash, with all my heart."

"Since it seems a time for full disclosure, I have a confession as well. I wasn't asleep when you came out of that bathroom. You, standing naked in the moonlight took my breath away. I wanted you then as I want you now, but the time wasn't right. And like you, it was important to me that I remain pure until this moment. It was worth the wait. I love you, Cordy, with all my heart. There will never be anyone else."

With the promise of a lifetime in her eyes, Cordy sighed, "You, Ash, only you, until death do us part."

CHAPTER 59

Dreams Come True

After saving the world, Jon was getting settled into his new position at NASA. He was going to have his hands full running the Lafitte family's U.S. operation and keeping Mindy happy as well. He didn't know which one kept him the busiest.

Sam was ready to take the reins of the European operation of the Lafitte business. Jon was stepping aside and letting her take the lead. There was no one he trusted more than his sister to run their business and continue its growth and profits. He drew comfort in that unbeknownst to her, she would not return to France alone.

As Sam prepared her ship to leave, Jon pulled into the parking lot. He and Mindy got out and waved to her as they walked toward her. "Oh sister, sister," he called out to her, "I see you changed the name from 'Who's Your Daddy' to 'Dreamcatcher.' I like it!"

In a way that only a younger sister could, she responded, "Oh brother, brother," and gave him a big hug.

"Well, the day has come to start a new life on the high seas. Are you ready?"

"I was born ready, brother, you know that. Hi, Mindy. Has he been behaving?"

Mindy smiled. "I've tamed the wild man. I think he likes it."

"Is that so, brother?"

"Well, Mindy has many hidden talents. I don't think I'll find another one like her."

"Mindy, someday you will have to tell me about those hidden talents but today, the ocean and a faraway land calls to me, and I must follow. I was about to give up on you, brother. I was getting ready to cast off."

"Mindy and I had to stop and pick up your going-away present. It was important that you not leave without it, and there was a delay. But it made it, and here we are."

"I don't see anything in your hands. What is it?"

"Oh, I think you're going to like this present. No, I take that back. I'm sure you will love this present."

Jon lifted his arm into the air and waved. The back door of his car opened and out stepped Peter, wearing mirrored sunglasses, cut-off jean shorts, a white cotton shirt, flip-flops, and an ear-to-ear grin.

Sam couldn't believe her eyes. She hadn't seen him for weeks. She had never missed a man in the way that she had Peter. She had never felt the loneliness that she felt in his absence.

"What's he doing here?"

"Well sister, sister. Peter seems to be quite smitten with you. Right after your first date at the Dragons' headquarters, he asked me if he could court you. I asked him what his intentions were, and he said to make you his life partner.

"When he found out that you were sailing to France to take over the European business, he started taking swimming lessons and asked me to teach him to sail. He was a good student and has become a great sailor. He is fully aware of what it will take to sail across the ocean with you. And by the way, he now swims like a fish."

As Peter walked closer, Sam's careful smile expanded to a full glow. She started bouncing up and down with excitement. Not wanting him to become smug in her reaction, she settled and decided to play it cool.

"If you're going to sail with me, you'll have to lose the mirror sunglasses. I know what you were watching bounce up and down."

Peter responded, "I don't think so, Sam. I kind of like my glasses. Besides, I think your best asset is when you are walking in front of me or when I'm looking into your beautiful eyes. I missed you, too!"

"No one has ever fallen in love with my back side. They could never get past my front. You never cease to surprise me, Peter. You are different from most men that I've known."

"Yes, Sam, I am different. Get that in your head! I appreciate your assets, but I love you! Do you understand that? Do you believe that?"

"I'm working on it," Sam responded softly.

"Work faster! Permission to come aboard, captain."

"Yes, yes, of course! Permission granted!"

Peter boarded the ship like a seasoned sailor and strode straight to Sam and embraced her, kissing her passionately.

Breathless, Sam broke from Peter's embrace and ran to her brother and jumped into his arms, "Thank you, thank you, brother!"

Jon returned Sam's hug and lowered her to the deck. "Your welcome, sister, sister. Don't break him. I have a lot of time invested in this one.

"And sister, sister? You are right, he is different. I think you have met your match!"

"We have to go, brother. The sea is calling. I love you!"

Jon and Mindy got off the ship and waved as they cast off the lines.

Peter called out, "Thank you, Jon. Thank you for everything!" Then he turned and smiled at Sam. "Well, captain, what's my first task?"

"Come here and give the captain another kiss and then get to work," she commanded.

He tenderly kissed her. As he started to step away she clung to his arms and looked into his eyes and said, "Peter, you've made all of my dreams come true."

"This is looking to be the ultimate magical mystery tour," and he kissed her on the nose.

Sam steered the ship out to sea while Peter contentedly stood beside her watching the sunset.

She started reciting a verse that held a special place in her heart from the book, *The Prophet* by Kahlil Gibran:

"Let there be spaces in your togetherness and let the winds of the heavens dance between you. Love one another but make not a bond of love: Let it rather be a moving sea between the shores of your souls"

Peter and her eyes met. "One of my favorites too."

That evening when everything had been battened down for the night and the crew was down below, Sam and Peter were alone on the deck. Sam placed the ship on auto pilot and turned to Peter, "Do you want to steer the ship, or shall I?"

Peter was lying back on the seat cushions, and Sam came to join him.

"I like it when you steer the ship."

Sam sat up and untied the strings to the top and bottom of her swim suit and they fell down around her. She rolled over on top of Peter. "I like to steer!" *Tonight, I want to explore, dream and discover.* And that is just what they did!

CHAPTER 60

Chris's New Friends

All of Chris's comrades in battle had departed, taking their treasures with them. He remained on top of the mound holding Goliath's Sword. When he turned around, he was shocked to see that the Neanderthal soldiers continued to kneel.

"Hey guys, what's up?" asked Chris.

"I am Goliath. You wield Goliath's Sword. You are our commander. We wait your orders."

"Well first of all, stand up. I don't want any man kneeling before me. And let's clear something else up. I'm not you're commander. I'm your friend.

"I have a new gig in New Orleans. Jon Lafitte has offered me a management position at one of his casinos. I could teach you to be dealers and bouncers. Would you boys want to join me in this new adventure?"

They didn't quite understand their new friend, but he wielded their ancestor's sword. They would follow him into any battle or casino, whatever that was. They nodded their heads in agreement.

"I'm coming home, Queen Marie, with my new family. Alright, boys, we're headed for New Orleans, home of gumbo and the best shrimp dinners in the world. I'm taking you all to Bourbon Street for world class hurricanes. Goliath, can you drive?"

Goliath laughed, "Yes, I can drive. You'll be surprised at what we can do. The Dark Watchers underestimated us and treated us like slaves. You've freed us from them. I'll get the truck that we used to arrive here. That will accommodate all of us."

Once they were settled in the truck, Chris leaned over to adjust the radio, "What kind of tunes do you like, Goliath?"

The big guy leaned back in his seat, adjusted his mirrors, and said, "How about some jazz and blues?"

"Guys, get ready! You're headed for heaven! New Orleans here we come!" They drove off with the music blaring.

After a ten-hour drive, they arrived at the New Orleans casino famished. The temporary manager showed the Neanderthal men to their rooms and Chris to the penthouse. After they were settled, Chris took them to the casino buffet. Chris was amazed at how much these boys could eat! Good thing it was all-you-can-eat!

Along with being manager, Chris kept his promise. He taught his giant friends how to be dealers and bouncers. Their tables were full every night as the guests were intrigued by their height. As bouncers in the lounge and bar areas, their physical presence deterred many a potential altercation

Chris's new buddies became very adept at their new vocations. They loved their new life of freedom, independence, and prosperity.

Where once they were slaves to do evil, now they were free men to live lives of their choosing.

Although Chris felt like all of the Neanderthal men were his brothers, he developed a special bond with Jolly. Who would have guessed a man of the tribe of Dan and an ancestor of the Nephilim could be friends and live in harmony?

The Heavenly Council was pleased to get reports from the Guardian of the peace and friendship between them.

Alexander Pope said it best, *Hope springs eternal in the human breast; Man never is but always to be blest.*

The future was looking up for Earth and mankind!

Epilogue

Balloons and party decorations hung everywhere in Chief Saunhac's home in Nova Scotia. Aziza and Han had invited the family for the twins' first birthday party. Mary and her granddaughter had baked a cake and prepared a feast. Little Louie had been commandeered to help hang the decorations. It had been a while since the family had been together. They anxiously awaited their guests' arrival.

Ash and Cordy, carrying Isis, arrived first. Han and Aziza hurried to the door to hug them in welcome.

Han said, "We are so glad you came. We've missed you."

Aziza winked as the twins toddled into the room, "It will be nice to have extra hands to chase these little ones."

Little Louie, a tall Mi'kmaq man, entered into the room, "Hello, Ash. Do you remember me? I was in the teepee with you when Chief Saunhac initiated you into the tribe."

Ash laughed, "Yes, I remember you. How could I forget a giant of a man named Little Louie?"

"Then you remember Chief Saunhac gave you the name Little Rabbit. I wonder if you know what the chief meant by giving you that name as your animal spirit totem. I carved a rabbit from the oak trees near Saunhac's house. It signifies strength, intuition, great courage, and speed. I believe Chief Saunhac named you well." Little Louie handed Ash a wooden rabbit.

"Thank you, Little Louie. I'll treasure this as a gift from you and a memory of Chief Saunhac."

Little Louie teased, "So are there any little rabbits yet?"

Ash patted him on the back and answered, "Much to my mother's disappointment, no little rabbits yet."

Another knock on the door brought Grandpa Bill to the party. Seeing an old friend, Mary dashed to greet him. Hugging her, he asked, "How are you, Mary?"

"Busy, Bill, very busy. The house is filled with laughter and young children. A new generation of Pure of Heart have come into the world to help protect it. Generation after generation through man's history, they will continue the fight. The war is not over, but what we have is a moment of great peace and joy. These children are our hope for the future. The chief would be so happy to see his family all together."

Cordy saw her grandfather and rushed to him. "Grandpa Bill, you made it! I didn't know if we'd be able to pull you away from the river and your boys. How's the fishing?" she teased.

Bill embraced his granddaughter. "It's so good to see you Cordy. The good old boys and I just take the boat out and talk about old times. Every once in a while, we'll catch a big one. Retirement has been just great. How are you doing?"

"My vet business is booming. Ash loves his job at the university, but we'll be leaving for Egypt in a few months."

Bill's understanding eyes met hers, "You knew he would want to go back to Egypt, it's his passion."

Cordy responded, "Yes, I know it is. I could never and would never stop him from pursuing his love of all things Egypt. He suggested that I stay home so I didn't have to give up my vet practice. But, I told him no way! We're one! Where he goes, I go.

"Egypt is a magical place. He found the Keys of Life there, which sent him on his quest. It's like Sir Galahad looking for the Holy Grail, and on the way, he found true love, me!"

"I'm so happy that you've found your soulmate!"

One of the twins waddled over to Cordy with hands outstretched and a snaggled-toothed grin, babbling, "Up, please."

Cordy melted. "How can I resist that?" She picked up Gabrielle and snuggled her neck. Looking at her grandfather they shared a thought, *We're finally a family!* The loneliness and estrangement they had felt over the years was gone. Now, only love filled their hearts.

Cordy looked around the room and beamed. It was mayhem. Michael was running around on his wobbly legs. Grey Wolf's offspring chased Michael. Isis lay on the high book shelf with her new friend Minnie, an energetic kitten, aloofly watching all the activity. Family and friends were engaged in conversation. Chaos yes, but, at last, this was family!

As Cordy started to put down a squirming Gabrielle, there was another knock on the door.

Ash opened it to see a tall Welsh Native American smiling down on him.

"Well, hello, Remington. What a surprise to see you! Come in and meet my wife and the rest of the family. We're having a celebration.

"What brings you here?"

"Do you remember Uriel telling me to go to my homeland and find a sacred relic?"

"Yes, he told you that just before telling you to make a swim for it."

Remington laughed in memory, "That's right. Well, I found it."

Han came over and introduced himself, "I'm Han, Ash's father."

"It's nice to meet you, sir. I have something that I think you and your son might be interested in." He opened the large package that he had under his arm. Inside were two blue stone quartz tablets.

"I believe I have found the Tablets of Stone."

Han and Ash were speechless. Han found his voice and uttered in disbelief, "Oh my goodness! What a find! Let's give this a look over in a little bit when we have more time and less distractions. Come join us. We're just about to sing 'Happy Birthday'."

Family and friends gathered around the birthday cake and sang to the twins, who reluctantly wore party hats. To everyone's amusement and expectation, the one-year olds smeared their cake across their faces.

They watched as Aziza opened the presents. She got to the last one which was a small package from 'Aunt Dirty Dottie.'

"Dirty Dottie. Isn't she a friend of yours, Ash?"

Ash smiled fondly, "Yes, Dottie is a friend of mine. She saved my life many times during our quest to defeat De Villiers and protect the treasures of the Pure of Heart.

"I guess she remembered the twins' birthdate from the picture you sent me when I was hiding on her boat. I noticed her new title of 'aunt'. It looks like she's adopted our family as her own. That's OK with me. She is one special woman!"

Cordy warned, "Be careful, Aziza. Be very careful when you open that package. Dottie is a bit on the wild side."

Ash laughed and put his arm around his wife, "A bit?!"

Aziza gingerly removed the paper and opened the box. She pulled out two matching sippy cups. They looked like round breasts with nipples to sip from. Michael clapped and reached for one of them.

Han started to stutter and turn red. He tried to be polite for he knew they owed a great deal to the twins' new-found aunt. "Oh, aren't those nice. How sweet of her. I see there's a disk, too. It's labeled, 'Dirty Dottie sings Happy Birthday.'"

Aziza distracted Michael and returned the cups to the box. "Oh, thank goodness. She sent a gift receipt. From the Sex Toy novelty shop?"

Everyone broke out into hysterical laughter.

With twinkling eyes, Ash consoled his parents, "It's probably the only toy shop she visits on a regular basis.

"We better check out the disk before we let the babies hear it."

Bill cackled, "It's only 'Happy Birthday'. What could she do?"

Ash picked up the disk and inserted it into the CD player with trepidation, "I warn you, they don't call her Dirty Dottie for nothing."

Han urged Ash, "Well, the suspense is killing me. The twins are the only ones here below the legal age. We'll cover their ears while we listen to it. Push the button already!"

Placing their hands over the twins' ears, they listened as Dottie sang in a seductive voice that would have made Marilyn Monroe blush.

Grandpa Bill, patting his heart, and in a strained voice, panted, "I stand corrected! You have to admit, she has a helluva voice."

The doorbell rang, startling them. "I wonder who that could be," Mary said as she went to answer the door.

Cordy announced, "What would a party be without a surprise? Wait 'til you see who our special guest is!"

In sashayed a smiling Dirty Dottie wearing her signature plunging neckline, skin-tight dress and stiletto heels.

"Oh my gosh!" exclaimed Ash as he lifted Dottie off her feet and swung her in a circle of happiness.

"Cordy and I are so happy to see you. Everyone, this is the infamous Dirty Dottie. My sweet lady, to what do we owe the pleasure of your visit?"

With a hitch in her voice, Dottie said, "This is all Cordy's doing. Cordy, you can't imagine how happy you made me by including me in your family celebration. When I got your letter, it made me feel as if we've been friends for a long time. Many women don't get me, but you my friend, do.

"And it is so good to see my Ash man again!" as she smiled wickedly and squeezed his back side.

Grandpa Bill approached Dottie and took her hand, "I don't believe this! Do you remember me, Dottie? In the war you saved my life. You hid me from the Germans. We were a bit younger then and used different last names."

Dottie stared intently into his eyes, "Bill, is it really you?"

"Yes, it is. I didn't put two and two together until I saw you. You are as beautiful now as you were those many years ago. Welcome to the family, Dottie! Give me a hug for old times' sake."

Tears ran down Dottie's face. For the first time in her life, Dottie felt a part of a real family.

"Isn't it amazing how everyone and everything is connected!"

ABOUT THE AUTHORS

Carolyn Schield and Tom Vorbeck are a unique brother and sister team who decided to write a thrilling, adventurous, and mysterious trilogy. The Keys of Life, the first book of the trilogy, brought them together after they had drifted apart over the years.

Carolyn writes articles for alternative media and international magazines. She lives in Texas with her husband and children.

Tom is an award winning artist. His work can be seen at the Holocaust Museum in Washington, D.C.

Carolyn and Tom hope to share with their readers their passion and excitement for life.

Their first book is Keys of Life: Uriel's Justice. The book has been a #1 Top 100 Amazon best seller. Their second book Keys of Life: Sword of Fire has also been a # 1 Top 100 Amazon best seller.

For more information are readers can visit:
www.facebook.com/urielsjustice/
www.amazon.com/gp/product/B00JHV5TEK/ref=series_rw_dp_sw
www.amazon.com/gp/product/B01N3YONEB/ref=series_rw_dp_sw
twitter.com/UrielsJustice